OUR <u>SHIT</u> CHANGED 2

DERRICK JACKSON

Printed in the United States of America

Street Credibility Publishing
P.O Box 14523
Cincinnati, Ohio 45250
Website: www.streetcredibilitypublishing.com

Street Credibility is a federally Registered trademark
Library of Congress Control Number: 2024918013
ISBN: 979-8-9888270-2-3 (Paperback)
ISBN: 979-8-9888270-3-0 (eBook)

Editing by Derrick Jackson
Cover design by Sienna Arts

Published by Street Credibility Publishing

DEDICATION

I dedicate this book to Candice Jackson for nobody knows the blood, sweat and tears put into what we do, all the hard work done behind the scenes to place this beautiful art into the world for all to see. I appreciate your love and patience while I make my dreams a reality...

To new beginning.

Myona:

Beep, beep, beep, beep, beep, beep, my alarm clock was driving me crazy, frustrated I threw my pillow at it as hard as I could, trying my best to knock it off the dresser. Damn I was irritated, the alarm clock woke me up out of one of my most beautiful dreams I could ever have about Chris Brown, the love of my life. He has always been my superstar crush every since I was a little kid, that's my baby for sure, what's crazy is I been having these dreams about him almost every single night and I do mean, those real sweet dreams where we would be making sweet, sweet love every time I hear his name, I just can't help it my pussy gets so wet, sometimes I get so caught up in my dreams, I want to stay there and today I really wish I could, I threw the covers back on the bed in an attempt to take on the world, a world that seems to crumble every year for the last 10 years to this date, June 12TH , I lost my mom and my dad, both murdered in cold blood, and every since they been gone, there has been a big hole in my heart that feels like it could never be repaired, my dad was a major part of my life, even at an young age, he taught me and my brother about the streets, what to do and what not to do, and I still move by a lot of his teaching still to this day. What I didn't learn from my dad or mom my grandmother stepped up and laid the footwork on the rest. But life was still hard, I never shared a father daughter dance at school and my father will never get to walk me down the aisle if I ever get married, after my mom and dad was murdered, we almost went to foster care because nobody didn't want to take us in, but grandma Vickie was there for us, she loved us and made us feel safe, she was my dad's grandmother, sworn in by the game, it isn't nothing you could get pass her, one of her favorite sayings, seen it all, done it all, nothing is uncommon to man. I give thanks for her without her in our life we would be in the system. I got up and headed to the shower, as all my thoughts built up in my brain, I just wanted to feel the hot water run all over my body before I stepped out into the world to face this day. Every year it's the same old shit, any minute now, I'm going to be getting a call from my friend London, bugging me, asking me all types of questions about how I'm feeling and shit, and it's cool, I know my girl really cares about me and truly means well. Me and London been friends since we met in middle school. She always been like a sister to me, she has always had my back whenever I needed her. After I took my hot shower, I dried off with my bath towel, laid back down for a while just to try to relax for a minute, while I checked my messages there was an unknown missed call on my caller ID, instead of calling it right back, I figured I'd call them back after I got ready, I have to get Jyel up and ready to go to school, every since we was kids I been taking care of my Lil brother, making sure he's doing good in school and staying out of trouble, keeping him out of the streets, I remember one time before my parents died me and my brother got into a fight and I left him at the store, I got in trouble by my dad then my mom, they both took turns using the belt on me and the main thing they was saying the whole time was, look out for your brother, they didn't just tell it to me, they beat it in me, so his success is a weight on my shoulders and I am not gone lie, the older he gets, the harder it gets to control him and make sure my shit is straight at the same time, this is my last year to graduate, then after that, I'm going to move out and get my own place. It's finally going to be my time to show my independence, I been waiting on this for a long time, as I walked up to Jyel room, his door was slightly ajar, I knocked and the door popped open, the odor of old gym socks and unwashed ass smacked me in the face, like I asked a disrespectful question and got put in my place real, quick! I tried to hold my breath but the smell was unbearable, boom, boom, boom, Jyel get up it's time to go to school, I didn't want to go in no farther, Jyel boom, he snatched the door all the way open. Damn Myona what the fuck do you want? don't you see I'm trying to sleep.

There won't be no more sleeping in here this morning, it's time to get up and go to school, you know you can't miss no more days.

Excuse me! Do you know what the fuck today is?

Yes, I do, and!

And that means, I don't want to be bothered, so leave me the fuck alone.

He pushed the door as if he was going to shut it in her face, she quickly placed her foot in between the door way to stop it from closing completely.

Come on now, move or we about to have a serious problem, Jyel said while putting all his weight on the door trying to force it closed.

Ok! If a problem is what you want then a problem is what you gone get, she said as she began to push through the door with all her might pushing him back with ease, don't forget that you my Lil brother, not the other way around.

He seen that his hold was breaking so he just let go, and what's that supposed to mean, Myona we aren't kids no more, I'll beat your ass! He said as he stepped up ready to show her his words came with action.

Boy! You heard your sister, get your ass up and get out of this house before me and you have a problem.

Yes, ma'am, Jyel said while passing Myona off a crazy look.

My grandmother stepped in to referee and I'm glad because Jyel could be hard to deal with sometimes, if he doesn't listen to me, Grandma Vickie always put him in line, after everything got situated with Jyel I called London to make sure if she was going to meet up with me later, to my surprise it took her a while I rang her phone over and over again before she ended up picking up.

Hello!

Girl what's up! Why you aren't picking up the phone for me? I got to call you a million times now before you answer?

Damn Myona I was doing something, plus you be acting like we fucking or something!

Bitch if we were fucking, you would definitely be in check, you would be answering on the first ring.

Ok what's up, I'm kind of busy, she said as she popped her lips.

In the background I could hear a sucking sound and a soft moan, like she was trying to hide the fact that she was doing something altogether.

Bitch what is you doing?

I'm trying to get this dick together if you don't mind, London said as she pushed the dick in her throat the far as it could go, while making loud spitting sounds, showing that it isn't no shame in her game.

London has always been a free spirit and don't have no shame in anything that she does, it's been times she would even try to have sexy with men in front of her, and not only did she get a bad reputation but it made a lot of people think we was one and the same, even though that was her friend, she made it clear to the world they were nothing alike, they were day and night for sure.

Girl why are you so nasty! You didn't even have to answer the phone if you were going to be doing all that!

Because you weren't going to stop calling me if I didn't, now, bye, I'll talk to you later.

Bye! Love you, I said as we hung up the phone.

After talking to London I figured I finally call back the unknown number that called me a couple of hours ago, as I called it didn't take long, they answered on the second ring, all business.

Lyon Family Financial.

Huh what? I said checking the number to see if I made the right call.

May I help you, ma'am?

Yeah, well, I don't know, but somebody called me from this number, I'm just returning the call.

Ok ma'am, can you give me your first and last name please?

Myona Wright, I said feeling out of place with the call altogether, I know they can't be looking for me I haven't even went to open up a bank account yet, plus I never heard of them, I know I don't have an account with them unless somebody stole my identity, otherwise this got to be a mistake.

The caller came back on the line after having me on hold for at least 30 minutes, Ms. Wright.

Yes!

We got you down in our system as you having a birthday coming up soon, is that correct?

O I see what this is, no I'm not interested in your services! Whatever it is that you do!

No! no! no! Ms. Wright I'm am a Fiduciary.

A what? Listen I am not accepting no loans, that's gone take me forever to pay back no I'm good!

No listen Ms. Wright, I was hired by your father before he passed to be your financial manager to oversee the Trust he set up for you, now I have a check for you here and a video message from your dad, now you have to be 18 years old to receive everything, so I want to meet up with you the day after your birthday so please place me in your schedule don't make any other plans, and I'm also looking for an Aiden Wright, he is listed as your older brother, do you know where I could reach him?

No I don't have a number for him, I actually haven't seen him in years, I was hoping you could give me a number for him.

No ma'am unfortunately I don't, but when I do, I'll be sure to get that for you, I know your father would have wanted you guys to stay together,

Yes, he would.

So you will be here to meet me a day after your birthday, I need an email address so I could email you the address so you know where we are located and details to what you will need to bring with you.

Which is?

Not much Ms. Wright, just identification to verify who you are, we can't make no mistakes here,

I don't want to lose my job, he said with a light laugh to lighten the mood.

Ok yes, I'll have my ID and birth certificate with me, I'll be there and thank you.

Your welcome Ms. Wright, see you soon bye.

As soon as he hung up the phone, my heart was then released from my stomach, not only was my mind blown that my dad set all this up, but also to hear my brother's name for the first time, Aiden Wright. Nobody talked about him, or every time I would ask about him, it would make everyone angry accept my grandmother. I just never understood why they were so angry, but he had to do something that I don't know about, I just don't know what, my birthday is next week so I know it's going to drive me crazy waiting to hear my dad voice and see him after I haven't seen him in all these years, and I wonder what message does my dad have for me.

Ace:

I woke up to the sun, poking through my curtains, and my head pounding out of control, from all the bottles I poured down my throat last night, I flew in from Miami, and decided to go to a couple of bars, to shake the pain of my dad's death date. Even dough I was the one who took his life, I loved my dad and miss him more and more each day, As fucked up as it sounds, I just couldn't let him get away with killing my mom, damn! Life has been everything but a win, win for me, I got my life together financially, invested in a couple businesses, so I'm not hurting on no money, I always told myself that the only reason I would show my face in Cincinnati, is to get some money, but it's not, I been running from my past for a long time, and I know my family know that I either murdered my father or that I had something to do with it and I feel once Grandma Vickie gets the chance to see the journal my dad wrote, she will understand why I did what I did. I hope she is still alive, I haven't seen or talked to her in years, I still got her number, the guilt has placed a heavy weight on me over the years so I never called, but I have to talk to her, I owe her the truth but first I got to get this bitch out my bed and get myself in the shower, I got a lot of business I got to handle, as I looked at her, still laying in my bed, I couldn't remember her name but damn she sole is sexy as fuck, I walked over and tapped her on the ass, as soon as my hand tapped her on the ass, she tooted her ass straight up in the air, pussy siting all the way out, I wiped my dick out, rubbing my dick in between her wet lips until I slid inside her, real slow, gripping her tight not wanting to let go, she started moving her hips to the song that was playing in the background dropping it back on me, weakening my knees with each stroke, I got turned on more and more, watching my dick fill her up, pushing as deep as I can go, damn this feels so fucking good, I started to feel my toes curl, o my god I'm about to cum, her juices was pouring all over me, I couldn't stop I have to keep going, I pounded harder and harder until my load exploded all inside of her. Damn I'm tripping, right after I Cum, my common sense popped back in. damn I don't know her and I'm fucking her raw and Cumming all in her, man yeah I'm tripping, the thoughts instantly made my mood change.

A baby, look I had fun, I hope you did to, but it's time to go baby, I got to get up and make some moves.

Damn, and it's just like that huh! She said, as she gave him one of the nastiest looks she could give.

What!

Fuck me and then flip, I guess all you told me was bullshit!

What did I tell you baby? Look! I don't even know your motherfucking name, and we just had a good time and that's it.

So you don't want to get to know me?

Know you! Shit I know you already, you a little slut whore, chasing scene to scene, what else is there I need to know.

You can tell by the look on her face, every word he spoke cut a hole into her soul.

So that's what you think of me, that I'm just some hoe?

You aren't, Lol, you aren't huh! You didn't just fuck me and you haven't known me for even 24 hours so you tell me, you aren't, bitch get out my house, you got what you came for, and if I see you out in public you can speak, don't make this weird.

Fuck, you, motherfucker!

Baby don't trip, that shit good, I'm gone call you! he said as he threw her the remainder of her clothes.

She got dressed, tears running down her face, confused, because she really thought that he liked her and then he flipped once he got what he wanted, his actions left her hurt to the core, she pulled for the door.

Baby, baby, baby, he said as he called for her before she went out the door.

What!

Baby what is your name!

She was more than embarrassed and didn't want to give out her real name, so she made up one,

My name is MoMo

MoMo is your name? Lol come on get serious! What's your real name in case I got to find you?

MoMo that's my name!

Ok, is what he told her, after he slammed the door on her back, glad he got rid of her, he made sure he proceeded to call one of his guys, a friend of his told him, he would hook him up with some dude making major moves around the city. He felt he could trust him so he called him to let him know he was now in the city and needed his help, he told Ace that he got him and that everything was everything, so Ace began to put all his plans in order, and it all started with a call to his Grandmother Vickie, so he could let her know that he is not only alive but that he is also ready to set shit straight. As the phone rang, he pondered on how this conversation was going to start, then she answered.

Hello, Hello, is anybody there?

Grandma!

Recognizing his voice instantly, she called out his name.

Aiden is that you baby?

Yeah it's me, he said not knowing what to say next.

Come home baby! Whatever it is, we can fix it, we can talk about it baby.

Grandma I'm alright, and I'm going to be coming to see you real soon.

How soon baby? We miss you, we love you, I need to talk to you, your brother and sister need you, it's time baby.

Then the phone went silent, that was it, he couldn't take no more, he hung up, something just didn't feel right, his thought began to run wild, like what if she trying to set me up or something, no! what would she have to gain? Shit! All he knew is no matter what they were going to be meeting up really soon. After the phone call, he sat and stared out the window, frying to put everything together in his head, he didn't aspect his Grandma Vickie to react to his voice the way that she did, he thought that she would hate me, to his surprise she even told him that she loved and missed him, it got to the point he didn't know what to do next.

The emotions he felt, had him all over the place, he didn't know whether he could trust her or not, all he knew is he had to get the truth out one way or another so it would no longer eat him alive, like it's been over the years, every since that day, life has been a tough pill for him to swallow, but once the truth is out, he can finally feel free, once he could tell them the reason why he did the things he did, it would put an answer to all this madness!

Jyel:

Today is an important day for me, even dough a part of me didn't want to get out the bed, because of my mom and dad death, I had too, today I'm going to sign up for a junior

Detective spot at District 1, it's going to help me with my school credits for me to graduate and will look great on my resume for college, every since my family was murdered, I wanted to be a cop, I always felt that maybe if I were a cop, I would not only make this world a better place but I could also find out who killed my parents so I could bring them to justice. So when I heard about this program, I had to sign up for it, over the years I have kept in touch with the lead Detectives on the case, one has even ended up being a great mentor to me, but every time I would start asking questions, it's always ended up being the same old dry ass lines every time, sorry there is no new leads, but when we find something out, you will be the first to know, 10 years and you haven't found nothing out yet, fuck that, it's time for me to start putting in my own work. As he walked into District 1 , he approached the officer working the desk at the front, she had big brown smiling eyes, that would be hard not to notice.

Hello, how are you doing? How can I help you? Are you here to report a crime?

No ma'am, my name is Jyel Wright and I'm here to sign up for the junior detective program.

As she looked in the computer for his name, she came across it, ok great, did you come with all the proper paperwork?

Ah the proper paperwork!

The puzzle looks on his face, opened him up for a conversation he wasn't sure he even was ready for or wanted to hear, but he braced for it anyway.

Yes, sir, you have to fill out an application, then once we process your paperwork, we will contact you if you qualify.

If I qualify?

Yes, if you qualify, we just don't let anybody into the junior detective program, you have to have certain requirements to be accepted.

Which is?

He could tell the officer was becoming more then a little impatient with him, but it didn't matter, he needed the program and would stop at nothing until he got it!

Look Ms. Officer!

Officer Kelly!

Ms. Officer Kelly I really need this program!

And what is the reason that you want to do this program if you don't mind me asking?

He told her about his parent's being murdered and how that alone, made him want to be a cop, instantly he could sense compassion come from the officer, she looked around the room, and then motioned for him to move in closer.

I'm not supposed to do this but I'm going to pull some strings together for you so you could get in this program, but now Mr. Wright, I don't want to go through all this for nothing, don't let me down now you hear me?

I won't, believe me, I won't!

Now it's one more thing I'm going to need from you.

And that is?

A signature from your guardian, showing that they will give consent for you to join.

Those words cut like a knife, he knew it would be hard to get that signature, mainly because his whole family are pro street and anti-cop. he doesn't know how they are going to react to the news, as he was in thought, Ms. Officer Kelly could tell that something was wrong, because it was written all over his face.

Mr. Wright, is there a problem?

Well yeah kind of!

Your family doesn't know you want to join this program?

Well, no, I

No, no, no, Mr. Wright, if you want to join the Junior Detective program, I am going to need that signature you understand? Now I have done all that I could do now it's time for you to do your part.

Yes, ma'am I understand, I'll get the signature.

Good! Now, leave me a number that I could contact you on after I get everything together and we will go from there.

Myona:

She was going to tell her Grandma Vickie about the call from Lyon family financial but she got off track a little bit and couldn't afford to be late for school, this is her final year of high school, so there was no way she could be late, she figured if she just caught up with her Grandmother after she get out of school, it would be no big deal. As she pulled up to the school, in her 528i BMW, everybody would always break their necks to stare, she admired that car. she got it as a gift for her sweet 16 birthday, she was so happy when her great uncle Pat pulled up in front of the house with it, she loved it the first time she laid her eyes on it, she treated it like it was her baby she didn't let anybody mess with that car it's all black and when the bought it they wrapped it with a big red bow on it, she bugged her Grandma Vickie for four years for a car, she would always ask for black because it was her and her dad's favorite color, and BMW is one of her mom's dream car's she would always talk about when getting when she was a kid, so by her being able to have both together, it just made her feel like they are always with her, watching 14 over her, plus she has always pretty much been spoiled growing up, she has always gotten whatever she wanted as long as she followed her Grandmother's rules, which wasn't hard at all, all her grandmother wanted for her to do was go to school, take care of her business in school which came with good grades and take care of things that needed to be done around the house, stay out of the streets, which she didn't get since she didn't have to many friends. And when she tried to branch out to meet new people, her Grandmother would always say let the dead bury the dead, although she knew it was something she got from church, she didn't know quite what it meant. Her Grandmother has always been a very spiritual person who would recite a lot of different scriptures from the bible, but she still was waiting on her to break one of the scriptures down for her so she could get a better understanding of what it is she exactly is talking about, and the last rule but not the least was, keep them boys out your face and you get whatever you want, which was another easy rule for her to follow because when it came to boys she always experience some type of deep trust issues, mainly because of the way her mother died. She always wondered how could somebody rape and murder her mother in the house while her kids were close by in the other room, then leave her there for her kids to find her. The picture of her mother's eyes staring wide open looking back at her will be forever burned into her head forever, they cut her head off her body and laid it right on top of her naked body, no matter how hard she tried to get it out of her head, it just kept playing in her mind over and over again, and for the longest she hated the idea of men altogether, the only way she could change her image of them even in the slightest were because of her relationship she had built with her great uncle Pat, he raised her as his own so she was able to restore some of that trust back to the other side. There were times she wanted to step out of line but she never broke any of Grandma Vickie's rules, and the reason way was simple she loves being spoiled, so if she ever did meet somebody down the road, in order for her to break the rules, they would have to spoil her the way that her

Grandmother does, and that would be a big pair of shoes for them to fill. Plus, she has seen how her friend London has always spread herself then when it came to guys, that alone turned her in the opposite direction. Every time she turned around it were always somebody talking about her behind her back, saying this hoe did this and this hoe did that, and the truth is she just didn't want that type of reputation for herself. Her Grandma Vickie didn't like her hanging out with London at all, but being that it's been her best friend for a long time, she knew that Myona wouldn't just turn her back on her friend regardless what reputation she carried, from the way she sees it, that's London life, just because she hangs with her, doesn't mean they are into the same things together. As Myona were getting her things together, getting ready to get out of the car, she seen some guy approaching her car, not knowing his intentions she quickly reached in her purse to put my hand on her masa.

Hey baby what's up can I talk to you for a minute, he said with a deep lust for her in his eyes, she knew where this was going and even dough from tho looks of him, he was kind of cute, all games aside she really didn't have time for small talk, she had to be in class before she became late to Mrs. Wood class, she hated for people to be late.

Look I really don't got time; I'm going to be late for class!

Not willing to back down just yet he tried his best to still slow her down on her path, well maybe I could get your number and we could talk later.

As she searched his face for the answers, of what might he really want, she couldn't find nothing that would stand out at this moment, so she came right out and asked.

So what is it that you want to talk about? she asked watching his body language and his answer closely.

He wants to tell you how small his dick is and how his sex is shitty, or maybe how broke as fuck he is London said as she walked down between the middle of them, snapping her neck and twisting or hips.

Fuck you bitch! Why you keep going around trying to dog me out to everyone you can, at least I am not telling nobody how bad your pussy stink and believe me I should because it does!

She couldn't help but laugh at both of them as she finished grabbing her things from the car and started heading towards the door of the school building, leaving them both behind while they argue with each other, before she got to the door, the guy raced in front of her to bet me to the door so he can open it up for her leaving London behind to stand and watch.

Hey so w hat's up! You gone let me get that number or not?

Are you serious? she said not believing If she heard him out right, you really want me to answer that question? DE cussed that he would even try such a thing with her, knowing he had been with her friend.

I mean what, shit what I do, he asked.

You think I would even date you after you fucked my best friend, that alone tells me right off the back what you think about me, I'm sorry I'm not what you looking for.

And what is that? What is it that you think I'm looking for?

Obviously a hoe! she walked pass him not willing to share another word with him as London laughed in his face, to see if she could push some more of his buttons as she walked pass him as well.

Hey girl wait up; I need to holla at you about something! London said as she tried her best to catch up.

Myona stopped so she could let London catch up to her, what's up girl? You know I got to hurry I can't be late for Mrs. Wood class, she been acting like I'm her worse enemy if I'm just a couple minute's late, calling my grandmother, sending me to the principle office, just doing a lot of extra shit she doesn't have to do.

Girl hold up it won't take long, look I been having a lot going on and I need you to have my back on something, just in case my mom calls your phone.

Girl what! Come on now, why would your mom be calling my phone? Myona asked

Well I kind of told her that I spent the night over your house last night and that's the reason I didn't come home.

And she believed that shit?

Yea, I told her we both have a real big test coming up and we have to pass if we were going to graduate.

She just laughed, thinking how most of the shit London gets off on her mother is crazy, if it were her with her Grandma Vickie, hands down she would have been beaten into another world by now, but London has always had the type of mom who barely pays her any attention because most of her attention focuses on the different man that comes in and out of her life. Stating the facts, it's been a lot of men, she is with a different man, damn near every night, to the point her pussy barely ever gets a break, it's like dick is the woman drug or something. From where

Myona is standing all London's mother did is pass that shit right down to her daughter, and the sad part is its clear London thinks that the only way she is going to be able to find love is through sex.

Yea, it's cool girl, if she calls I'll cover for you, but where the hell was you last night, if I might ask!

Girl I stuck in KT's last night and I met this fine Lil mixed brother, he wined and dined me and we ended up going back to his house for the night.

Is that right, did you fuck him? she asked searching her eyes for an answer that I already knew

We danced and laughed and he held me, girl he was so sweet.

Girl did you fuck him or not? Cut to the chase and cut the shit, she said putting on her serious and impatient face.

Yea, girl I fucked him, damn is you happy now, is that all you wanted to know?

That's something I should be asking you, she said as she tried her best not to show just how disappointed she was in her once again.

Yes, and no!

Meaning?

Well he had a big ole dick girl, he fucked the shit out of me all night, tore my walls down, I'm still sore but he ended up being a real dick when the morning hit, she said looking sad and like she actually expected a different outcome.

Aren't they all? And girl what did you expect, giving him the pussy on the first night, what is there to respect in the morning?

Girl damn, here you go judging me again, like I can't have no fun, she said as anger crossed her face.

Having fun don't have nothing to do with giving yourself up, to every man you come around.

At that moment, she could tell she had hit a nerve, but she couldn't help it, she loves London, and felt that somebody should at least try to tell her the truth about the consequences of her actions but everybody can't handle the truth so some shit is better left unsaid.

Alright girl I'll holla at you later, she said as she turned and walked away.

London, London, I'm sorry, come here, I didn't mean it like that I said but she just kept on walking not turning around not even once. I guess I'll dill with London later, I have a lot on my plate right now, I don't have time to pay attention to her bullshit as well. They have always had their disagreements, so she knew eventually she would come around. As she walked into Mrs. Wood class a couple minutes late, she tried her best to avoid eye contact as she made her way to her sit.

Ms, Wright, I'm so glad that you can bless us with your presence today, Mrs. Wood said most sarcastic voice she could display.

Mrs. Wood, I'm sorry I really don't want any trouble I been having a rough day from the start, I woke up late and it's just a lot on my mind.

Your sorry huh, you shouldn't be telling me your sorry, that's an apology that you owe to the class, for coming in here late, interrupting the lesson I'm teaching all together. So why don't you stand up and apologize to them for being rude to them, this has nothing to do with me.

She really didn't want any problems, but the teacher was making it hard for her not to respond with anger and even dough she held it together, it took everything in Myona not to snap on her and walk out the class, but all she could hear is her grandmother's voice telling her (this is your last year, don't let that lady trick you out your spot) so she took the high road and stood up and apologized to everybody then sat back down in her seat. All through the class she could barely keep focus on anything the teacher had to say, all she could think about was the call she got earlier and the message her dad has for her, there is nothing she could do but be patient and wait.

London:

After she left Myona, she was so angry at her for how she is always ended up judging her and her life. She felt Myona was starting to become more like everyone else, throwing shade and talking down on her because she was the popular one who got all the good looking man who wanted her and not Myona. Damn she dogging me and she supposed to be my best friend, she said to herself in thought. She couldn't get the thought out her mind how played she felt by her best friend and only wished she could pull her off her high horse and make her feel that same pain she was experiencing or worse. As she was going into the class room she felt someone violently grabbing her arm slamming her into the hallway lockers.

Boom!

What the fuck! Poured out her mouth as she looked to see who was putting their hands on her.

Bitch why is you going around, telling motherfucker all that weak ass shit about me?

Lol, what's so weak about the truth Frank? And you better keep your motherfucking hands off of me, before we have a problem we can't fix.

Whatever bitch!

Call me another bitch she said as she walked towards him fist balled ready to throw a punch on the next wrong word that came out of his mouth.

London don't get yourself hurt fuckin with me.

I bet you won't call me another bitch!

Look chill with all that bullshit you been starting around school, spreading lies and shit about me.

Frank, you tell me what part of it is a lie, you do have a small dick and your sex game is whack, and you looking real dusty today, so you don't have no money, I was just trying to save my girl from wasting her time.

You didn't say all that when I was digging in you, your toes were curling and your eyes was rolling, like act I was fuckin killing you or something and if I was so much of a broke as nigga, why was you eating this dick like I was the richest man in the world then.

Let's just say I'm a good ass actor, and you a fool for trying to get with my girl, you knew that was my girl.

True, true I knew, but I felt it was fair game since you fucked my home boy.

Frank I told you I was sorry for that; I didn't know he was your friend!

It doesn't matter if you knew if he was my home boy or not, you act like we were together, so even if he wasn't my home boy, you still would have been fucking dudes behind my back and that's fucked up, I thought you cared about me, maybe you right.

He turned and started to walk away, she ran up and grabbed his arm, turning him back around to face her.

Right about what?

He looked her in the eyes, snatching away from her, you are a good actor, he said, as he turned once again and walked away.

As she watched him walk away, she was hurt that she were hurting him and even though she tried her best to hurt him the way she was hurting, she knew she was wrong and that he really didn't deserve everything that were being done to him, she really loved and wanted to be with him, she just made a big mistake sleeping with the other guy who ended up being one of his best friends. She wished she could fix it, but just didn't know how, she went to class and the whole time, instead of working on her class work all she could do was think about Frank, a part of her wanted to do whatever it would take for him to forgive her hoping that maybe they could get back together, but every time she tried, she always ended up messing things up between them. Then she thought about how he had just tried to get with her friend Myona, she wondered what he seen in her and she replayed the comment she said after she turned Frank down on my account, (you are kind of cute) she thought of what would of happen, if she wasn't there to interrupt their little conversation. Myona probably would of gave him the number. She was tired of how she was being judged by everybody, now Myona, the more she thought about everything the angrier she got, she couldn't focus so she decided to just skip class for today, as she was walking out the class she noticed Frank talking to Myona in the hallway, so she ducked back behind the wall out of sight so she could watch them from a far.

Frank and Myona conversation:

Myona wait let me holla at you!

Hey what's up, look I told you,

I know, I know and I respect that, I know you a good girl and even though I really like you, I really didn't mean no disrespect, but that's not what I wanted to talk to you about.

Ok, so what did you want to talk to me about? She said looking for the answers in his body language. She wanted to hurry up and get away from him, not only was he fine but she knew how her girl felt about him and didn't want her to get the wrong impression if they were seen talking together.

I been having some problems with my math and if I don't get it together I'm not going to be able to graduate, I really need your help, can you tutor me? The teacher referred you to me, that's the only reason I'm asking.

Look I can't, I would if I could, but I can't!

Why? Is it because of this morning? Is it because of London? He said with a deep disappointment in his eyes.

Well yes, and no, look I just don't really want to cause no problems between me and my best friend.

So what I'm supposed to do? Fail because of a friendship I am not trying to break up in the first place or you just afraid to admit you kind of like me, so if we study together you might not be able to handle yourself.

That comment made both of them laugh, but mostly on her part, because what he was saying was kind of true, but she was going to stick to her guns no matter how much she liked him, betraying a friend was a line she would never be willing to cross.

Lol, boy don't go there, I told you I would never cross that line, and what is your name, we been talking this whole time and I don't even know what they call you, she said with a smile dancing in her eyes.

My name is Frank, Myona

Ok, well Frank, I won't be able to tutor you, but I also don't want you to fail either, so I'm going to give you the number of a great tutor she has helped me through some of my toughest times I have been in myself. Just when you call, tell her I was the one who referred you and tell her your situation and she should be able to help you a lot and hey she might even be single! She said as she pulled the small piece of paper from her book bag writing down the tutor number handing it to Frank.

The problem is she isn't you, he said as he stepped in to get a little closer.

Bye Frank have a nice day, she said as she stepped away from Frank, taking off down the hallway not looking back in his direction, not even once.

Frank watched Myona walk down the hallway, he was stuck in a daydream, thinking about all the things he would do if he had her and not to mention too keep her, if they were ever together, he could tell she likes him, she is just really playing hard to get.

London:

This dirty ass bitch, she thought as she watched Myona and Frank laughing and giggling, she wondered what they were talking about, what was just so funny. She seen how Myona looked at him, why would she stab me in the back like that, she knows how I feel about him. The more she watched the more the anger built up inside of her, out of nowhere she watched Myona pull a piece of paper out her bag and write what looks like her number down, damn behind my back you gone creep with him behind my back. She wanted to step out and confront the both of them, but decided not to, she had a better plan, one where Frank could feel the pain she was feeling and one that will pull Myona off her high horse once and for all. After Myona walked pass, she decided to walk down on Frank to see if his lust for Myona would make him fall in place with her little plan.

Frank come here, can I talk to you for a minute?

Damn, what London, what?

This won't take long, look I just want to apologize for how I been acting and I won't do that no more.

Cool, I accept your apology, man just let that shit go London, you know you are really bugging out on me.

I know and I really am sorry, I know you're a really good guy and I know you don't deserve any of that, I really like you but I made my mistakes and I guess I just got to move on.

Yea, we got to move forward London, because I really liked you to but I can't move past what happen with my boy but we can still be good friends, maybe with even a little benefits every once in a while.

It hurt her more than ever to hear him say out his mouth, that he just wanted to be friends, that it will never be a relationship between them ever again, she did her best not to show it.

I could really see that you like my girl!

Who Myona? She alright, he said trying to stay away from eye contact.

You don't have to lie, I just seen how you looked at her when she just walked down the hall, Frank I am not gone hate or get in your way, I just want to see you happy, even if it's not with me, as a matter of fact I'll even help you get with her, I know she likes you to, she even told me!

I'll give her my blessing, yawl could date.

He could have passed out, hearing them words come out of her mouth, it was truly a surprise.

So what's up Frank, do you forgive me?

He looked her in her eyes, checking to see if she was really sincere with her words, and he seen no flaw in her, even though it was hard to believe, he really believed her.

Yeah I forgive you London! I'm willing to put the pass behind us, Frank said, as he reached in to give London a friendly hug.

Ok, so I could help you if you want my help! She searched his eyes for an answer.

London, how are you going to help me? I really don't need any help. You giving your blessing for us to date would be enough for me.

I got a little information that would be useful for you when it comes to my girl, she is everything but normal, you know we tell each other our deeps and darkest secrets, but if you don't want my help then I understand I'll stay out of it, you know, just let you do your thing, see how that works out for you, she said as she turned and started to walk away.

Frank watched as she walked away, but her words replayed in his mind over and over again. He didn't want to dismiss her, he had to at least stop her to hear what she had to say, so he chased her down, to get the juicy information she had about Myona.

London wait, he said as he gently grabbed her arm to get her attention.

What Frank! I thought you didn't need my help!

Well I thought about it, and I really like her, even though I got a little game and the ladies love me, I just don't want to mess this up, it's just something about her, she is just special to me!

She seen the look in his eyes and realized that he was really serious about her and that really made her sick to her stomach. He said she was special, she wanted so bad to ask him, what made her so special? What did she have on him? Being that they never touched, kissed, or nothing! How could he feel that way about her? So many questions she wanted to ask but she couldn't, she just had to keep it together.

Ok look so Myona is my friend, so you know she tell me almost all of her secrets!

Yeah well! Frank said as the look on his face was starting to show irritation.

You not going to believe me if I tell you!

Come on London damn! Just tell me!

Ok! Myona is kind of a closet freak on the low.

A closet freak, what the fuck is that?

Frank you serious? You don't know what a closet freak is?

Hell no! I actually have no clue about what you talking about!

She likes really weird sexual things, like having sex in weird places and she also talks about having rough sex all the time, where she wants the man she fuckin to choke and smack her around, I don't know why she likes that type of shit but she does.

What! Get the fuck out of here, I don't believe that! She doesn't look like that type of girl. Your lying, Myona is a good girl, Frank said brushing London off.

You don't know my girl, like I do! She is a fuckin freak! One time we were talking, she told me she would like to role play one day like she was being raped, she wants the person to rough house her, even go as far as choke her while he forces himself inside her, something about, she wants to feel powerless in the moment. When she told me that, I couldn't believe it even came out her mouth.

Frank didn't know what to say, he couldn't believe what he was hearing.

But don't tell her that I told you, because she is really shy around people, plus she would get mad at me if she found out I told you!

So why are you telling me in the first place then London?

Frank I know she really likes you, so if you play your cards right, you could be that lucky person,

London said as she checked his eyes to see was he going for the bate.

Damn you really think so?

Yeah, as a matter of fact I'll put my word in for you, you know the school prom is coming up, I could see if I could make it happen by then.

You serious! London I would love that; you think she would

want to be my date?

Frank if you're going to be her date, how will you make her fantasy come true?

What should I do then London?

Ok look, if she wears a black short tight mini skirt, then that means she is game, that's going to be the signal you need to give her what she wants.

London that sounds crazy! Frank said while shaking his head in disbelief.

Frank I'm her best friend, you think I would just lie to you for no reason? Do you want to be the special guy or not?

You know I want to be!

Then do what I say and she will be your girl for sure, but remember what I said, you can't tell her I told you, ok!

Ok! Ok! I won't tell her.

As London walked away she smiled, thinking to herself damn, men could be so stupid when it comes to the love of pussy.

30

Ace:

I pulled up to club 360 to meet this nigga named Low, I met him through a friend since I been back in town, we connected real quick because of his love for money, I did my homework around town and a lot of people say he is a real stand up dude, eventually I'm going to have to put that to the test, I don't need nothing but loyal people around me, my daddy use to always tell me, that every man is pulled down by a weakness, you just have to keep your eyes wide open so you don't miss it and so far I haven't seen it, the time is ticking and so I think I'm going to put him up under my first test tonight, I'm gone see how good he do under pressure. As I stare out in deep thought, my passenger door popped open, knocking me back into reality.

Hey what's up big bro?

Man you better watch what the fuck you doing, you can't just be hopping in people shit without notice, you fuck around and get yourself killed out this bitch!

Damn, big bro! my bad I'm sorry nigga, I thought you seen me coming!

No I was in this bitch deep in thought, I said as I stared off.

You know what they say big bro!

What's that?

Don't nothing come to a sleeper but a dream.

Is that right? I said as I reached for my Glock 17 with my free hand, wondering if this nigga was giving me a message or a hard time.

You my guy big bro, just keep your head up out here, shit I am not the problem, you can put your gun away, I fix problems for you. If you ever need me just call, big bro I'm hungry, you keep the food on my plate and I'll keep putting in the work.

Low, I got you, I'm gone make sure you and me both eat. I got a lot I want to talk to you about.

Talk to me about what big bro? shoot the breeze I got time.

Just hold off till tonight! We can sit down and have a couple drinks, then I could tell you everything, but right now, I got to go handle some business, I don't have the time right now!

Well that's cool, you got what I asked you for, do you?

I got half of it!

Half! Damn bro I need more than that, I told you this shit is in high demand, this gone be gone in about an hour.

Good! That way you can get my money back to me fast.

Why wait, he threw the money in his lap after he counted it in front of him, neatly stacked and wrapped in rubber bands to hold it together.

Ok now that's what I'm talking about.

What you thought I wasn't about my business? Bro I'll see you tonight and when you come, bring the whole brick, so we won't have to run back and forth, it makes shit hot.

Alright, I got you!

As he got out the car, I placed my gun back up under the seat and I popped the trunk so he could retrieve the half of brick of heroin from the back. As soon as he shut the trunk I pulled away from the curve, pulling out my phone to make a call to the one and only Ms. Ebony Ford, AKA E-B, I met her through one of my close partners Hell Rell, when I first started moving cocaine, I didn't know where to start, so for a discount on his purchases, he turned me on to all the licks around town, when I ran into E-B our connection was strong, her boyfriend was locked up at the time, so she would always call me over to buy a little coke and talk my head off about him, when she got real lonely, shit I didn't mine, at the time I would do anything to get close to her Lil sexy ass, she had these pretty brown eyes, nice full pink lips, big tits, and a Lil bitty butt that went just right with her Lil nasty walk, she really had me going, playing hard to get, till she finally gave in, I would feed her coke all night, while I work that tongue between them pretty Lil pussy lips, I would eat it all night long, by the morning, I gave her the dick, then left, I ghosted her for about two weeks. That shit drove her crazy, she was blowing up my phone, sending me all these crazy text messages about how she misses me and can't stop thinking about me so I slid over there. As soon as I came through the door I made her get on her knees, she told me she didn't suck dick and I had to be her man. All that changed when I turned and started my way to the door. After she stopped me at the door that day changed our relationship forever. I poured the coke on her tongue and fucked her face all night, through time and patience, I made her a pro, I couldn't keep her off the dick, she loved it so much, I passed her around, she became my top bitch for testing weaknesses and exposing nigga's locations. She was down for any mission as long as she got a

Lil bread and it kept me happy.

She answered on the second ring.

Hi daddy I miss you.

Lol, I miss you to baby.

You miss me, like you trying to see me tonight?

Well, it has been a while, so yeah we gone spend some time.

Why I got the feeling that isn't the reason you calling.

Baby, listen, I really need your help!

See here we go with this shit again, it's like that's the only time you call me now, when you need a favor! Damn baby what about me? What about my needs? We don't nearly spend time together like we use to and I'm still mad at you for leaving the club with that Lil dusty bitch the other night, why you didn't call her and ask her for a fuckin favor?

Baby please don't trip!

No Ace answer the fuckin question!

You know what bitch! Fuck it! I'm tired of going through this shit with you. I don't have to explain my motherfucking self to you, you are not my bitch! As a matter of fact, you don't have to call me no more.

I hung up, thinking about who I could call next to put my plan in place.

Ring, ring,

E-b was calling back.

Hello, what the fuck you want? I told you to lose my number!

Baby I'm sorry ok, stop tripping I'll do it for you.

Why the fuck we got to go through this, every time I need something handled?

I just love you baby, and you know it kills me when I see you with somebody else. But I'll do it, but can we spend some time soon?

Yeah, where you at now, I want to pick you up and take you shopping, I want to make sure you look extra nice tonight.

You know I'm up in price hill, just swing through,

Alright, I'm on my way and baby!

Yes, Ace

I love you too!

Low:

When he got out of Ace car, he signaled for one of his guys to follow him, after a while he made a call to check his progress.

A Juice, what's the deal on homie?

It hasn't been too much so far, I seen him pick up some Lil fine little bitch up on the hill, and when she got in the car, she didn't waste no time putting her head in his lap.

Fuck all that! Are you checking his stops?

Yeah I'm with him right now, by his car, they just went into the mall.

Why the fuck is you waiting by the car? Stupid ass, he could be going to meet up with his connect and you gone miss it all!

Bro why would he do that with a bitch with him?

Nigga's do all types of crazy shit around hoes, bro get in there and lay eyes on him. He makes a move I need to know about it!

Alright I got you, I'll send you something if I find it.

Right after juice hung up, he wondered what juice might find out about Ace, one thing for sure is he had to be sure on who he was dealing with. He didn't need to bring no police into the circle. It's crazy how he just popped up selling bricks on the street but don't nobody know him, usually you start young working the pack on the low level, and that's how you get a name, hell that's how Low got his name from working all the Low level blocks. Nobody just comes straight in and move straight to the top, all he could think about is how he has to find out the guy angle. He also wondered what he had to talk to him about tonight, if Juice can't deliver any information he was just going to have to just wait and see.

Ace & E-b:

As E-b searched through the clothes racks, she noticed that Ace had a real concern look on his face as if something was bothering him.

What's wrong baby?

It's crazy, but I got the feeling we being followed!

What makes you think that! E-b said as she moved her eyes around the mall to see if she could catch the vibe herself.

Bitch don't be so obvious, but it's the real black ass nigga with the heavy beard.

As she looked for the guy that could fit that description, she saw a dude who fit and looked real out of place.

Ok, I think I locked eyes on who you're talking about but what makes you think he is following us? E-b said as she searched his eyes for answers.

Because this motherfucker been behind me the whole time, I really noticed him when I picked you up from your apartment.

Damn! And you just now saying something?

I had to be sure, I could have just been tripping!

So that's why you came all the way over here to this mall when we had one way closer to the house, and here I am thinking you was trying to treat me extra special when you really were just trying to shake your tail!

Well I'm sure he's on me now, I'm just wondering how or why, don't nobody know me or my movements from around here.

That's the point! Someone sent him to find out a little more about you I guess but fuck that just keep your eyes on this ass, I'll find out what's his angle.

They stayed in the mall for hours as she went into dressing room after dressing room, trying on dress after dress trying to tire the guy that has been watching them out as much as she can so he can eventually want to leave the mall.

Ok baby he just left, now I want you to hung back for a minute I'll call you and let you know what's next.

She left Ace at the cash register and tried her best to catch up to the unknown man.

As she came out the door leading to the parking lot she spotted him getting inside of his car, no shopping bags in hand, as she headed to the car she checked her surroundings to see if the watcher had a watcher to watch his back. To her nothing seems out of place, so she walked up to the passage side and tried the door, it was open. She slid inside.

Hey! Hey! What the fuck is you doing? Juice said as he reached for his gun, looking to see if Ace was with her.

Relax! Relax! Baby, I wanted to catch up with your sexy ass and make sure we do a face to face.

I been watching you watching me.

What makes you think I was watching you?

Shit! Either you were watching me or the dude I was with and if so, I don't fuck with gay nigga's, she said as she made a move for the door to make her exit.

Naw! What the fuck! Hell Naw, I am not gay!

So you were watching me? She shut the door back and moved in a little closer to him.

So what's your name daddy?

Juice, a hold up where is your dude at? You were just in there with him and now he isn't nowhere to be found, but you out here with me.

Well Juice, if you must know I told him I had to run out to the parking lot to meet my mom, she needed some extra money for my daughter, she keeping her for the weekend for me.

Ok, so what you want?

Pull off before he come out here and see me and you together, and then it's going to be some shit, he is the jealous type and that nigga crazy as hell.

I thought you told him,

Pull off damn! I'll tell him I went with my mom and she dropped me off at the house, that way I could spend a little time with you.

She reached over and long stroked his dick, through his pants, turning him on instantly like a light switch.

Aww damn baby I see you real aggressive!

Yeah I am! When it comes to something I want, I seen you watching me, and I am not gone lie, it turned me on, my pussy got so wet, thinking about it.

Damn baby! But you don't even know me.

But I want to get to know you, if you let me.

She took his hand and let him rub his fingers through her dripping wet pussy, just to show him she was being for real, she moaned as he played with her clique.

Damn baby you are wet as fuck!

You like that baby? E-b said as she searched for the passion in his eyes.

Yes, baby shit!

Taste me!

He licked his fingers like he just got finish eating a piece of BBQ chicken.

Do I taste good baby?

Damn, yes!

Pull off so we can finish this at my house.

Juice pulled off anxious to get to her house, he thought about all the things he was going to do to her and the positions he was going to put her in, before he knew it they had pulled into her apartment complex.

Hold on baby! Pull over there by the dumpster, I see my mom's car is in the parking lot, we might have to continue this for another day.

If it is, does that mean we aren't gone be able to chill, I want you real, bad, I got a Lil money so we can go get a room if worse comes to worse.

She could see the thirst was in his eyes real, bad, he would follow her to the moon and back, so she asked without hesitation, let me see your phone so I could give you my number, I don't want us to ever lose touch, you gone be my bay, after he gave her the phone, she put her number in and gave it back, Juice called while she was still in the car to make sure it was the right number.

Damn, you don't trust me?

I do, I'm just salty you got my dick all hard and now you about to bounce on me.

We could hook up tonight! If you would like.

Darm that feels like a long time from now, how about you give me a Lil something to help me while I wait.

What you want me to taste it, E-b said while she licked her lips.

Everything she did turned him on, it was just something about her that had his nose open.

Yeah baby, just taste it a Lil bit for me, you got my dick throbbing, please don't leave me like this!

E-b slowly reached over and rubbed his thigh feeling for his dick through his pants.

Pull it out, let me see what you working with.

Juice rushed to get his pants down to his ankles.

E-b leaned over and began to lick and pop her lips on the tip of his dick.

O shit baby yes, just like that, he said as he used both hands to push her head down forcing his dick down her throat, she gladly opened up receiving every inch, not holding back drooling all over him as he fucked her throat, he leaned back and pumped as hard as he could, trying his best to empty his tank.

Damn baby I'm about to cum!

E-b reached for the switch blade out of her panties, right as she could feel he was Cumming into her mouth, she cut his dick right off, then spit the cum in his face and threw his dick out the window.

Ahhh you bitch, what the fuck you bitch!

She placed the switch blade to his throat,

I'm the last good nut you'll see nigga, now tell me who sent you!

You crazy, ass bitch you cut my dick off, screaming in pain barely able to move.

I'm gone kill you if you don't tell me what I want to know, now hurry up and spill the news.

The longer he took, the deeper the blade pressed into his neck.

Alright, Ahhh fuck, alright!

Who nigga? And I am not gone ask you again.

Low, it was low who sent me!

On what business? E-b said as she pressed his neck and reached for the phone at the same time.

He wanted me to check up on your dude business, to see if he was straight.

Give me your phone code, as she tried to look into the phone, she decided to shoot more questions, and on what grounds? See if he straight how?

The code is 3318, and he just wanted to see if he was the police, look please just let me go, I got to get to the hospital, I'm losing a lot of blood.

Lol, today you losing a lot more than that, E-b said as she sliced his neck from ear to ear, the more he tried to fight to stop the bleeding, the more she sliced in other places, opening him up all over the place, after he had taken his last breath, she checked his phone to see what type of messages had been sent, she seen nothing out of place, she wiped everything clean, got out in walked to her apartment when she got up stairs, she knocked on the neighbor's door.

Boom! Boom! Boom! Angel, come to the door.

Girl what!

Call the police, I just seen somebody dead in the parking lot girl hurry up!

Neighbor ran out to check for herself, and when seen him, you could hear her screams from a mile away, while her neighbor was making a scene, she went into the house and call Ace.

Hello, girl where the fuck is you?

Baby, it's done! And you were right he was following you, for some dude named Low.

Is that right?

Yeah he wanted to see if you were working with the police so he sent a tail to keep an eye on you!

And this motherfucker told you all this?

Yeah, after I cut his dick off and threw it out the window.

What! Where are you! Feeling sick of the thought of what happen to the guy.

I'm at home, about to roll up and watch the coroner come pick this nigga up, he dead in my parking lot, he fucked up by taking me home without asking for directions, I couldn't risk it, but I got to go, I love you love, I'll see you in a couple hours please don't be late.

She hung up watching from the window as the ambulance pulled Juice out the car trying to give him aid, and just thought to herself what of a waste of time that was. There was definitely no way they were going to be able to bring him back.

Jyel:

I was happy once I got my application filled out by my grandmother, for a while I was scared that she wouldn't support my decision, because of the profession I chose, I mean she wasn't too happy about me wanting to fight for my country but she told me as long as I go to college and stay out of the streets, she would be behind me 100% percent. I turned the application in and to my surprise, the lead Detective who teaches the program, called me back immediately and wants me to start the class today, after I shared the news with my grandmother, I went to my sister room to make sure I could tell her the news as well, but on my way, I heard a knock on the door, which stopped me in my tracks, so I ran to the front to answer.

Boom! Boom! Boom!

Who is it!

Boom! Boom! Boom!

Who is it! I still got no answer, so I snatched the door open to see who it was, London stood on the other side playing with her phone.

Hello, didn't you hear me ask who is it?

Yeah and! She said twisting her neck.

What the fuck you mean yeah and, when somebody ask who is it, you say who it is, I shouldn't have to teach you the basics every time you come over here.

Boy shut the fuck up, where is Myona, I got some shit I got to tell her, she said as she moved right pass him into the house.

He didn't know what it was about the girl, but she always rubs him the wrong way whenever he sees her. He doesn't know why his sister insist on being friends with her. Every since he has known this girl, she has had a bad name and stayed in some shit. he wanted to talk to his sister about her but he knew she would do nothing but get mad and now was not the time to give her the good news about the program because he didn't want London in his business, so he figured would just catch to her later. He grabbed his things and went out door early. He couldn't stand to be late especially for his first day in the class. He took the bus early in hopes he would make it their early to make a good impression on the instructors and as he looked out the window, the sight of the world around him hurt his heart to see all the ran down buildings in the neighborhood, he was embarrassed to say those are some of the same building he started his growth in life in. The parks he used to play in is now filled with drug pushers and users, used needles litter the grounds. Chicks selling pussy out in the open. Nothing is a secret any more, people use to look out for the kids, now all they care about is there selves. Whenever he would look on the news, all he would see is young guys getting murdered for either being in the wrong place at the wrong time or mainly because they became the target for stepping out on porch, running in the street, they lose their lives because they did it without looking both ways. It's a big lost both ways, as his thoughts fell into place all he knew is that he wanted to be a part of the change in his community. He knew in his heart he could connect with them a lot more than anybody else because he came from where there from and seen hard days in more ways than one. As he pondered on his past he thanked God for his great grandmother who took him in when both of his parents got murdered, if she didn't, there wouldn't be no telling where him and his sister would be. He thought about his brother all the time, wondering if he is alive, is he a part of the streets or did somebody take him in like their Grandmother did us. He wondered how things would be if he ever got to meet his big brother. As the bus were coming up on his stop he could see to young boys, pushing and old man around, instantly he got upset and felt in his heart he had to step in.

Hey old man, where the fuck is my money?

I don't have no money, the old man said as he tried to keep his balance from falling.

I need my money, you smoked my dope, I need my shit, I am not going to keep running into you and you come empty handed every time I see you, I am not going to keep sparing you!

I am not giving you shit motherfucker, that shit you gave me was weak!

Right after the old man's last word, one of the young guys punched the old man in the jaw, knocking him to the ground, cocking back ready to deliver another blow to the old man's head.

Hey what the fuck is you doing, beating on this old man like that! Jyel said as he caught the guys hand in the middle of him delivering another blow, throwing him back to the fence.

Young man, stay out of this! The old man said as he tried to pick himself up off the ground.

Yeah nigga, you better stay the fuck out of it, before I fuck you up, he said as he reached in his pants, pulling out a Glock 17, laying it to his side.

And what you gone do with that besides make me mad, Jyel said as he moved in closer to the young dude with the gun.

Nigga you must be stupid, the young guy said as he pointed the gun to his face, ready to pull the trigger.

Stupid! No! I'm not as stupid as you! Answer this question, how the fuck you gone pop that bitch if the gun is on safety.

The young dude pulled the gun in to see if what he was saying was true. That was just enough time Jyel needed to spring into action, as they fought for the gun a patrol car pulled up to the stop light watching from a distance.

Right as young dudes friend was about to jump in and help his friend seen the patrol car at the stop light, which seeming to be looking their way.

O shit Joe! We got to get out of here the fucking police at the light.

Yeah Joe you better get the fuck out of here before you lose your life, Jyel said as he overpowered the young dude to the wall, trying his best to make sure he doesn't end up on the wrong side of the barrel. As they continued to wrestle for the gun, the old man had finally got to his feet and began to wave down the patrol car.

Officer help! Please help!

The young dudes friend took off running, leaving his friend Joe behind, the old man caught the attention of the officer, they hit their patrol lights and rushed over to where the old man were standing, the young guy Joe had finally got his hand on the trigger and began to squeeze, bullets started flying wildly through the air, one striking the wall, another hit the patrol car which made the officer jump out the car with his gun pointed at Jyel and the young guy Joe as they continued to fight for the position of the gun.

Freeze and get on the ground now! Freeze and get on the ground now or I'll shoot the officer said not taking his eyes off the suspects.

One of the shots landed in the old man leg sending him to the ground screaming in pain, as soon as Jyel seen that the old man had been shot, he pushed the young guy away from him as hard as he could, throwing him off balance enough so he could get on the ground following the officer's orders.

Drop the gun! Get on the ground now! I'm not going to tell you again!

As the young guy caught his balance, he finally got the chance to try and dump a shot into Jyel body for causing all this bullshit, he raised the gun in his direction.

Put the gun down!

POW! POW! POW! The officer shot the young guy before he could even get a shot off, all three shots landed in his chest area, knocking him off his feet off the impact, with no strength left in his body, all he could do is watch around him, while he tried to catch his breath, Jyel and him locked eyes as they lay next to each other.

I told you, get the fuck out of here before you lose your life, now look at you, Jyel said as he cracked the biggest smile he could, watching the young guy life slowly slip away. As the ambulance was pulling up to help the young guy and the old man, the other officers had rushed in to put handcuffs on Jyel, as they picked him up off the ground, the old man started screaming from a distance to get the officers attention.

He didn't do nothing! Stop! Let him go! He saved my life! The old man said over and over again as he fought to get out of the ambulance care.

As they were just about to put Jyel in the patrol car, hc was recognized by the police chief that just pulled up on the scene.

Officer Kemp hold on! Wait a minute, I know this young man, let me have a minute with him.

Chief Detective Cooper grabbed him by the cuffs and moved him away from the officer so they would be able to talk in private.

Jyel Wright, what are you doing? I stuck my neck out for you to get into the program and you out here doing this shit! Getting into trouble, this shit is a mess, this young man is dead, another has been shot, what the hell happen Mr. Wright?

Look calm down! I didn't do anything, well kind of.

This young guy is dead and you say you didn't do anything, you think I'm stupid, Chief

Detective Cooper said as he snatched Jyel up by the shirt making sure he had his full attention, this shit isn't no game son this is serious!

The officer stepped in and separated Jyel from Chief Coopers strong grip.

Chiefl Calm down, I just got word this boy is a hero!

Huh what! The Detective Cooper said as he searched the young officer's eyes for some answers.

I talked to the older guy who got shot, and he told me that this boy saved his life, he even fought the ambulance first responder from taking care of his wound until he made sure we Imew what was going on with him.

Did you get his full statement on everything that happen from beginning to the end?

Yes, there is another officer, riding to the hospital getting the full statement right now as we speak. I just wanted to make sure I let you know what's going on, so you can release this young man, he's a hero, and by the way great job young man.

Detective Cooper looked at Jyel ready to make an apology.

It's ok Chief, Jyel said as a bright smile covered his face.

Why didn't you tell me? Why would you just let me go off on you like that?

I tried to talk but you wouldn't let me get a word in.

Thank you Officer Kemp, I got it from here, I'm going to take Jyel downtown so I could get his statement.

Ok Chief, the officer said as he turned then walked away, then stopped in his tracks to turn and face them once more.

Hey kid!

Yeah, Jyel said as he turned towards the officers.

From what I heard, you truly are a hero, I don't know what you want to do when you get a little older, but I know you would be a great cop someday, you might want to think about that.

Thanks Jyel said, as he turned and walked away with Chief Cooper, the Chief wanted to know everything from the beginning to the end, he scolded him in a way a father would his child. He made the drive hard to bear, he questioned him at every turn he made, he was beginning to feel like shit was a little deeper then he leads on.

Answer me! I need to know Jyel, what's your intentions in joining this program, he said as he kept his eyes on the road.

I mean, my intentions are to have a better life, I don't want to earn my worth on the comer, I want to have a career, make sure my life means something.

Is that right? Huh? Or you sure this isn't about trying to solve your mom and fathers case? Chief

Cooper said as he watched his every movement.

Yea and no, I mean if it was you, wouldn't you want to know who killed your mom and dad?

What type of question is that?

Yes, I would, but Jyel we been working on that case for over 10 years now, what makes you think you're going to come in and do anything different!

Excuse me! But fuck what you think, it's not your mom and dad, it's mine!

Look Jyel, I'm not trying to offend you, it's just a lot you don't know about your dads past.

So! And what's that supposed to mean? He doesn't deserve justice? What you gone tell me next, that I'm better off without him! That he was so fuckin horrible that him and my mom deserved to

Jyel calm down, now nobody deserves to die, I'm just saying before your dad died, he was being accused of some stomach turning crimes, that I know all too well, I worked some of the murders in my earlier years of joining the force and I am not going to lie, when I close my eyes at night, I still see that Cassie Humphrey girl, Chief Cooper said as the tears began to build in his eyes. Then it was a witness on the case and hours later him and his mom was murdered as well, then after that, it just seems like bodies just kept dropping all over the city with your dad's name on them, damn! It was like everyone that was around him just kept on dying. Things slowed down after he had his first son, but he put a lot of fear, in a lot of people hearts, it was a lot of people glad to see him go.

You knew my brother?

Yeah I seen him, everywhere your dad went, he went also. But I haven't seen him since your dad got murdered. I wouldn't be surprised if he isn't dead too, shit word is your dad had something to do with your brother mothers death, I don't know how true it is, but that's what I was told!

You make it seem like my dad was a monster!

Chief Cooper laughed at the top of his lungs, like he was sitting front row at a comedy show, while wiping away the tears he gained from the painful memories of Lamar Wright, he spoke on the comment he felt the best way he could,

Monster is an understatement! He had to be a worshipper of the devil himself, and I know you don't want to hear this but he either was the reason your mom got killed, due to revenge from something he did or he probably had something to do with it himself.

Man fuck you! Pull the fuck over!

The anger was building inside him the more he sat around Chief Cooper, he couldn't take being around him anymore, he had hurt him to the core with every word he spoke, rather if it were true or not, he felt he really crossed a line, the more he talked the more he was starting to lose respect for him. How could he talk about my parents that way, then call himself a friend, and could my dad have been that bad, did my dad have something to do with all those murders, could he be the reason for the murder of my mom? He started to second guess everything his grandmother had told him about his dad, and it hurt.

Jyel I'm not pulling over, now I'm truly sorry if I offended you, but I still want you in the program! I could take you being mad at me but don't throw away your future for it, you wouldn't be using your head.

Jyel stared out the window, staying clear from any eye contact, deep in thought about everything that were being placed in front of him.

You right!

About! Chief Cooper said as he tried to wait patiently for him to answer.

It's not about you and I'm going to find out who killed my mom and dad with or without your help, no matter what type of guy you say he was, because everybody deserves justice, no matter what he did, he didn't deserve to die!

Chief Cooper took in every word as he continued to drive to the district.

London & Myona:

After London entered the house she busted right into Myona's room without even knocking.

Bitch what the fuck is you doing? She said as Myonajumped, startled from London's rude and obnoxious entrance.

Bitch what the fuck is you doing busting into my room like that? How did you even get in my house? And I told you, you can't be running around my house like you run this motherfucker, if my grandmother seen you, you Imow she would trip.

Girl Jyel let me in before he left, damn chill, you act like I broke in or something, and G- ma isn't gone trip, you know this like my second home, but I have to talk to you about something, it's important! She said as her face was covered in a strong sense of urgency.

About what! What's wrong? Myona said as she rushed to the other side of the room to see what it could be that's bothering her best friend.

Girl nothing serious like that! I just wanted to know what you were wearing for the prom. I got some ideas, you know we got to show out this year.

Bitch you scared me, making me think something was really wrong and all you talking about is what we wearing to the prom, I am not worried about the prom, hell, I might not even go, I got more important shit on my mind then that!

Girl don't start that shit, you going! You going to be going off to college soon, leaving me here without my best friend, so the least you could do is go to the prom with me before you disappear out of my life.

London, you act like you can't do the same, college would be good for you, you don't have to stay here, there is nothing here for you but a waste of time and life, plus I don't know, shit I don't even have a date, nobody has asked me out yet!

Myona, first of all, you know that college shit isn't for me, so cut the shit, and you would've been had a date if you weren't so damn picky when it comes to men!

You mean, little boys! None of them dudes are my type, I just can't chill with somebody if I'm not feeling them.

Bitch you so dramatic, how you know if you feeling them or not if you never give them a chance? The question is, what the fuck is your type?

The opposite of yours, that's for sure, Myona said as she walked pass London to go sit down on the bed.

O so now you shooting shots, you trying to say I don't have no taste when it comes to men? She said, unable to hide the anger on her face from her friends deep cutting insults.

Don't get mad bitch, I'm not trying to insult you, or how you say it, shoot no shots or nothing, we just like different things in life, it's not necessary a bad thing, just a fact.

Yeah ok! So what you going to wear?

London I told you I don't know; my mind just really hasn't been focused on none of that.

Ok, well you focus on everything you got going on and I'll focus on what we wearing, ok!

London said not willing to take no for an answer.

What about our dates?

We don't need no dates, we can go with each other, as two big lesbians.

Damn bitch you suck pussy too? Myona said while laughing shaking her head to the joke she just laid down.

Huh no but I will try it, shit hell I'll try anything once!

Girl you are so nasty!

London just sat with Myona as she did her class work, deep in her thoughts about everything Myona said about them liking different things in life, though she said she was not frying to insult her, it sure felt like it, but it's ok in the end she knew she would be the one to get the last laugh.

I was thinking we should dress like twins to the prom or you don't like the way I dress either?

London you still holding on to what I said earlier? I told you I didn't mean nothing by it, you know I love you, I don't know why it's so hard for you to let things go.

Ok then, if you didn't mean nothing by it, then you will let me pick out our outfits for the prom.

See now I don't know London.

What so you gone criticize everything about me now?

Feeling guilty Myona let up,

Ok London go ahead and pick out the outfits, just please don't go crazy!

As London looked on the laptop, she ran across a couple of miniskirts and dresses that sparked her attention, she thought about what dress would be easy access not just for her but for Myona on her special night as well.

Myona can I ask you something? And I want you to tell me the truth.

Girl haven't I always kept it 100 with you?

Are you a virgin?

Myona paused not knowing just how to answer the question all together, but she has never lied to her best friend, so why lie now.

Yes, I'm a virgin, she said as she put her head down, showing her embarrassment with her answer, knowing she probably lose some cool kid points.

Bitch I knew it! You are so lame Lol, that's why you been acting all uptight, because them walls haven't been knocked down. Girl what's up with you? You better get with the program!

No, I will not get with the program, I'm saving myself for marriage!

Marriage! Girl you need to stop watching all those damn romance movies, she said as she shook her head in disgust.

Like I said, we are two different people who likes different things! Myona said raising her voice, losing her cool to the conversation.

Hoe we aren't that damn different, if so, we would not have been friends for so long.

Bitch you sound stupid, Myona said as she shook her head to the comment.

After a long time of searching through the dresses online, she finally came across one of the most scandalous one she could find.

Girl I found the perfect dress for the both of us, check this out, Myona.

She turned the laptop around so she could see.

Girl hell Naw! You trying to dress me up like a whore for the night! What you trying to do, pimp me out?

Girl don't start, you said that I could pick out the outfits, so you can't turn around and change your mind now!

Yeah I did say you can pick out the outfits but bitch, there isn't much of an outfit there, you know I don't dress like that!

Well you dressing like that for that night! For sure for sure and I'll even pay for it.

With what money?

The money I got from pre-pimping you out, so watch out bitch I got a lot of money and it's gone be a line wrapped around the corner for that virgin pussy.

O no not this pussy Lol, you better go handle that then, we both know you could.

Ok bitch we gone fight, one more hoe joke, say one more word.

They both laughed as she went ahead and bought the two dresses, one in red for her and one in black for Myona, after they was purchased, she got up and got her things, said her good byes and headed for the door. Once she made it outside, she texted a picture of Myona dress to Frank and once he didn't reply, she decided to give him a call.

Hello,

Frank what's up did you get the picture?

Yeah I got it, but what did you send me that for? You want to show me dresses and shit now, what I look like one of your girlfriends?

It's the dress that Myona is wearing to the prom.

Word, damn! Get the fuck out of here! She must really be ready to turn up wearing that shit, as he thought about her sexy ass squeezing into that tiny little dress, he grabbed himself as his dick got harder and harder.

I told you she gone be ready, I told her about the plan and you should have seen her, she was so turned on, that shit even surprised me. We dressing like twins that night.

Twins damn, is you going with a date?

She is my date,

Damn she fuck with girls too?

She moved the phone away from her ear, trying her best not to laugh, she could see he was thirty and she had him right where she wanted him, so to seal the deal, she put a little icing on the cake, she pushed him a little bit harder.

Boy you nosey!

Well does she?

A little, look if everything goes right with my girl, you just might get real lucky, she told me she always wanted to do a threesome, so you might can get me too.

Together! At the same time! I could hook up with both of y'all together in a threesome on prom night!

Frank you moving too fast, it's all about if my girl is satisfied with your performance and then we can go from there on the threesome thing, but what I'm saying is after you get finish fuckin the shit out of my girl, like you use to fuck me, then after you through then maybe, I might want you to bring that dick over my house so I could suck all her juices off that motherfucker, ok!

There was a long pause, so long that she had to ask him the question again?

Frank ok! Baby is you there?

Yeah I'm here, baby don't worry, I'm gone take good care of her.

Ok good!

Low:

As Low was getting ready to hit the club with Ace, he turned on the news to see what the weather would be looking like for tonight. He had been hitting juice phone for hours and still not getting any reply. Right as the weather man was sharing the news about the weather. Breaking news came across the screen, instantly catching his attention.

Today a man was murdered in the Bakersfield Apartment Complex in the Westside area, the man has been identified as Julius Reed 26, was found fatally stabbed in his car behind a dumpster in the complex, right now there is no information on how the man got in the apartment complex, when I asked around, nobody seemed to know him or have ever seen him in the complex before.

As we speak, Detectives are on the scene investigating, trying to find out just how the young man ended up here?

Kelly are there any witnesses? Did anybody see anything? The other reporter asked.

As of right now Bill, there are no witnesses, I was told a woman was walking past when she found him but there were no sighting of a suspect fleeing the scene, I'm going to stay on the scene for a little while longer and if I come up with something I'll be sure to update you.

Alright thank you Kelly, this is channel 9 news, I'm Bill Walters reporting.

Low couldn't believe what he was watching, he wondered if Juices mother knew the news, a deep sadness mixed with anger fell over him. He made a promise to Juices mom he would always look out for him, keep him out of trouble. He had failed at both, after he made the call to deliver the bad news, he wondered was this all his fault. Did Ace have something to do with this? All he knew was the last mission he sent Juice on and he never heard from him again after that, besides the odd text he sent with this phone number, he wondered if he was trying to send him a message, no matter what, all he knows is he's going to do a little investigation of his own. After he got dressed he headed out the door on his way to the bar to meet Ace.

Ace:

After Aiden watched the news a smile came across his face. E-b was starting to show her love more and more for him every day. Even though she showed her loyalty to him, he knew he had to keep an eye on her, she exposed her hand on just what she could be capable of, plus he had to clean her up from her mistakes, the wrong mistake could take his ass down with her. As he pulled up into her apartment complex, he realized he might be making a mistake by just pulling into their after everything that just happen here today so he quickly turned back out and parked down the street at a distance from the complex. He reached in the back seat of the car and grabbed the bags of the things he bought for her at the mall, then eventually started making his way to her door, but before he could knock, the door instantly swung open.

Baby damn, what took you so long? I missed you baby!

Girl stop it, it only been a couple of hours and you know I had to wait till shit cooled down over here and baby answer this question.

Yes, daddy, she said seductively as she made her way towards him, rubbing on his body, trying her best to grab his full attention.

Hold on, now why and the fuck did you kill this motherfucker in front of your house?

I had to make him feel comfortable baby!

Damn couldn't you do that away from your house? And I saw a couple cameras on the wall when I came in, what if it caught everything? Are you sure nobody seen you?

Baby just relax, everything is straight, I dotted all my I's and crossed all my tee's, nobody seen a thing. To be honest, I wasn't going to kill him until I noticed that I never gave him my address but yet he still drove straight to my house.

And the Camera?

They don't work, they haven't worked in months, I got a girlfriend I lick on from time to time who work in the office, and if she would have seen something, she would have hit my line so don't trip we good.

How in the hell did he know where you live? Is this dude somebody you use to mess with and you don't remember or something?

E-b pushed him and headed towards the kitchen.

O you trying to play me like I'm just some big ass hoe huh, grab a ticket and get in line ass bitch huh, you know you starting to be real fuckin disrespectful, talking about you love me, you don't love me, you only love what I could do for you, you gone keep stepping on my heart till it isn't going to be any good for anybody else.

Baby don't say that, I do love you, it's just crazy that dude knew where you stay, did you check his phone.

Yes, I did and nothing really stood out besides he kept texting and calling this dude name Low.

O yeah,

What baby, she said as she watched his movements to see if he would clue her in on the what was the importance of his name.

That nigga Low must have had us followed, that's has to be the way he found out your address, he followed me!

Ok! Who the fuck is he?

He the one, I'm taking you to meet at the bar tonight. He must be trying to put eyes on me to see how I move.

And why would he do that, is y' all at war or something?

No, he been buying a lot of work from me, and it's probably what you said in the first place, he thinks I'm the police or he trying to find out who my supplier is, maybe both!

Ok what do you want me to do daddy?

I want you to get up under him and find out his weakness, he acts like his shit is tight and I just don't believe that, because everybody got a weakness.

Yeah baby! Then what's yours? She said as she looked for the truth in his eyes.

Why do you ask shit that you already know?

If I knew motherfucker, I wouldn't ask!

You my weakness baby, always have been and always will be, he said as he walked away to look out the window. And E-b I need you to find out where he lives. We can't have him running around here a free spirit, with no ties to where we could find this dude.

Is there anything else you would like for me to do master, E-b said showing her sarcasm.

Bitch stop playing, this shit is serious!

I know it's serious, the question is why you doing all this if you aren't frying to free yourself from a war!

I got a lot on my plate, so I need a Lil help while I move business around, I did my homework on him, I just got to do a little more before I give him the keys to the city.

Now that's funny, because I'm surprised you got any keys to give to the city in the first place. You use to talk about how you hate drugs and drug dealers because drugs were the main reason for your mom and dad dying, now all of a sudden, you want to be the kingpin of the city. And speaking of keys, I'm gone need some myself after tonight, I see you getting use to claiming my pussy on your taxes, I might as well get some of the benefits!

Now my personal business is my personal business, so stay in your place when it comes to my mom and dad, don't speak about them, that shit isn't cool, I told you all that stuff in confidence, why would you throw it back up in my face?

Baby I'm sorry but,

No buts Ebony, it's either you got my back and trust my judgement on things or not!

You know I do, she said as she dropped her head, feeling bad that she spoke out of place about his parents.

Well stop asking all these motherfucking questions then, and you know I'm gone take care of you now put one of these dresses on you picked and make sure you wear the best one for tonight, I want this nigga to lose his mind when he sec you.

As he talked, he watched her undress, which he loved to see her do, she has an amazing body. Her shape is real petite but demands attention in any room she walked into, her tits set up like a young woman in her first year of college, she has these pretty little feet he would suck on any day. Her hair falls to her shoulders and she got these puffy little lips that drive him crazy when she looks at me a certain way, and she has a little bitty cute ass that sat just right. As he watched her put on dress after dress, he could tell she loved the attention, her body language filled cups for his thirty ass to drink. As she tried on everything he bought her, nothing stood out until the very last one, it was an all red dress, so tight it looked like it was painted on her body, red hills, with the red D&G frames to match. Damn she was hot.

I like it! That's it baby, that's the one!

O so you like what you see huh?

Hell yeah! Ace said, the more he watched her the harder he noticed his dick had gotten in the moment. He tried his best to stay away from keeping eye contact, it was the only way he could keep his composure, the temptation was strong he had to keep looking away!

Does it look good enough that you want to rip it off of me?

E-b of course it does, but we got to go, we can't be late.

You never explained our approach for the night! E-b said as she bent over looking back to see if he was watching.

What you mean? He said as he got side tracked from the view.

Arn I your date for tonight, and I act un loyal to you because I'm so turned on by his charm, am I the ex-girlfriend who is hating on you, giving him information to see if he is loyal to you, if he is, he would run back and tell you I was throwing shade.

Naw nothing like that!

Ok so tell me what you got in mind then daddy.

I want you to act like you don't know me, that way once you spend a little time with him, he won't mind opening up.

A little time with him, damn daddy how long is this shit going to take?

Could be a week or a couple of months, just until you find out where he stays, how he moves, and what his weaknesses are!

Sound like to me you want me to be this nigga girlfriend or something. You trying to hook me and this motherfucker up in a relationship so I could leave you alone or something? Damn you frying to pass a bitch down to your homie? That's a lot of dick sucking and pussy pushing to get that type of information, especially if he anything like you.

And what's like me like?

Secretive and tight lipped, you still haven't eaten a bitch pussy yet, but that's gone change today, I need this pussy licked and don't forget to run by that ass hole either!

Damn you nasty, I said in deep thought about her request, the fact that she demanded me to eat her pussy made me want too even more, shit, closed mouth don't get fed.

So lay down, E-b said as she pointed in the direction she wanted him to go.

Hold up, hold up, I didn't say if we had a deal or not, he said as she pushed him back on the couch climbing on top of his face, pulling her dress up to her chest.

You gone give it to me whether you like it or not, she said as she straddled his face, making him taste her sweet juices one lick at a time, pussy to ass, ass to pussy, she came all inside his mouth, dammit he was turned on and he couldn't turn it off if he tried, after she was done, she got up and fixed herself in the mirror.

Caught up by her moving on from the situation, like nothing never happen.

Baby what is you doing? You got my dick hard as hell, come fix it! Ace said in a begging tone.

Huh uh and fuck up my makeup I just spent hours getting ready! Not a chance and if we get into all of that we are going to be late remember, if you really want some of this, then after the bar, you'll come back through tonight and see me, she said as she cut out the living room light and headed for the door with her keys in hand. As they drove to the bar it was a complete silence between them, as Ace lay deep in thought.

Baby is you mad at me? She said as she batted her eyes at him in a playful manor.

Yeah, I don't even know why you asked, you know I'm mad as hell, why you asking them stupid ass questions!

E-b began to laugh so hard, the tears began to pour down her face, how are you going to get mad at me when I suck your dick all the time and you don't do nothing to please me in return me, hey I got to win one day, why not today.

You told me you cum when you suck my dick, that's a two for one special, you should thank me.

I do cum, but that still don't mean I don't want to feel your touch, I'm a woman every once in a while I need these walls tore down, but your just like any other man I know, nothing matters but what you want, it's all about what you could get, fuck me huh!

Put your head in my lap, hurry up, put your head in my lap, he said over and over as he reached for the back of her neck.

I said no motherfucker, what the fuck you don't get?

O shit get down, do it now, Low's car is pulling up on the side of us, I don't want him to see us together.

As He grabbed her head forcing it into his lap, Low's car pulled up on the side of them, trying his best to get his attention.

A yo, Ace, roll down the window!

As Ace rolled down the window, Low could see he had somebody in his car, who looks to be giving him head while he is driving.

Damn my bad my man, I didn't mean to interrupt your moment, I just seen your car and thought

I flag you down.

Naw it's cool, I was just about to call you after I was threw here.

We still meeting up at the bar right?

Awe shit, yeah, yeah at the bar no doubt, as he moaned from the pleasure he was receiving.

Low laughed at Ace reaction, alright make sure you don't leave me hanging, Low said as he drove off, not even waiting for a reply

E-b you can get up, he's gone now.

She lifted her head, quickly fixing her hair in the mirror, if I would have stayed down there any longer, you probably would have got what you wanted, you always keep them balls smelling really good, damn what you Zest fully clean, that shit drive me crazy.

Girl whatever, you got to stay on point, dude almost pulled up on us.

How was I supposed to know that shit was real, you could have been just trying to trick me into sucking your dick, she said as she popped her lips and twisted her neck.

Girl please, I don't have to trick you to do nothing, if I want it then I'll get it.

Low:

As he rode off he raised the window, so he could make a call.

Yo what's good fam,

What's up Baby Yee, is everything good for tonight? I just caught Ace at the light and he told me he was going to meet me at the bar.

Did he act funny like he had something to do with Juice getting murdered?

No, he didn't act funny at all but I do think I need just a little more time to fill him out, but I know he had to have something to do with it, shit just don't add up, I tell Juice to keep an eye on him and then hours later, he ends up dead, you tell me what you think.

That does sound suspicious, well you already know I'm up for the job, just give me the signal and I'll air his ass out right where he stands.

Yeah just wait for my word, don't do nothing until you hear from me first.

Ok, how am I going to know who he is?

We gone meet at the bar, I'm gone walk up and give him a hug, then signal for the bartender to get us some drinks. That's going to be the sign I'm with him and we on track, just make sure you stay close and keep your eyes open, I don't need you getting side tracked fucking with them bitches.

Bro I got this, you don't have to worry, now let me get off here and finish getting ready, then I'm going to be on my way.

Now you sure you got this Baby Yee? Because if you can't handle this I could get somebody else to do it!

Low I got this, don't trip, I put that on the crown, king!

Alright

After they hung up Low laid back in his seat letting the guilt overpower him from Juices death, all he knew is he has to make Ace pay for what he did, he told Juices mother he would take care of it and one thing he has never done is broken a promise, he couldn't just let his cousin death be in vain. He knew that if anybody could get the job done, it would be Baby Yee, he been one of his number one hit man from the crown for years, his loyalty is no mistake, whenever he called, he would get it done and do it clean, where shit wouldn't trace back to the team, after tonight he could bury this shit with Juice and move forward with plans on taking care of Juices kids, making sure they straight. He felt like that was the least he could do.

Ace:

Before Aiden dropped E-b off with her friend around the corner from the bar, he gave her the details about him meeting Low at the bar and how he felt would be a good approach for her to pull up and talk to him but not without putting some type of secret code in place to let her know that he was ready, so she had to be in the right place so she could keep an eye out. As he pulled up to the front door of the bar, he shot her a text to let her know, that he everything was falling in place. As he stepped out the car he checked his soundings to make sure he wasn't being watched then he headed into the bar. Once inside, it looked like the whole city came out tonight, some guys pulled out some of their finest rides, washed up and ready to go. So many sexy ladies were everywhere, it was hard to keep his head in a straight line. Even though he hasn't been in town literally since he was a kid, it still felt as if he had never left, like he never missed a beat as if he has been there for years, everyone he came across were starting to embrace him like he was family, as he walked in, the bartender motioned for him to come in her direction.

Hey handsome how you doing tonight? She said as she batted her eyes, showing her strong interest in his presents.

I'm doing alright Ms. Carly, how about yourself?

I'm doing a whole lot better now that you here,

Is that right, he said as he smiled at her, noticing her flirtatious ways over flowing like champagne from a fresh poured glass, trying his best to let her down easy, without hurting her feeling, even though she was a very attractive woman, older women had never been his type.

Come spend some time with me before you get out of here tonight, she said as she turned to make a drink for a customer, showing whoever wanted to see that amazing shape she was in possession of.

Ok I'll try, he said as he took a quick peek, then he turned to walk away. She called for him one more time, yes Ms. Carly.

Ace I won't bite, unless if that's what you like.

As he smiled and turned around to scan the room he seen Low walk in the bar, looking around trying to locate him, it was time they had that talk.

Myona:

As she sat on the bed reading her history books a deep loneliness came over her out of nowhere, for a while now she has been feeling like she has no life, just school and home, her intention are to do more, but she didn't know what it was that she really wanted to do, and it really didn't matter all she knew is she just wanted to do something, as she picked up her phone, she hated the fact she didn't have any friends, but London, she even thought about being in a relationship but just couldn't find anybody that could match her taste, which only made her feel worse, she began to question herself, was she really too picky, what was it that draws her more away from men then towards them? Was it the way she was raised or the lack of trust she had for them because of what happen to her mother, she fought for an answer between the two. Right before she let her thoughts get the best of her, London began to call her.

Hello,

Bitch what are you doing?

Studying for my exam I have to do on Monday, why what's up?

You always studying, get your head out that book for a minute and come outside with me for a while.

And do what London? I am not going with you to hook up with no lame ass guys.

Who the fuck said anything about a motherfucking dude, I said come outside with me, enjoy the fresh air on your face, you can continue to be a book worm tomorrow if you like.

I don't know if fresh air is the only thing your ass want to feel on your face, Myona said as she laughed, then quickly turning back to serious, I still got a lot to do here, we might have to go out some other time.

Girl! Not only do you got jokes, I knew you was going to act like this, I wasn't even going to call your ass, you boring ass bitch!

I'm not boring, don't say that, at the end of the day I just make sure I take care of my business, my daddy, use to always say business over bullshit, and I carry that model with me every day.

Myona when is you going to start living your life having fun? I am not getting on you for taking care of your business but damn, you got to give that shit a break sometimes, can you honestly say your happy right now? Always locked in your room with your head in a book.

Yes, and no!

Yes, you lying and no you're really not, so come on come outside with me tonight, we going to have a lot of ftm, just you and me, shit I'm started to get depressed myself from heartbreak and loneliness because my only friend don't want to be my friend when I need her. So come on Myona!

Ok, ok, I'll come out with you but if this ends up being about a dude and not about us, then I'm out, you hear me!

Yes, mother I hear you, London said as she closed her eyes on the other end of the phone trying not to get irritated.

You promise !

Yes, I promise, it's going to be all about you and me, now hurry up and get dressed, I'll be there in 10 minutes we going to the fish tank tonight.

The fish tank, the adult bar, girl we aren't old enough to get in there, now I said I want to come out but I am not for, getting in no trouble.

Once again girl, don't trip I got a Lil friend that work at the door, he gone be able to get us in and if he can't, we are just going to have to go somewhere else, so like I said, hurry up and get dressed I'm on my way, I got my mom's car for the night.

73

As much as she wanted to tell the girl no, she didn't want to end up on the other end of another lonely night, so she said ok and got off the phone to get ready.

Ace:

As I set at the bar, Low walked up and gave me a hug, which was odd and ordered a couple shots for us to start the night, as I watched his body language, I could tell that something was on his mind, so I tried to throw some questions around to see if he would be willing to open up.

So what's up brother, how you feeling tonight? I said searching for an answer, as he looked at me like he was trying to look deep into my soul.

I'm alright, it's just been a lot going on with the family, he said as he looked away, trying hard to fight back the tears from flowing.

Bro, if it's something on your mind, we can talk about it, real talk, I'm here for you, I know how it is, when it comes to family,

Well, yeah, it's just that my little cousin got murdered today and it's been bothering me really bad, as he spoke he watched to see if Ace body language would change and when it didn't, he tried his best to just change the whole subject altogether, but I am not here for all that I want to know what is it that you want to talk to me about?

Bro we could just chill and throw down some more drinks and focus on the business part of things later, I need you focused and I know that's hard to deal with, I'm sorry for your lost.

Naw I'm good, Ace man I need to focus on business because without it, ain't no telling what I would be doing right now.

Once again I know about family lost, my mom and dad got murdered, well my dad murdered my mom then he got murdered the same night.

Karma is a bad motherfucker, damn that's fucked up, in the end nobody wins that war, that is most definitely a lose, lose, situation. I wouldn't know how to feel after that, like do I get mad at my dad for what he did? And should I feel like my dad deserve it because of what he did, I don 't know, that's just a fucked up situation to choose from, the pain alone I don't know if I would have been able to get through that Ace.

Well, I did and you will too, Ace said as he leaned over and patted him on the back, so what I wanted to talk to you about was, changing your position in our involvement.

What you mean changing my position? Low said at the same time making it his business, to get his hand on his' gun, which is located in his jacket pocket, trying his best not to draw attention to the situation.

I mean just that! I want to change your position, I want to bring you in as a partner in my business operation, I been checking around on your name and all I could find, is a good track record and I need that type of business and a loyal friend around me, that type of love around me.

Ok that sounds good but what's the catch? Low said as he looked around to check his surroundings.

Why would it be a catch?

What makes me so special? If I got this right, you just going to come down here and hand me the keys to the city, just off my name, just off a couple of questions you asked around town, men lie and bitches lie too and the real truth is you don't know me from a can of paint.

You right, I don't know you but I frust the word of my people and from what I could see about you, you got a good heart, so I'm going to give you a chance. Plus, I have a lot of business to take care of while I'm here and I don't want to spread myself out to then, so I need you to run this part of the business while I take care of the other business I have lined up, I got to keep my hands clean for a while, is that a problem for you? Can you handle that or not?

Low looked at Ace shaking his head in disbelief, then shot a slight smile and said, yeah I could handle that, the question is when do I start?

I'm going to cut right to the chase I'm going to start you off with 10 bricks, if you do good with that, the next one would be about 50.

50 what! 50 bricks? Low said as his eyes lit up like a Christmas tree, he couldn't believe what he was hearing.

Yeah 50 bricks! Is that too much for you to handle? If it is, let me know now.

No hell no I could handle it, I got you, believe me, I won't let you down.

I hope not, if you stick with me I am going to make you a very rich man Low, I just need you to be loyal to me and I will be loyal to you, I could be the brother you never had, but look man, I have to use the bathroom, I got to piss really bad, then we can go out to the car and switch shit up, I brought the 10 bricks with me.

Ok cool, as Ace was walking away, Low's phone started to vibrate from an incoming message to his phone via text, before he could read the message, a young lady approached him out the corner of his eye. Before she walked up, he had noticed her staring at him the whole night from the other end of the bar, now she had come to speak.

Hey handsome, are you here with somebody?

Naw, how about you? Are you in here with somebody?

No, and you know not to ask me that!

And why not?

If I was in here with somebody I would not be in your face right now!

And how do I know that?

I'm not that type of girl!

Too bad because that's just the type I like, Low said as he looked down to his phone to read the message that Baby Yee sent.

Low stay clear from the bathroom, I'm about to leave him in that motherfucker, no love, I put that on the crown!

The message nearly snatched all the air from his body,

Well if that's your type I can't fix that!

Accuse me Ms. Lady, what's your name? Low said as he scanned the room looking for Baby Yee, he caught him out the corner of his eye making it his way through the crowd towards the bathroom.

My name is E-b and what does it matter? I'm starting to feel like I'm not your type.

E-b I want you to stay right here I got to use the rest room, then when I come back maybe you can change my mind on what I do and don't like, all I know is you are beautiful enough to talk me into a lot of things I wouldn't usually do.

Is that right?

Yeah, now stay right here I'll be right back, as he moved pass her, he tried to place a call to Baby Yee to tell him to stand down, he couldn't kill Ace just yet, he had to get in deep then knock him down when the time is right. As he called Baby Yee, his phone was going straight to the voicemail, which made him pick up his pace even more to try to stop him before he went too far.

Ace:

As Ace went into the bathroom, he had to use the restroom so bad that he thought he was going to urinate all over himself, so he ran to the closet stall that he could, so he could relieve himself all of his problems. As the door were closing behind him, somebody stepped in behind him very quietly closing in on the space between them, Ace instantly notice that it was a figure that stood by the door waiting for him to come out, not thinking of the worse, he just assumed they just wanted to use the stall next, after he used the bathroom, he went to step out so the next person can have their turn and he heard the gun cock, then the bathroom door flew open,

Bitch, don't you motherfucking move, you know what time it is, he said as he aimed the gun straight at who he knew to be Ace's head.

Come on man what you want? You can have all the money I got on me, just don't pull that trigger, I got a family!

Baby Yee laughed and proceeded to reach for Ace pockets, as he was in motion, the bathroom door flew open and before he could look up a shot rang out. POW! Striking him in the chest, sending him instantly to the ground. As he looked up he could see it was in fact Low who shot him. Ace stepped outside of the bathroom stall and reached down and snatched the money back out of Baby

Yee hand, that he violently snatched out his pocket not even a minute ago.

Gone! Get out of here Ace I'll take care of the rest, you got to keep your hands clean I don't want you in here.

Naw I ain't going nowhere, I wouldn't miss this for the world, as a matter of fact, he pulled his gun from his waist and aimed the gun at Baby Yee head, we could do it together so we could be bonded by blood.

Low moved in closer to Ace, his mind was racing not knowing what to do next, should he up the gun on Ace to save Baby Yee life, or should he put his boy in the ground and secure his future, while Low was fighting with his thoughts, Baby Yee was not only fighting for air, he was fighting for words as well.

Lo, Lo, please Lo

What motherfucker, speak up I want to hear this, Ace said as he stepped in closer to hear what he had to say.

Before Baby Yee could say another word, Low quickly deliver a couple of shots into Baby Yee his head and chest, finishing him off.

Low why the fuck you shoot him yet? That motherfucker was trying to say something!

Ace, we don't have no time for that, we got to get the fuck out of here, clean without making a scene now let's go!

As Ace put away his gun and walked back out into the crowd, Low hurried up and tried to check

Baby Yee pockets for his phone, he had to have it, he just texted him a few minutes ago, It was important that he find it because he knew that would be the one and only thing that could link him to his murder. As he checked all of his pockets they were empty, not a phone in sight.

Fuck! He thought to himself, if he didn't have it then who the fuck did, as he got deep in his thoughts, he knew deep in his heart this would come back to haunt him later, he hurried up and fixed himself and went back out to the bar to meet Ace, as he approached him, he was sitting at the bar with the two chicks he left at the bar before he went to go save him in the restroom.

Low I'm so glad you could finally join us, is everything cool with the family?

Huh, he said threw off from the whole conversation altogether.

You said you had to call home and check on the family, is they good? Ace said as he stared at him up and down to see if he could keep his cool.

Yea, everything cool, he said as he took his seat back by E-b.

Damn baby what took you so long? I was beginning to think you was going to stand me up, E-b said as she betted her eyes at him in a seductive way, trying her best to get his full attention.

Naw baby you to damn sexy to stand up, Low said as he pulled her in close, making room for her to sit on his lap, so what you doing tonight?

I don't know, it depends!

On what baby, Low said as he searched her eyes for the answer.

It depends on if you really trying to get to know me or if you just trying to fuck.

Low laughed as hard as he could, ok, Ms. Lady, so what is it that you think I want to do?

See that's the problem, I don't want a man that makes me go off my thoughts alone, I need one who can tell me what he wants, I hate guessing, E-b said as she pulled away, showing that she was ready to make her exit.

Hold up, baby where you going?

Away from here if you can't be straight up with me, right now you looking like the normal guy

I'm use to and I need more than the normal treatment baby, I'm a queen.

So that means you not going give me no pussy tonight?

Finally, a little honesty, but the answer is no, you can't get no pussy tonight, I just am not like that, but you are more than welcome to get my phone number, then we could chill another time.

Usually he would tell a bitch to keep it pushing, especially if she wasn't fuckin on the first night but it was something about her that drew him to her, that made him want to get to know her, for the first time in a long time, he was willing to chase.

Ok, I'll take that number but I am not ready to go home yet, will you stay out and kick it with me for a little while longer?

Before she could answer, a loud scream came from the back of the bar.

O my God, call 911, somebody been shot!

The whole crowd shifted to the door, frying to get away from the scene as fast as they could.

Ace let's go bro, somebody got shot, we got to get out of here.

Ace finished his drink off and headed out the door behind Low.

Myona:

As London was pulling in to the parking lot, it looked as if the bar were closing because everyone was exiting the front.

It's still early, I know the club isn't about to close already, London said with a disappointed look on her face.

Girl it must not be meant to be, let's get out of here and slide somewhere else, I know you aren't trying to chill out here!

Naw we can go but I got to pee really bad, I'm going to see if they will let me use the bathroom before they lock the door.

London pulled in a parking spot, jumped out and ran to the front door, as she was going in Ace was coming out.

Ace, she said as she passed by, she got no reaction, so she called his name again and pulled his arm to make sure he sees her.

Damn what! He said as he snatched away looking to see who it was so badly trying to get his attention.

You gone act like you don't see me? You just gone walk right pass me Ace?

As he stared at her, he tried his hardest to try to remember where he even knew her from or what's her name, the look on his face gave everything away,

Damn you don't know my name! it's MoMo, she said as she snapped her neck showing her attitude.

As soon as she said her name he remembered her, the chick he met in the bar the other night who sucked his dick all morning, damn near had to beat her off the motherfucker with a stick. He also remembered kicking her out right after, so he thought when he seen her again they wouldn't be on good terms.

Yeah, I do remember you MO baby, I were just on the move, so I didn't see you, don't beat me up baby.

You lying Ace but it's cool, that's probably why you didn't call me because you forgot about me so quickly, you must have a lot of hoes on your team.

Don't trip baby, look what you doing tonight, he said as he thought about how the liquor was making him feel, and how he could sole lay back and let her do all the work all night until the morning.

I don't know why?

I want you to come over tonight, I lost your number and I was hoping I see you again.

Ace bring your ass on we got to go! Low screamed at him from his car.

Before he could walk out of her life again, she asked him for his phone then hurried up and called her phone from his, so she could make sure he wouldn't get away this time, then she added her number personally to his phonebook.

Come on Ace!

I'm coming damn! Hold on!

Make sure you call me tonight, I'm gone be waiting on your call, London said as she seductively walked away, working her switch because she knew he would be looking.

As he walked away shaking his head, to the thought of MO, he looked up and seen this bad Lil cutie stepping out of the car trying to fix herself. She had an amazing shape, with the prettiest little toes any man could ask for and wouldn't have no problem sucking, from head to toe, she was beautiful, for once in his life, he believed in love at first sight. He started walking in her direction, there was no way he could leave without at least trying to get her number, before he could speak, the girl took the wrong step and lost her balance, trying her best to grab onto something to break her fall, Ace rushed to her aid catching her before she could hit the ground. As he helped her up, she turned to look at the person who was holding her tight, then they locked eyes and suddenly he got lost for words.

Thank you, I'm so embarrassed, I can't believe I fell, like that, these damn shoes tend to work against me sometimes.

Naw you cool, you don't have to explain, I'm just glad that I was here to help break your fall, I would have hated to see something like that happen to a pretty girl like you. If I had the chance I would catch you every time you fall.

Caught off guard by his response, she stared him down to make sure she heard what, she thought she heard.

What's your name? she asked,

Ace!

What's yours?

She thought about giving him her real name, and sexy, but she wanted to make sure she would be safe just in case he is the weird type, so she made up one but not giving it to much thought, so it just poured out her mouth.

Meme,

Meme! That's your name?

Yeah it is, do you got a problem with that, she said as she chased his reaction.

No, I was just expecting something like Lisa, or maybe Tiffany!

O so I tell you my name, you don't like it and so now you want to change it, just like a man!

And what's that fucking supposed to mean Lol?

That you probably just want to try to control me, like all the other man do and if so, that isn't happening.

Lost for words, he just smiled, as he helped her get back in to the car.

Ace what the fuck is you doing, is you fuckin, crazy motherfucker, we got to go, Low screamed from outside his car window as he pulled up on the side of him.

As he was about to speak, she stopped him right in his tracks, just go ahead, I'll call you I don't want your boy to have a heart attack.

Call me! I am not playing.

Or what! What you gone do if I don't? she said but at the same time she watched his body language showing that he didn't want to leave, it made her smile, no go ahead, as she seen him turn back around, I was just fucking with you go, I'll call you.

She watched him as he went in his trunk and handed the guy who was scaring at him to hurry up and leave a big black duffle bag, it was then it became obvious how he gets his money. Right then and there something told her to get rid of his number, that she didn't need to be involve with people who move in them types of life styles, nothing good could come from it, but the other part of her wanted to find out what he is truly about, it was just something about him that made her get butterflies in her stomach. She continued to watch and After he handed the dude the bag, he said a couple of words, jumped in his car and drove away, right as he was almost out of sight, London came running up to the car with her face covered in panic.

Bitch we got to go, she said as she jumped in the driver seat, not looking for a seat belt, flying out of the parking spot, headed for the street, on her way to the express way, not saying a word.

What is the fuck going on London? Who are you running from?

Bitch I went to use the bathroom and found out somebody got killed in the motherfucker!

What! You know who it is?

I heard it was Baby Yee, and if it is, it's most definitely going to be some shit that's about to pop off behind that.

Sounds like he was well known!

Well known isn't the words, the crown got a lot of love for that dude for sure, I been heard he up in the ranks.

Who is he and what is the crown? Is that a gang or something, she asked as the confusion poured out in her facial expressions.

Well no and yea, it's really some hood shit.

Hood shit! I said not catching on to anything   saying.

Bitch just forget it! Damn you are such a fuckin white girl, she said as she laughed at her as hard and as loud as she could.

Anyways, so where is we headed now? I asked as I tried my best to just change the subject altogether.

Bitch I seen my boo, I'm about to drop your ass off, as London spoke, the car began to pick up speed.

See that's the shit I been talking about, ready to jump up and leave me at the drop of a dime over some dude, with all that talk, it's about us, we gone say fuck chilling with the guys tonight talk!

Where did I lie Myona, huh! Where did I lie, it is fuck'em tonight, that's why I'm dropping you off so that's what I can go do bitch is fuck'em, I can't fuck you, you going to try to fight me as soon as I try to eat that pussy.

And bitch you damn right too, I'll punch your gay ass right in the face, you know I don't get down like that.

So how you get down? London said as she ran her tongue over her wet juice lips, you want to eat it, I'll let you eat this big motherfucker.

London quit fuckin playing with me! You know I hate when you do that shit, don't play with me like that!

Alright I'll stop playing with the little baby, she said in her baby voice, trying her best to piss her off even more.

Man damn I swear if you weren't my girl, I would most definitely would've punch you in the face!

So who was the dude you were talking too when I was walking back to the car? I could see somebody, but I couldn't make out his face, London said as she leaned in real close to make sure she could be as nosey as she possibly could.

Myona thought really carefully before she gave an answer to her question, because ever since she has known London, London would only want to know who she was talking too so she could try to date the guy herself, so instead of telling her friend the truth, she just decided to lie.

Girl it wasn't nobody, just some lame ass dude with some hot as breath, blowing fire on me, trying his best to get my number, I sent him on his way.

Lol believe it or not, you should of gave him the number,

And why is that?

The ones with the hottest breath, eat the best pussy!

Bitch I bet you would know

O you know I know, 101!

As Myona leaned back in her car seat, staring out the window, a text came through to her phone from a number she never seen before, so she opened the text and it read,

I got the feeling, you really something special.

As she read the message word for word a big smile spread across her face.

Boy whatever, I bet you up to tell me anything right now, you been listening to that loud music and you full of that liquor, feeling good, probably thinking right at this minute, damn I need some pussy and some head, in my man voice Lol.

Lol no I am not, I was calling to see if you made it home ok, Ms. Know it all, every man doesn't always, just want pussy and head from a woman.

Rolling her eyes to the back of her head, she pushed a little harder to check his angle,

So what is it that you want? If you don't mine me asking!

I want to talk, and smile,

Listen don't start this shit tonight, I don't feel like being bullshitted around, you want to talk and smile, don't be fake, show me the real you.

To be honest, this is the real me, I just never had the chance to express myself to a real woman, I don't know why but, the feeling and vibe you give me is so different.

Aww look at you, we haven't been on the phone for five minutes and you already falling in love and shit.

As she laughed, a shyness fell on him that he has never seen before, it hasn't been even two hours that passed by, and he couldn't stop thinking about her.

Girl who is you texting, all over there smiling from ear to ear and shit, London said as she could barely keep her eyes on the road.

I might be, but look I'm tired of texting, let me call you so I could hear your voice.

She wanted to talk but didn't want London to be all up in her conversation, so she decided to decline on the offer.

Why! Are you with your dude right now?

Why in the fuck would I be even talking to you if I got a

dude? Do you think I'm that type of woman? Please let me know now, if that's what you think about me, because that isn't how I run my business !

Damn, I didn't mean to put the heat up under your wig, you don't have to be on guard all the time, chill, learn how to let loose.

I bet you do want me loose, so I could be another one of your hoes that you knock down or better yet, you walk all on like a door mat.

As he smiled at each text she sent, showing how tough she real is, he began to fall for her more and more.

Don't worry about none of that, me and you in this for the long run, I'm going to make you my girl one day, not no door mat, I like you just the way you are.

How are you so sure? We haven't even been on a date yet, and who's to say I'm going to like you after the date, I might decide to just pass on you altogether.

No you're not!

How are you so sure?

Because I'm gone treat you like the queen that you truly are, all you got to do is give me a chance, that's all I'm asking for!

As he waited for Meme to reply back with an answer, the phone kept ringing over and over again with the name MoMo coming across his line, who the fuck is this? He thought as he tried his best to put the number with the name. Unable to recognize the two, he decided to just answer the phone.

Hello,

Baby what's up, it's getting late, I still want to come see you, what you doing? Where you at?

I'm still out taking care of some business, I'm going to have to hit you back a little later. Just make sure you up!

How later? Look you am not about to have me up looking for a call and then you stand me up.

Look before it gets too late, I'm gone slide you an address, so you can go and relax and wait for me to get there.

Ok, I could do that, if you shoot the address now, like I said, you are not about to have me up looking stupid.

Alright, I'm about to shoot you the address, but I got to go, I'll see you in a minute.

After he hung up, he went right back to texting Meme,

Baby I want to hear your voice; can we make that happen?

Liking the thirst, he was showing, she decided to submit just a little bit.

Ok, just give me a minute I'm almost home, I would answer now, but I don't want my friend to be all in my conversation,

O so I'm your little secret?

I wouldn't say that you a secret, I just don't like to mix my relationships with my friendships, I'm more of a private person.

As he listened to every word she spoke, he could sense her realness, he had the feeling that he would be in good hands with her, she might be the one, he just might hand his heart too.

Ok cool, there isn't anything wrong with that, just call my

phone when you get home, as a matter of fact, I'm going to call you myself if it takes you longer than an hour.

O so you my daddy now, you sound like my brother or something.

Good I like that about him, he looking out for Lil sis!

You mean big sis, he my little brother, but I'll call you when I get home and you better answer.

Yes, ma'am, he said as a smile crossed his face.

E-b & Low:

As they rode in the car, they rode in complete silence, that was until E-b broke the mode.

Ok so tell me, what's your greatest fear?

As he leaned back in his seat, for the first time, he didn't speak quick, he actually gave the question some real thought, not able to come up with what he felt was the right answer, he decided to just speak from the heart.

To tell you the truth, I don't know what I fear, what about you, what's your greatest fear?

Me not finding real love, just because it's so hard to connect with someone, who I think would truly love me, who would put me first.

And that's something that you fear? Not ever finding love? Shit, nobody has ever loved me all my life and I'm doing just fine, what the fuck you need love for?

Love rules the world; I need love to feel safe, to know for once, somebody has my back and I won't be the only one looking over my shoulder, it's hard out here alone.

As Low listened to what E-b had to say, he began to get a strong vibe that she was going through something and for some reason, he wanted to know what that was.

I hear you baby, but I don't know how that feels, everything in my life, all my life, has been take, take, take, let alone give, me some love, Low said as he stared off into space, letting the words, build his emotions one at a time.

As E-b sat and watched him, it became very clear to her, what was missing in his life, and the only reason she could find it so quickly is because it's the same thing that's missing in her life as well, to really feel loved, the more they talked, the more she seen, they weren't that different at all.

Trying his best to keep his composure, he asked her where she stayed and the car broke into complete silence.

Baby do you hear me? He said as he tried to stare in her eyes to get a vibe on how she was feeling at the moment.

Yeah, I hear you, I'm just a little deep in thought.

About? What you don't trust me?

Could I trust you? Could you control yourself because if not let me know now!

Damn, you act like you spending the night with me or something.

That's what I was planning on doing, but if you don't want me to stay over then it's cool, I'll find some where to go, all I know is I just don't want to go home right now.

Why? You on the run? He said as he cracked a smile to try to lighten the mood.

Laughing from the question, but her face went right back into a strong seriousness.

I'm just tired of being alone, I don't want to be alone tonight, I don't think I could take being alone tonight but I don't want to wrestle you off the pussy all night because you can't keep your hands to yourself, and you seem like an alright dude but this isn't that type of tonight and if that's what you want then I am not tripping, I'll go, I could catch up with you later, I might take you out to dinner or something, but I don't want you to catch no mixed signals, I'm letting you know everything up front.

The more she talked, the more he could feel, things he once had a strong hold on, weakening, he wanted her, he placed it in his mind, he would do anything to make her his girl and I do mean anything to make that happen.

Baby it's cool, I'm gone keep my hands to myself, I really don't want to be alone neither.

After hearing those words, E-b put her hand on the back of his head and began to give him a nice massage, so nice that his eyes began to roll in the back of his head.

Damn, that feel so good, you got a, way with them hands, baby, it only makes me wonder about that,

Low! Don't start, she said stopping him before he could even finish his sentence.

Lol, he turned up the music and he leaned back and enjoyed the ride, he usually would just go to his little apartment in the hood but he couldn't, not this late with this much dope on him, he had to go to his main house. A part of him knew he should of dropped her off before going, but she seem like a good woman and plus he figured that she would never remember the way, because he made sure that he took the longest route he could, as he looked at her from the side, she was just so damn comfortable, like she didn't have a care in the world, didn't even question the drive even though they had been driving for about an hour now, it was like in his mind, she trusted him, but he fought against the thought, saying to himself that she couldn't possibly fully trust him when she just met him, it made him wonder even more, what was her deal.

As they kept driving they finally pulled up to an all-black gate with L&L on the front.

Where are we, E-b asked with amazement pouring out of her eyes as she looked all around at the beautiful home they just pulled up too.

It's nice huh, Low said as he watched her reaction slowly.

Shaking her head yes, she said I'm gone get me one of these one day, while smiling the brightest smile she could have smiled,

Low laughed,

One day! Why does it got to be one day? You can get that shit now fuckin with me, shit you want this house that bad, I'll give it to you, I own about six more, some that look like this and some far better.

She acted like she believed him but in her heart, she knew he was lying, he was just trying his best to impress her, she seen it a million times before.

And you would just give me this house?

Yeah, if you fuck with me, baby I'll do whatever for you.

Do you tell every woman you come across, that you will give them a house and that you'll give them the world if they fuck with you?

No I don't but,

But what makes me so special? She said cutting him offin mid-sentence, you only known me for a couple of hours but yet you offer me the world, now that's what makes me think everything you are saying is bullshit.

I know it sounds like bullshit but it's something about you, I can't put my hand on it, you give me a feeling that I haven't felt before, so I want to get to know you and if we work out, just know I come with a lot of perks.

We gone see if you like to bullshit or not!

After Low showed her around the house, they sat out back by the pool, drank a little wine and talked about everything going back as early as their early childhood, there connection was getting stronger and stronger by the minute.

Jyel:

As Jyel sat at home watching TV, his phone rang taking his attention off of the television.

Hello! Who is this and how can I help you?

Jyel this is Detective Cooper,

Hey how you doing Detective Cooper,

I'm doing alright, but hey I want you to come in and see me today,

Why what's going on Chief?

I want to talk to you about your future in the junior Detective program,

Ok, he said as he became excited and had a loss for words,

And Mr. Wright,

Yeah, Mr. Cooper,

Wear something nice,

As he walked into District one, he headed to the clerk's desk to let them know he was there and out of nowhere a rush of reporters stopped him in his tracks.

Mr. Wright, I'm the reporter with WLWT channel 5 news and I were hoping you could give me a little of your time, so I could interview you.

Interview me, for what?

Mr. Wright, we heard how you saved the old man's life, you did a very good thing, we just would like to get a couple questions from you on the record.

Ok,

How did you know that he was in trouble?

Before he could even speak one word, the Chief popped into the room, throwing his arm around him, guiding him towards the back of the building.

Chief what is going on, what is all this?

Well the Mayor got word about what you did and just wanted to shed some light on the situation, he said that you are a real hero and the city of Cincinnati wants to reward you for it.

Chief, you should have told me, so I could prepare for this, I am not ready for any of this!

Come on now, if I would have told you, then how would it be a surprise, now come on everybody is waiting on you.

Everybody! Everybody like who?

The press is here, every local news channel in the city, hell I even think I seen that one dude who be doing the world news, David Mummer, or something like that, you know who I'm talking about.

The chief pushed him ahead of him, so he could be the one to lead, they entered from the back and onto the stage in front of hundreds of people, the lights were shining, cameras and microphones were everywhere.

As I walked out on that stage, I could feel my heart making its way to my stomach, as soon as I made it to the microphone, all the questions began to start pouring out.

Mr. Wright, how does it feel to be a hero?

Can you break down the very moments of your rescue?

Did you know the old man you rescue before today?

Did you risk your life to save a friend, could you consider him a friend?

Question after question, and I didn't have the answer for not one.

The chief noticed that Jyel was lost for words, he felt sorry for him and thought, maybe he shouldn't have put him out there on the spot like that, so he decided to step up and be his voice.

Ok now people, this is his first time in front of a camera, please take it easy on him, shoot him one question at a time now, and give him some time to answer.

Chief what's next for the young hero?

I'm proud to say he has joined our junior Detective program, so we can get him on a good path to college and who knows, he might even join the police academy one day.

Mr. Wright, was it your choice to join the junior Detective program? And if so, why?

Yes, it was my choice to join the program, some of the reasons being college and building my career for the future, but also in truth, growing up I always wanted to be a cop.

What inspired you to want to be a police officer?

When I was younger, my mom and dad got murdered, and the case has been unsolved now for 10 years, I want to find out who murdered my parents so I could bring them to justice.

Mr. Wright, are you the son of Lamar Wright?

The audience got quiet, like that one question sucked all the air out of the room.

Yes, I am, how did you know?

Mr. Wright are you aware of your fathers past?

His past! What about his past? he said as he fought to get closer to the microphone as Chief

Cooper had begun to pull him away.

That's enough questions for now, we going to let the boy rest, maybe if it's enough time we will answer some more.

As he pulled him away from the stage, he could see looks in their eyes, it went from proud to petty real petite really quick, and he didn't like it at all.

Myona:

When she woke up, the need for more sleep, had a hold on her body, the first thing she did was grab her phone to check her messages, she began to search all through her phone for his messages and calls unable to stop thinking about him. After she just got his number last night, it was surprising how fast to her the infatuation she built up for him so quickly and it was clear that's was not normal for her to think about a dude longer than five minutes, but she was and just really hoped he's a nice guy. As she rolled over to turn on the news to catch the weather, she were instantly caught off guard to see her brother face plastered all over the news for rescuing some old man life from getting killed in some robbery, she jumped up and rushed downstairs to tell her grandmother, what was going on.

Grandma! Grandma!

Girl, I already seen it, you don't have to tell me, obviously your brother has taken on a side job, now he thinks he batman, out fighting crime and shit.

He didn't tell you nothing about this?

Not a word, he been walking around here like nothing never happen, he gets that part from your daddy for sure.

Speaking of daddy, I saw they brought daddy up in the news press today when Jyel was answering questions, the question is why?

Grandma Vickie walked away like what she just heard

scared the hell out of her, as soon as she passed through the door to exit, she turned back around.

I didn't want to answer all these questions when it comes to your dad but fuck it, it's in my face I might as well confront it.

Confront what! Grandma what are you talking about?

It's a lot you don't know about your father, that now, I feel that your old enough to understand if you want to talk about it.

Of course, you know I want to know anything that has something to do with my parents.

Grandma Vickie sat directly across from her to make sure they could engage in a serious eye contact.

You know your dad wasn't a model citizen!

Grandma just tell me !

Ok look, ever since your dad was a young boy he ran the streets. He was real smart and sharp for his age and your daddy didn't hold no hands, he was the type to try to get ahead by any means.

Lol Grandma stop talking like you a mob boss or something.

No serious Myona!

So by any means necessary huh, so would he murder somebody? she said as she searched her face to see if she could find some kind of truth in her Grandmother's eyes.

Yeah, as a matter of fact, that's statement itself is really an understatement, he had a lot of skeletons in his closet.

If it was that bad, why isn't he in prison instead of dead?

The question crashed her heart like it was in a car accident, and yet she was still careful with her words.

Like I said before, he was very smart and sharp for his age, the police had a lot of information on him but no real proof so they couldn't really lock him up with no evidence and their witnesses kept coming up missing, I think the most sensitive murder they said your dad was involved in was this girl name Cassie Humphrey everything went downhill after that.

What happen to her?

She was raped and murdered in the park, some jogger ended up finding her early in the morning during their run.

My dad would do that? Damn he sounds like a real monster!

That's just something they were saying, like I said they had no proof, if somebody would get killed, they would tie his name to it, plus if he did it he would have told me, I been covering up murders for him since that boy was 9 years old, No matter what he done, he was my baby, he made sure that we could have a better life, even if it would have costed him his own.

Grandma, I got a call from this place called the Lyon Family Financial company.

O yea, I know a little something about them, what did they want?

Daddy had set up a trust for all three of us and he left a video message that he wanted us all to see.

I am not surprised, that's just the kind of shit he does, I do want to go with you, if you don't mind.

The man told me it was a private meeting, so I don't know if you are going to be able to come.

Trust me baby, me coming won't be a problem, but I do need to tell you, your brother called me the other day.

Who Aiden?

Yeah,

What did he say?

Not much, but I think he gone be showing his face real soon,

Is that what he said,

No but I got the feeling, it's going to come to that, I could just feel it!

Low:

As I woke up, E-b was still lying next to me, her smell like an alarm clock in my nose, beautiful was the only one of the words I could use to describe how I feel with I think about her, I can't believe just how good of a woman she truly is, she so far has passed all the test. I left my phone out to see if she would check through it, she didn't touch it, I left out $450.00 on the dresser to see if she would steal it or at least some of it and she didn't touch that either, I even acted like I had passed out off the liquor, to see would she try to Rome my house to see what she could take.

I rolled back the cameras and she never moved but once and that was to go to the bathroom and she didn't even do that alone, I remember her waking me up, talking about the house was too big, so she is scared to walk around alone. In fear she might get lost. So I could tell off top she is not into no funny business, so maybe she does want to get to know me. I got up and went to the kitchen so I could make us some breakfast and I saw breaking news come popping up on the screen so I hurried up and turned up the volume so I could hear what they were talking about on the TV, some young boy was getting a reward for making a citizen arrest, this instantly made me shake my head, thinking, what has this world come too. But then the reporters began to rush him with a parade of questions, questions that stood out like crazy, they mention the name of Lamar Wright, a name everybody that has ever moved around in the hood would recognize even if their head was held under water, even though they say he's dead, nobody knows if it's true or not because the family made sure they kept the funeral private, no outsiders could get in, it's been 10 years this year and I could still say he still places fear in the hearts of many. But it been clear to me that the great legend is as good as dead or he would have been showed his face by now.

People saying, he just laying low because of all the different murders he committed, every time I turn around they keep making this motherfucker out to be like some urban legend or something. Say his name like Candy man, three times and he will appear. I still remember the beef I had with the motherfucker and a part of me don't know why I want revenge so bad but I do. What he did to my reputation was unacceptable, I just never had the chance to make my mark. As I continued to listen in on the news report, the young boy stated that Lamar Wright was indeed his father. That was another tall tale that people always wondered about, did he have kids and if so how many? From all the stories I heard of him robbing and putting in work in the streets, I know he left them with a nice Lil piece of change.

He wrote down the young boys' name and called one of his young boys who run under the crown to put in some leg work to find out where the young boy lives. He answered on the first ring, like he been waiting on a call all day.

Big homie, Low, what's good? He said showing a little excitement in his voice.

I need your help with something, it's some good money in it for you so don't trip, I am not asking for nothing for free.

O yeah like what?

I got this Lil dude I want you to check out for me.

I will but what's the deal.

I got some old business I got to take care of but I don't have the time to chase them down so what's up, you up for the job?

He paused before he could give a direct answer, causing Low to check to see if he were still on the line.

Hello you still there?

Yeah I'm still here and yeah, I'm with it, I got you, but Low, what happen last night?

What you mean?

How did Baby Yee get killed on your watch, on a move he was busting for you?

Bro shit was crazy last night and we lost connection and the nigga moved without me.

So who was it that killed him? Was it the dude you sent him to get? And if it was, how would have dude would have known that Baby Yee was on him, unless somebody gave him the heads up and only a few people knew what was going on.

I don't know Boone; I don't know who did it!

Low that shit sounds fishy as hell, he was with you but you don't know nothing.

Boone he wasn't with me!

Cut the shit Low, all I know is blue chip looking for some answers, so you gone have to set up a meeting soon, to make shit right with the crown and by then I hope you got some better answers then the ones you giving me.

Alright, I'll set the meeting up.

Look Low, he told me he just wants to talk, you know your family man, I guess he just want to get your side of the story, when it comes to things, but don't stand him up, it's going to make shit look funny, not just to him but to the crown as well.

Every word put Low deep in thought, his head was in outer space, only the repeating of the calling of his name, snapped him back to reality.

Low what's up, you hear me Low!

Yeah, I hear you Boone, I told you I'll set it up.

As he hung up, a lot of shit crossed his mind. He knew that he might end up in a war with the crown, especially over the death of Baby Yee, he was a top rank official for the crown, he knew that they would not just walk away easy from this. Now that his back is against the wall, every way there is to get to the money, he became willing to take by any road, in order to get ahead of this situation that he has now found himself in. There was no backing out now, the war he created has been put in full motion without anybody in knowledge of what's going on, in his mind he drew a line, it's my side or there's, what was clear to him is that money brings power, he loved the taste of power, the only thing that was missing is the money. He thought about how important it is now to stay strong up under Ace, he knew fuckin with dude, he could make some real money, and I mean really fast, but the heat is turning up in the streets, he now faced obstacles that he didn't have before, how could he hustle in peace when he has beef waiting for him on every comer. So far he knew he could move the drugs through a couple of people that he could trust, but that wouldn't last long, because fear might take over and cause them to back away, once it comes out that the crown is looking for him, he thought about paying the crown off to switch sides, he knew nothing really depends on loyalty anymore, now and days everybody comes with a price, you just got to name it. He also thought what would be up for gabs, when it came to Lamar Wright son, he knew it had to be millions involved, maybe first the son then Ace or vice versa whichever comes first. As he wrote down the young hero's name and did a screen shot of his picture, E-b was starting to wake up from her sleep watching Low run around the house excited like he just won the lottery.

What's up bay? She said as she tried her best to fully wake up and get the sleep out of her eye.

O so I'm bay now, it's only been one night and I was drunk, but I know your fine ass didn't give me none of that sweet little pussy you got the lock and key too.

How you know motherfucker? You said you was drunk!

For one, I couldn't smell you on my breath when I woke up and I was drunk but I know we didn't fuck because two, if we would have, I would still be in it right now, laying that pipe, putting down the law, morning sex, is the best sex!

Lol, that shit all sound good, talking all that shit and that dick probably isn't nothing but two inches.

O so you gone play me like that, he said as she was about to stand up, he wrestled her back down on to the couch.

Stop Low, Lol, I got to pee!

Go ahead and do it, as a matter of fact do it right here, because from this moment on I'm not going to ever let you go.

Aww shit, you another one of them!

And what is that? He said as he waited for her to unleash her answer.

A big ass pussy whipped momma's boy, who hasn't even got the pussy yet, I might need to go to the court house right now, to go get my restraining order, might even have to beat you off the pussy.

They both laughed as they laid there holding each other staring out the window at the beautiful view the 20 acres of land the estate sits on.

Baby can I ask you a question? E-b asked as she turned around so she could face him.

Go ahead baby, I'm an open book, ask me whatever you want, Low said in his playful tone.

First thing I want to know, is have you ever been serious with any woman?

What you mean, like in a relationship or something? Well no, unless you gone count my mother.

Be serious!

No I have not been in any real relationships because up until now I have not met anybody as special as you.

Ok, I see you got a little game, I bet you tell all the bitches the same line the morning of.

First of all, you got to be some kind of special to me for me to bring you to my honeycomb hide out, if you weren't, we would be in a hotel, motel, room right now.

Whatever! I was hoping we could spend some time together and just lay back and get to know each other, pick each other's locks.

Ah huh, Low said as he ran towards the kitchen to see can he catch the phone before it stopped ringing, just as he was about to answer E-b slid to the bathroom to relief herself and make a phone call of her own.

Hello, Latrell, I just came from downtown viewing Julius's body, she said as she tried her best to try to hold back the tears from pouring down into the phone.

Aunt Jackie, I told you I would have went down there for you or I could of at least went with you. You should have called me; I really didn't want you to see him like that.

I had to see my baby Latrell, that's my baby! These motherfuckers' killed my baby, o lord, help me, she said as she could no longer hold her strength together or hold back her tears.

I'm sorry Aunt Jackie, I wish it were something that I could do, I just feel so helpless right now.

Sorry! Your sorry alright motherfucker, you better get off your ass and find out who did this shit to my baby, you hear me!

Yes, ma'am,

Now when I went down there to view the body, they gave me his property, so I need you to come see me sometime this week so we could go over a couple of things.

Ok but what's wrong? Low said as his interest began to build more and more from her weird request.

It's a couple things I want you to see,

Like what?

Boy we aren't going to talk about none of this shit over the phone, so you just make sure you make it over here as soon as you can.

Ok I will,

After he hung up, he just sat and reflected on the conversation, he just had with his Aunt J wondering what it was that could be so important, that she couldn't say it over the phone.

As he came from the kitchen, he noticed that E-b was nowhere to be found, so he decided to look for her.

After Low walked onto the kitchen, she grabbed her phone and ran to the bathroom to make a call to Ace to put him up on the details of what's been going on at Low's spot.

Hello,

Ace, listen to me, I don't got much time to talk, but I had to bring you up to date on what's going on.

Ok, what's good, did you find something out?

Yeah, I'm at his house now, and I know it's his main crib because he even admitted it to me.

Damn he took you to his house already, how do you know it's really his main spot and not just some throw off spot, telling you anything to keep you off balance.

Believe me this is far from some throw away spot, he brought me to a big ass house in Indian

Hills and,

Cutting her off in mid-sentence, there ain't shit cheap up that way, ok cool, bring me a piece of mail so I could lock in his location.

Why do you need his mail, I could just text you the information right now!

No don't do that! If anything goes wrong, the police can pull up old text messages and link us together, and start trying to fill in the blanks.

Ace what blanks? I did what you asked me to do, my job here is done!

No it's not! Showing his anger through the phone, I told you to find out his weakness for me, plus I need you to make sure that it's his main spot, we don't want to jump out of pocket and not know for sure!

Matching his tone she shot back, what do you want me to do Ace, fuck him, huh! What do you want me to fuckin do?

Don't do this right now E-b calm down, this will be over soon I promise, I just need you to stick to the program, I'm going to make sure I take care of you.

E-b, E-b, where are you baby? Low said as he called through the house trying to see where exactly she was located.

I'm in the bathroom baby I'll be out in a minute.

Look I got to go, but we aren't done with this conversation Ace!

Yeah we done, you just need to hit me up when the job is done and not a moment before.

Ace hung up, sending her emotions up in a world wind.

Baby what you doing? You been in there for a minute!

I'm on my way out, damn a bitch can't take a shit in peace!

Threw off from her answer, damn it isn't no shame in your game at all is it, you doing the most, you do one more thing in this motherfucking house, I'm gone start passing your ass some bills to pay, while you moving around here like you own the place! Low said as he laughed walking back to the living room.

She tried to pull herself together but a strong rush of emotions began to overwhelm her, to the point she started crying uncontrollably, her wall to keep up her composure was broken. Low heard her as he was going down the hall, it stopped him right in his tracks, he turned around to walk back to the bathroom to see what was wrong, hoping it wasn't something that he said.

Is something wrong baby? You know I was just fuckin with you don't you?

The bathroom door opened, and E-b stepped out wiping away the tears from her face, trying to get her composure back together.

I'm sorry, I didn't mean to hurt you, I was just fuckin with you, just talking shit ok, calm down baby, Low said as he tried his best to comfort her.

It's not you! So you calm down!

Then what's wrong, one minute you laughing, then the next minute you crying, now I know women could get emotional, but this might just be a little bit too much for me. You sure you don't need no medication.

Shut up fool, she said showing a smile, trying her best not to laugh.

See I'm glad your ass putting it all on the table now showing me, how crazy your ass really is, now tell me what the hell is wrong with you!

I just got out of a long term relationship and he hurt me really bad, and even though I try to keep a smile on my face, it's been real hard for me because I really loved him unconditionally, we were together for 10 years, we had all these plans we created, like to get married and have children, I really was looking forward to settling down and building a family, you know. Now I'm back at square one, lonely, and just don't know what the fuck I'm going to do, that's the real reason I don't want to go home, it's to many memories of him there.

Why did you guys break up?

He only wanted to use me, he really never loved me, I thought we had something special but it was all a lie.

Everybody uses somebody for something, it's just all about if you are getting your needs met, Low said as he moved in closer.

And that's the point, mines didn't even begin to start getting met, I was cheated out of my happiness.

And what makes you think that? Low said, as he pulled her

in close to him, things happen for a reason, you could have been getting shaped perfectly just for me.

Ignoring his words, I found out he was married and had children already, he was never going to build a life with me, man I just feel so stupid, I don't want much, just somebody to love me for me.

E-b looked into his eyes, as she shared how she was feeling, not all that she was doing or saying was an act, the pain was real, the tears was real, she really was in love with someone who she didn't know would ever love her the way she wanted to be loved, Low could feel her pain, not in the same way, but in a way of his own, that's way he was so weak to her presents, because he had been on a lonely ride in life as well, he always wanted to feel loved as well, since his mother died at a young age, all he ever had was the streets, as they embraced each other, to find some type of comfort in each other's pain, E-b couldn't believe just how good it felt to be held, their faces brushed by each other's and instantly they began to lay down a long passionate kiss. Once they unlocked lips, it felt like the heat in the house had turned up to a hundred degrees or more, it began to get hard to control their self's, they both indulged in the feelings they were sharing and wanted more. E-b began to move from his lips slowly to his neck, then down to his chest, exploring his body, like he was a geographic map, becoming more and more generous with her tongue the lower she went. Nothing about today was normal, from the way she touched him, he had never been touched like this before, she pushed him back to the wall, at the same time pulling at his belt, forcing his pants to his ankles, she could feel his heart jumping through his chest, as she pulled out his long rock hard dick, her mouth became moist, as she run her tongue around her lips, she pictured how it would feel to have him inside her. She got down on her knees and stared up at him, pulling his soul to her through her eyes.

I want you tonight, in every way possible, I could have you, E-b said as she kissed the tip of his dick, driving him crazy, as she took her time teasing him, showing him that she was in control, grabbing more and more strength from his uncontrollable moans. His words spilled out in a soft erratic way.

Damn, yes baby, whatever you want, just don't stop!

Feeding into his words, she matched his energy,

I want you to hold my head and fuck my throat, can you do that? That's what's going to get my pussy real wet daddy.

Low couldn't believe what he was hearing, as he entered her mouth, he gripped her head as tight as he could, forcing himself to the back of her throat as far as he could go until he could hear her gagging for air, the whole time she kept her eyes open and on him, watching his every more, as he pulled out, he could feel her slob running down his leg.

Yes, baby I want it rough just like that, E-b said as she headed straight for his balls running her tongue all around them enjoying every moment.

She could feel the excitement building in his legs as they began to shake and the tightness in his grip got tighter and tighter, but she maintained her control, slowly her pace, deep throating every inch of him top to bottom, until his knees began to get weak and he couldn't take it no more, he snatched her up into his arms and carried her back to his bed, as he kissed her sweet soft lips he held her tight, once they got to the bedroom, he threw her down on the bed, and began to finish quickly undressing himself, watching as she did the same. The passion was building fast in the room, once they both were done undressing, E-b opened her legs open wide inviting him inside her space, showing signs of a fiend for her touch and to be inside her, Low tried his best to climb on top.

What are you doing? E-b said as she pushed him up before he could enter inside her.

Before he could say a word, she pushed his head down between her legs, licking her lips, motioning him to eat her pussy.

Low knew it was his time to show she wasn't the only one who could put it down in the bedroom, as she forced him in position, he took long licks to get her pussy acquainted with his tongue, each stroke put an arch in her back, sending chills up her spine as he went from running his tongue in circles to trying to suck her free flowing well dry, she tried her best to run from his grip, once he could taste her sweet juices explode into his mouth, he knew he had her right where he wanted her, the soft kisses on her thighs, brought her heart rate to a calm place as he made his way up between her thighs, once he entered inside, he started digging like he was in a mine in Africa, hands cuffed tightly on her ass cheeks trying to control his pace as he pulled her in from the bottom.

O yes, fuck me baby, o my god you feel so good inside me, E-b said as she held onto him for dear life, fuck me faster, pound the shit out this pussy baby, come on harder.

Low ignored her words, snatching her hands off his ass, pinning her arms behind her head, slowing his stroke to his liking, while he kissed on her neck, he began to whisper in her ear, erotic quotes,

I want you to cum all over this dick for me, come on, wet it up!

And she did just that, over and over again, she never felt like this before, he tore her walls down, stroke after stroke, then he switched positions, he pulled her hair and at the right times, he would even add in a little choking, strong but had a gentleness to it, after he pulled out of her he grabbed her hair swinging her to the floor and unloaded his thick sweet cum, all down her throat, forcing her to catch every single drop, and right when she thought they were threw, looking at her, he got right back hard and they started fucking again, the kisses, his touch, the way he held her, made her feel so special, something that was so unfamiliar to her, everything about this was different for her, usually it was finish your business then go about your business when it came to other men, even with Ace, so she began to look upon that as her norm, but with Low he was patient, his touch was tender, and it made her feel like for the first time she belonged to someone and not just a pass down. The more she was in her head, the more confused she became on what to do next, she developed feelings and couldn't turn them off or help how she was feeling, she rolled over and curled up into a ball, lost for words. After Low got out the shower, he climbed back in the bed with her, instantly he could notice she had for some reason became distant. He could tell something was on her mind, it was all over her face, so he crawled behind her, placing his arms around her, gripping her tight.

What's wrong baby? Low asked as he kissed her softly on the back of her neck.

Nothing! She said as she slightly tried to move away from his embrace.

Don't lie to me bay, I could tell something is wrong, we made all this good love, and now you want to be all distance now, like you aren't feeling me, when I know you do, now tell me what's the problem.

E-b turned to face him, so she could look him in his eyes.

Ok yeah, I am feeling you but I'm scared and I can't get hurt again, so you don't have to play no games with me, you got what you want, so we can just call it a day and go our separate ways, you don't have to fry to sell me no dream.

Low laughed as he pulled her into him even closer, closing the space, then he kissed her on the lips.

Just stop it, I'm feeling you too and I really want to get to know you, as a matter of fact, if you could, I want you to stay with me for a while, I think it would be good for the both of us.

Her face lit up like a Christmas tree, then quickly turned back to stone,

You mean good for you! All you want is some good in house pussy for a minute, then you gone throw me away, like you do all your other bitches, you probably got a drawer full of them hoes panties you save as victory trophies!

Do you always got to be so tough? Damn! Now listen, I know it's too soon to say this but it's coming from the heart and it's the truth, I haven't felt like this about anybody before, just stay with me please, I could only show you, one day at a time, I feel my actions will speak louder than words, you won't need for nothing, I'll take care of everything, we can even go shopping so you won't have to go home and get caught up in all them old memories, come on talk to me, I know you'll like that.

She smiled because besides the good sex he was putting down, shopping was definitely her other love language. Ok I'll stay, but I'm serious, I can't be hurt again so no games.

No games baby, Low said as he climbed on top of her again, ready to get the action started all over again.

Boone:

As Boone walked up to the front door of his house two guys came out the brushes, rushing him, pinning him to the wall.

Damn ok, I guess this how it's gone end for me huh? Boone said with the gun pressed to the back of his head, unable to turn around.

How you want him boss, on his i<iees or stuck in this position?

I am not getting on my knees motherfucker, you gone have to kill me, plain and simple.

Blue chip came from around the corner, grabbing the arm of the young thug, ordering him to lower his gun.

Calm down young blood, we just came to talk, no need to put in work, turn around Boone.

Boone recognized the voice and instantly turned around to approach him, with a strong anger building in his heart, for his so called friend.

What the fuck you on Blue Chip! You pull up to my house, planting guns to the back of my head, on what grounds.

Blue Chip looked him up and down before he moved in closer.

You know why I'm here, I told you I wanted you to set up a meeting with Low, me and that motherfucker got to talk!

You act like I'm dodging you or something, I put the word out.

And what did he say, Blue Chip said as he searched his eyes for the truth.

He said he was gone call you and set up the meeting, he said he didn't know who killed Baby Yee, I told him that shit sound fishy, being that he was going to make a move for him, but he assured me that he had nothing to hide and he was going to be getting in contact with you pretty soon.

And how long was this ago?

Not too long ago, he said he would call, that's why I didn't feel I had to rush back to you, I took his word for it, shit we all under the crown, I took it as, why would he lie.

Well something isn't right about this dude, how you don't know what happen when he was with you the whole time, so this is what I'm going to do, I'm going to give him until tonight to call me and set the meeting up and if he doesn't get back with me, I'm gone take it as if homeboy saying fuck me and the crown he swore an oath too, then I'm going send my young and up and coming soldiers to put in some work, you feel me!

Blue Chip I'll make sure I let him know!

Yeah you do that, Blue Chip said as he was about to walk away, then he slowed his pace, then turned back around as if a light bulb just went off in his head.

You know what, scratch that, instead of me looking high and low for this motherfucker, you know all his spots, how about you just take care of that shit for me.

Come on Blue Chip man, Low is like my family!

That's funny, I thought you was loyal to the crown Boone,

I am,

Well you got to show us, it's either him or us, you know I can't just let a motherfucker kill a member of this family and get away with it, if it was you, I would be at the next motherfucker head the same way, so don't have me guessing, I need to know what is it going to be Boone, him or the crown?

Blue Chips young goons stepped up, waiting for an answer as he tapped the gun against his leg, itching, waiting on the call to leave Boone right where he was standing.

I think you already know the answer to that, Boone said as he watched the young goon's movements.

If I knew the fucking answer, I wouldn't be standing here asking you questions, shit I would have just texted or sent you a call, but fuck that, I'm here now and I'm done guessing, so what is it gone be?

Blue Chip, I'm loyal to the crown.

Good! Blue Chip said as he patted him on his cheek, call me tonight to let me know if he is going to set up the meeting, if not, I need you to send his soul through a text, so we could clean our hands with this mess and get back to business, but until then, I won't be able to rest, I want to be able to face Baby Yee with some good news before the funeral.

Then just like that, they all disappeared back through the brushes from which they came. As Boone stood there, he played in his mind all the what if's, what if he doesn't set up the meeting with Blue Chip, what if he can't make it to him in time, what if he has no choice but to show his loyal to the crown, its either Low's life or his, so many thoughts flowed through his mind, it was hard for him to think, as he walked in the house, he pulled out his phone and tried his best to call Low but over and over again, he just would not answer, it was almost like he was sending him to the voicemail on purpose. He has never acted like this before, they have always had each other's back since they were kids growing up and they never lied to each other, until now.

Myona:

After she got dropped off by London, she wasn't quite ready to go in the house yet, and she wanted a little company, so she decided to call Ace to see would he be willing to come outside for a little while, he answered on the first ring.

Hey you, what you still doing up, I didn't expect you to call me anymore tonight.

Is there a problem? Are you busy? If so I could call you tomorrow.

No I'm not busy, what's up?

I was wondering if you would like to come outside with me for a little bit and grab a bit to eat.

Well yeah I could eat, what did you have in mind there aren't too many places open at this time of the night.

I want to go get some waffle house!

The waffle house!

Yes, the waffle house, it's my favorite place me and my dad use to go to a lot, so is you going to meet me there?

Yea, I'll meet you, which one is we going too?

I don't too much like the one in Covington, how about Clifton instead, is that one cool for you?

Yea, baby I'll be there in about 15 minutes.

Ok,

As they hung up, a message came through Ace phone, that read:

Baby I'm on my way, you better not fall asleep on me.

Damn, he just remembered he told the Lil bitch from the bar to slide through for the night, he shot her the address through a text telling her to meet him at his homie spot, because he had to run and take care of some business, she put up a little argument, so he could try to keep her off his phone for a minute, he told her about the key that he always hides up under the matt at his back door of his home. Once she is inside he told her to get comfortable, he will be there in a minute, that seem to calm her down, the only reason he sent her there and not where he was already, is because that spot was a little closer to the waffle house that they were going too, and who knows, he felt he might even get a little lucky, he didn't need nobody popping up, fucking up what he had going on.

As he pulled up to the waffle house, he stared through the window at Meme admiring her beauty from a far, watching as she played with her phone, then a text came through to his phone, it read:

This is Meme, are you still coming? If not, let me know

because I'm hungry and if you don't hurry, I'm about to order without you.

He smiled as he read the text, before getting out the car and walking inside.

Damn so now you ready to order without me, Ace said as he walked up to her, embracing her in a tight hug, they both laughed, sat down, ordered, ate and talked about a little bit of everything. The conversation was flowing like water. Ace was surprised on just how smart she truly was; he could tell she was nothing like the women he was use to dating. They were open about their likes and dislikes, what they wanted in a relationship and what turns them off as well in a relationship, and what for sure makes the relationship a deal breaker, but once they began to talk about family they both could tell the conversation was starting to show it needed space. It was a touchy conversation for the both of them. Changing the subject, Meme broke the ice.

It's crazy how we got so much in common, I would have never thought that from just looking at you, Meme said as she shyly looked away.

O so I see you the type who like to judge a book by its cover, now that makes me think, what do you see when you look at me then.

A heartbreaker, a big time player, a lady's man to a whole lot of ladies, do I need to say more?

No, you don't have to say more, I get the picture, and some of those things you said could be true, but that's only because I haven't met a girl like you, most of the girls I meet don't think with their brain, they don't know how to have a conversation, most of the time, they just think with their pussy, they never bring anything to the table but want you to be there superman or something.

Don't tell me you Mr. Captain save a hoe!

Ace busted out laughing, choking on the drink he just took a sip from, girl your ass play, too much, you always got jokes, he said as he tried his best to catch his breath.

Naw, for real, I know what you mean, my friend London act like that and I told her about herself but she doesn't see no wrong in her actions, everybody always gets on me about even hanging with her, people tell me what she does, they're going to think I do as well.

They might think that at first, until they sat down and talk to you, and then that would quickly change, you too bright for any of that, your light would shine right through, your daddy must have instilled some strong values in you, young lady.

My dad and my mom died when I was younger, but yeah I still carry a lot of our memories we had together.

May I ask how they died? Ace said as he leaned in showing interest in what she was about to say.

No not tonight, it's too much information to pass down to a stranger in one night, the first night at that.

A stranger!

Yes, a stranger, I just met you and that's hard for me to talk about, it makes me all sad and I don't want to be sad this morning after a good breakfast.

Ok, cool maybe once we get to know each other then we can talk about it.

Yea, maybe,

Her words had hit home, not only were they on the same page in life, they also suffered the same type of lost. A part of him wanted to know everything about her, he had the feeling for once in his life, he might have just found his best friend, the love of his life, the one and only for him, but only time will tell.

As she got up from the table, she went over and approached the waiter, Ace looked at his phone and seen what had to had been over a hundred miss calls and texts from MoMo, he was so interested in everything that Meme had to say, that he got lost in his track of time and forgot he even had her waiting on him. At this point he no longer wanted to deal with her at all, as he looked up from his phone Meme had a to go bag stopping by the table trying to get his attention.

Hey where you going, you just about to get up and leave on me?

Yeah, I'm a little tired, it's time for me to go home and crash, I paid for the bill, this one is on me, maybe you can get the next one.

Now you know, I would have got the bill, you didn't have to do that! And I'm not ready for you to go, me and you are having a great time getting to know each other, I don't want it to end, we can go to my place and just kick it, I promise I won't bite, Ace said as he pulled her in close to him.

She put her hand on his chest, to stop him from pulling her in any closer.

I had to pay for the bill, that's just how I was raised, now I can leave here feeling like I don't owe you something and you could leave here knowing I don't owe you nothing, and no I'm not coming to your house, but nice try, I could tell from the way your phone been going off, you won't miss me, you probably got somebody waiting on you right now.

As he started to put answers to his indirect questions, she placed a finger on his lips.

The worst thing you could do, is start anything good and pure off with a lie, she said as she pulled away and started heading towards the door.

When am I going to see you again, he yelled as she walked to the door, once she opened it, she turned back to give him an answer.

How about tomorrow, me and my friend is going to our prom, I would love it if we could hook up afterwards.

Say less, I'll be there!

I'll text you the address when I get home, you can just meet me in the parking lot once everything is over and then we could go do something, probably get something to eat and go look at the view over Fairview park.

Sounds good to me.

And just like that she was out the door.

London:

Once she told Ace that she was on her way, he shot her a different address that she had never been to before, out in West Chester, once she got there she noticed it was a very beautiful house that set at the end of a dead end street. At first she thought that he might be playing games and probably gave her the wrong address because the place was not easy to find, but then out of nowhere she seen it, it set out of sight hiding behind some brushes. Once she got out the car, she ran up to the back porch to see if the key would be where Ace said it was, once she found it, a strong excitement fell over her. As she entered, she noticed all the beautiful paintings on the wall, the more she looked around she noticed the house not only was amazing but it did show a little woman's touch here and there, but there was no pictures of a woman but one, which lay over a very large fire place, the woman looked nothing like someone he would be interested in dating and as she began to look closer, she could tell they shared a lot of features, so she took it as this must be his mother, as she continued down the hall, she seen a picture of Ace when he was younger, standing in a picture with a man, she decided to pick it up and take a closer look at it, when she looked on the back, it read: Son I love you, always have and always will, it was clear that this was a picture of him and his dad. Instantly she could see where he got his swag from, his dad had hood written all over him. She wanted to go through the whole house, looking and checking things out but she reframed from doing so, being that this is a nice house, he might have some hidden cameras, but she knew he wouldn't get mad if she took a shower, shit she had to make sure that the kitty was fresh, nice and right for him whenever he would make it there, she called him but didn't get no answer, so she sent him a text letting him know that she was there and to hurry up because she can't wait to see him, after she took a nice and hot shower, she was well relaxed in body but her mind was racing, she noticed hours had went by and it was still no sign of him, so out of worry, she began to call and text him over and over again until she passed out on the bed.

Exhausted from frustration, out of nowhere, the bedroom door slowly popped open, she slightly opened her eyes but didn't move, she continued to act like she was sleep, as Ace came into the room, he didn't say a word, but began to slowly undress, once he got down to his boxers, it was only then she could notice that his big fat hard dick was violently poking through his boxers, he began to grab himself, looking at her like she was a thanksgiving feast. Ace walked over to the bed and climbed inside right behind MO, pulling her in close making sure she could feel his presents in the room, with his hand he got straight to work, by spreading her legs and playing with her clique like it was a string on a guitar, the pleasure overpowered her to the point she could no longer pretend to be sleep, her moans began to pour through the walls of the whole house. As thoughts of Meme flowed through his mind, his mood turned aggressive, patience was no longer an option, he lifted her leg and forced himself deep inside her, causing her to fry to adjust to the pain, the more she tried to get away, the more it turned him on. He nibbled on her ear, pinning her in place as he pounded her walls as hard as he could, in his search he could feel her pussy getting wetter and wetter with each stroke. Which made her moan in enjoyment even louder, not wanting to break his concentration he grabbed her by the hair and forced her head into the pillow to muffle her screams as he shifted her body while still inside her, to a doggy style position.

Yes, baby, yes baby, o my god, pound this pussy, fuck this pussy baby, it's your pussy baby, I don't want nobody else, o god, I'm Cumming, fuck, cum for me baby.

You want me to cum all inside this pussy Meme? Meme tell me how bad you want me to cum in this wet ass pussy!

Ace stroked faster and faster until he exploded his hot and heavy load all inside of her, instantly his whole body became weak and he fell over to the other side of the bed. Feeling drained, trying his best to catch his breath.

MoMo jumped up and punched him in the chest as hard as she could, making sure she had his full attention.

Who the fuck is Meme? Ace! She said as she watched his eyes, demanding an answer.

Nobody you should be worried about, so why are you asking?

Why am I asking, bro you were just deep inside of me, making love to me, calling out another bitches' name, that's why I'm asking, who is she Ace?

Once again it isn't none of your business who she is, irritated by her pushing questions down his throat, he could no longer hold back and decide to take things a little farther, it ain't you! You just a fuck in a spare of the moment situation, and thank you by the way, Ace said as he rolled over showing MO his back, showing her his part in the conversation was over.

As she processed his every word, it felt like her heart exploded into pieces, sending tears uncontrollably down her face, not willing to give up just yet, she tapped him on the shoulder,

Ace rolled over angry because she stopped him from falling asleep.

What MoMo? What you want and why the fuck is you crying?

I thought you wanted me, you had my hopes up thinking you wanted to be with me, when really, all you wanted to do is use me, you just like all the other guys I been with, a user! You gone be the last motherfucker to ever hurt me, I could promise that!

Bitch whatever, you thought wrong and that's your problem, not mine, now get your shit and get the fuck out my house so I can catch up on some sleep, I been up all night and you fucking my sleep up with all that bitchin, sounding like a fatal attraction or something bye !

She jumped out the bed, grabbed all her things and headed for the door, trying to stop the snow from falling on her heart, turning her cold as ice.

Myona:

Good morning, birthday girl, Myona rolled over to the sound of her grandmothers Vickie's voice, I see you waking up late today, could it be because you been out all night last night, she said as she cut her eye at her, to let her know she knows what's going on.

As she adjusted her eyes to the clock, she seen the time and instantly jumped to her feet rushing to the bathroom to turn on the shower.

O my god Grandma where is Jyel? We are late, I over slept, I'm supposed to meet up with that guy from Lyon Family Financial. O my god I got to call him, Myona said as she ran around, searching through dresser drawers, trying her best to hurry up and get ready.

Myona calm down, Jyel is here and already ready and I

called the guy already as well and he's waiting on you, he told me he would give you a couple more hours to show.

Myona rushed into her grandmother's arms, embracing her with a tight hug.

Thank you so much!

You don't have to thank me, I know how important this is for you, just go on and get ready so we can go!

Yes, ma'am

Right as she was about to go into the bathroom, her brother came through the door, carrying a birthday cake and balloons.

What's going on birthday girl, I would say good morning but it's more like good afternoon, damn what you do last night get drunk, you look rough!

Jyel stop playing, you know I don't drink, super hero!

O now you got jokes! Jyel said as he fanned his sister off to her remarks.

Why you didn't tell me about you doing any of that stuff?

You know lately we both been busy, having a lot going on and I didn't want to bother you with all that stuff.

Myona walked over to him and wrapped her arms around him, placing the tightest hug she could on him, then she backed up and looked him in his eyes.

Baby brother we can never be too busy when it comes to each other, I'm only a phone call away, besides Grandma, we all we got and we can't never lose sight of that, ok! You got it?

Yea sis I got it!

Plus, what the hell was you thinking, doing something so dangerous, like that, you could have lost your life out there, don't just think about yourself when you make them type of decisions, think about the people who care about you as well, I don't know what I would do if something was to happen to you.

Now that's how it's supposed to be, family first, now both of y'all come here and give me a hug, Grandma Vickie said motioning for them to come in and give her a hug, you two is going to make me cry, you two have grown to be some very good responsible young adults, I know if your parents were here I know they both would be proud of you, just like I am, I love you.

They all embraced in a group hug, we love you to Grandma, they both said as they connected together, I love you too, y'all will always be my babies.

After all was said and done they all pulled up in front of Lyon Family Financial to go in and meet the man, she set the appointment with. Grandma Vickie and Jyel went to go sit down and wait while Myona went to go talk to the receptionist at the front desk to check in.

Lyon Family Financial, how can I help you today ma'am?

Yes, I'm here for my appointment.

Ok who do you have an appointment with ma' am?

I didn't get his name; I should have but it just slipped my mind I'm sorry.

It's ok, it happens, can you please tell me your name so I can check my appointment list?

My name is Myona Wright,

Ms. Wright, yes I see you have an appointment set here for you to see Mr. Scott Mitchell, if you have a seat, I'll let him know you're here.

Ok thank you,

As she went back to have a seat the receptionist called Mr. Mitchell to let him know they were there, after 10 minutes, he came out to greet them out in the lobby, he introduced himself, then asked them if they would follow him in to his office. Once they entered inside, he shut the door behind him and directed them to have a seat at a table in front of a large television screen and within two minutes, Lamar Wright popped up on the screen.

Myona Wright daddies baby girl, happy birthday baby, it's obvious if you're watching this video, that I'm no longer here on earth with you in the flesh, but my heart speaks strong from the spirit, I love you baby and I'm so sorry that I won't be with you to walk into your Journey from the young lady you are today, to the special grown woman I know you will someday become.

As he continued to talk, the tears poured down her face, she wished he was here, so she could hug him and tell him that she missed him so much, she would give anything just to have a couple of minutes with him. As she continued to listen, he gave her game about life's ups and downs, and how to get through them when they come her way. He even shared some embarrassing information about sex education and knowing when someone is right for you, and that love is patient, so never trust someone if they try to rush you into anything, he talked about setting her up with investors, and told her as long as she lives she won't have to worry about a thing. she had so many questions she wished she could ask him, so many questions she knew in her heart that only he could answer, that will never get answered, because his life on this earth is over with so her answers got buried right along with him. For once in her life, she could actually identify her feelings that she tried to but just couldn't do before, she felt so cheated and lost on what is it she was supposed to do next. As the video came to an end, her grandmother asked her was she alright as she embraced her with a tight hug. She asked Mr. Mitchell, can she have the video and he said that would be ok, as they were walking out, Mr. Mitchell yelled out for Myona to come back.

Myona, I need you to sign some paperwork before you leave, I have a check here for you.

She wasn't up for filling out any paperwork, after seeing her father on the video she just wanted to disappear into her room for today, so she asked if it can just be done another day.

Well Myona, by law we have to release these funds to you today.

How much is it? She asked still wiping the tears from her puffy eyes.

It's a little over 7 million dollars, it's just your first pay out from your trust fund, you get another one when you turn 25 years old and your last one on your 40th birthday.

What! She couldn't believe what she just heard, it felt like her head was stuck under water, she acted like her ears popped and she was fighting to hear the words he spoke clearly

Did you just say 7 million dollars?

Yes, i did.

Even Jyel couldn't believe what he heard, 7 million dollars, Mr. Mitchell did he leave her all the money?

Mr. Mitchell laughed a little, then shook his head in disbelief of the question, no he treated you all the same, you have a personal video and a check set up for you as well, on your 18th birthday.

Can I see my video now? That's to whole years from now, you can put a hold on the check. Just let me see the video for now.

Jyel, come on now you got to wait your turn, your daddy did everything he did for a reason, now you just gone have to be patient.

But Grandma!

There is no buts Jyel, now I don't want to hear it again.

As Jyel walked out he dropped his head, disappointed he couldn't receive his message from his dad early.

After she signed for the check she went home, and locked herself in her room, and played the video of her dad's last message to her over and over again. She let his words beat in her heart like a drum, as she sat by the window crying uncontrollably, she could hear a loud knocking at the door, it was her brother, he busted through, with a deep panic covered all over his face.

Myona, what are you doing, locked in this room, not answering, you know you heard me knocking!

Yea, and!

Answer shit! You scared the hell out of me, making me think you did something to yourself or something.

Jyel I'm sad, I'm not suicidal, crying wiping away her tears, she grabbed the remote control and started the video of her dad over again, so she could watch it from the beginning.

No! no! no! Myona you can't sit in here and do this to yourself, I can't let you do this, now I know you miss mom and dad, hell if anybody could understand that, it would be me, I miss them like crazy too.

Jyel I'm scared!

Scared of what? Jyel said as he sat down next to his sister on the bed.

I'm scared that I'm going to forget them, I could barely remember the memories, we shared with mom, we were so young and we didn't get to get enough time with her or dad, and it's just not fair.

As she continued to cry uncontrollably, he grabbed her and hugged her, trying to get her to calm down.

Sis listen to me, your right, it's not fair but it's just the hand we were dealt, we have to be thankful that we still got each other, if it wasn't for Grandma Vickie, think, we could have been separated, but we weren't, we grew up in a great home with love, besides our parents, we never wanted for anything and remember what Grandma would always say, God don't make no mistakes.

Every word set in that he said and her heart slowly began to calm, when she looked up, Grandma Vickie was standing in the door watching them in their special moment and it made Grandma Vickie proud knowing if she were to leave this world today she knew they would be here for each other. Once Myona looked her way, she decided to step into the room and have a talk with the both of them, she felt no time was better than right now to let them know about their father's past, that way won't nobody be able to fill their heads with things that are not true.

Myona and Jyel I want to talk to you.

They both looked her way, bracing their self as if they were about to get some bad news, about what Grandma, they both said.

About a couple of things about your dads past, Myona we talked about some of this before but I want to get everything out on the table today, to me really been overdue, I just been trying to find the right time and space to tell you.

Grandma Vickie sat right across from them and she didn't start until she made sure she had their full attention.

Ok now it's going to be a lot of things you're going to hear about your father and some of it is true.

They were surprise how truthful their grandmother started the conversation, not sugar coating anything in the middle.

What part is true, because Grandma the Detective told me a mouth full, the way they printed dad to be was a monster, they said he killed a lot of people Jyel said waiting for an answer.

Ever since he was a baby, he been in the streets, and a lot stemmed from how rough he had it growing up.

Why, I mean you were there right? Myona said wiping away the last of her tears.

Yea I was there, but somethings I couldn't fix that was broken in him, he took not having a father hard, so even though he had our love, he always was still looking for more, and in the mist of trying to find that love, he found it in all the wrong places, so it came with a lot of pain, so yeah, he did a lot of things that I'm not proud of to say, but I saw a lot of change in him once he had your brother Aiden, and I do mean a big change, he turned his whole life around, then you guys were born and all he would ever talk about was how he wanted to be a great father to you'll, one thing I know for sure is he loved y'all so much, I helped him set up all these different financial accounts, I truly think in the back of his mind, he knew that karma would someday catch up with him for all the things that he did.

Grandma do you think it was because something my daddy did, is the reason my momma got killed Jyel said dropping his head as the last word rolled off his tongue.

I wish I could answer that baby, even though I doubt it, he had been out the streets for years, by the time your mom got killed and they weren't even together when it happened, I just wish you didn't have to go through any of this baby, but what I do know is I'm going to be here for you till the day I die, I got your back!

They both said they knew and appreciated her every word, then each hugged her as tight as they could.

Jyel baby, you think you could give me a minute with your sister please, Grandma need to talk to her.

He said ok, then walked out the room shutting the door behind him, making sure he gives them their privacy, once Grandma Vickie noticed the door was shut she turned her attention to Myona.

Ok little girl, tell me what's going on with you?

I'm just a little down with everything going on, I really wish my parents were here.

I understand that but baby you got to live your life, you have to give thanks for all the blessings that you do have, you can't kill yourself over the things you don't, you're alive and well, it's your birthday and you just got a big ass check from your daddy, I don't know how you ended up in a locked room, crying your eyes out instead of being at the mall and isn't that school prom tonight?

Yeah, it is, but I really don't feel like going.

You got to go!

Why Grandma? I just want to lay here, eat ice cream and,

And watch that video of your daddy over and over again, o no you're not, Grandma Vickie said as she snatched her computer and ejected the DVD, then stood up ready to take it with her.

Grandma no! give it back.

Myona get up and get dressed, and go have some fun. One thing I know for sure is if you don't go you are going to regret it, you only got one shot at going to the prom, there is no more do overs, especially when you get my age, and I didn't get to go to the prom because I was pregnant and I really wish I would have,

Ok Grandma I'll go; can you please just give me my DVD back?

I'll give it back as soon as you get back home and tell me all the fun you had ok,

Ok!

Ok! This is going to be right here waiting on you when you get back, Grandma Vickie said as she kissed Myona on her fore head then walked out the room, letting the door close behind her.

As her grandmother left the room, she thought about the advice that she had giving her and decided that maybe she was right, so she tried her best to shake her depressed state of mind and get up and get ready to go to the prom, she did promise London that she would go with her and she knew if she tried to back out now, she would never hear the end of it. But before she called London to see what time they would be meeting up, she decided to call Ace to see if they were still going to hook up after the dance, she really liked spending time with him, he had a way with making her feel special, after two rings, he answered:

Hey what's up Meme,

Ok, now I'm really surprised,

And why is that?

Because you not only answered the phone on the second ring but you also said my name, don't try to make me feel all special, when the facts are you probably just got my name saved under new pussy or better yet, pussy I didn't hit yet!

Lol

First of all, you are special and if your name was saved under such a name, I would have called you just such.

Yeah ok and I would of beat your ass, they both laughed at her latest comment, then she jumped straight into her serious tone.

I wanted to know was we still meeting up after my school dance?

Yes, we are, and didn't you say, your birthday was today?

Yes, it is my birthday and I am not going to lie, I haven't been having the best day at all.

And why is that, if I might ask?

I don't know, I really don't want to talk about it, it's just hard to explain.

It's going to be ok, I have a Lil something for you, that I know will cheer you up.

Like!

It's a surprise, what I look like telling you over the phone, that's going to spoil my surprise.

Ok, well I'll talk to you later, I'm going to text you the address and I want you to be there by

11:45 pm, the dance ends at 12:00.

Ok anything else, Ms. Bossy lady?

No, see you later, she said as she hung up the phone, she was not able to hide her smile after she got off, her Grandma walked into the room and noticed her smiling instantly.

Ok now that's what I like to see, your friend London is here, I let her in, I hope you don't mind.

No I don't mind,

Ok I love you baby and once again I hope you have a good time, I'm about to head out I got to take care of some business but you be safe and make sure if you are going to stay out late tonight you text me to let me know you are safe.

I will and I love you too Grandma and Grandma,

Yes, baby!

Thank you,

For what baby?

Everything !

Low:

Waking up for these last couple of days has been different, but a good thing for me, being with E-b has made me view things from a different perspective. I woke up a little early just to watch her sleep, something I have never done with another woman, I'm finding myself doing with her, as I was sitting there admiring how beautiful she is, I got a text from Julius mom asking me did I find out anything in the streets about who murdered her son, I texted her back and told her I hadn't found out nothing yet but I would let her know as soon as I find out something, she texted back:

Boy, you owe me!

Each word I read touched me to the core, she was right, I did owe her, I got up and got dressed, so I could start a little investigation of my own, I walked over and kissed E-b on her forehead to let her know I were leaving and would be back soon.

Baby where you going? She asked as she sat up in the bed,

I'm just going to take care of some business, I won't be gone long,

Baby I could get dressed real fast and go with you, just give me a minute.

No baby I want you to just relax here until I get back, if you get bored how about you cook us a little something to eat, you can cook right?

Yeah I could cook!

Ok great, make us up something nice, Low said as he embraced her with a tight hug, kissed her then headed for the door. As he got in the car, he started to search for the news clip talking about his cousin's murder, so he could get the location where it all happen once he found it, he drove up to the apartment complex and instantly as he were pulling in, he noticed that there were cameras on the front of the building, pointing toward the spot they found his cousin juice, he decided to pull over into a parking spot, then walked into the main office to see if he could get some answers. As he entered, the secretary greeted him at the door.

How you doing today sir? Can I help you?

Yes, you can, my cousin got murdered in your parking lot a few days ago, I was wondering if you can help me with something.

Yes, I'm aware of the guy that got murdered that was very tragic, I'm sorry about what happen to him, how can we be of assistants to you, we told the police everything we know, which wasn't much.

When I pulled in, I seen that you have cameras on the building and I was wondering if I could get a copy of the video tape?

The secretary dropped her head as if she was trying to find some words to say.

I'm sorry but the cameras were broken and we just ended up getting them fixed about a day ago she said, without being able to keep eye contact, which made Low get instantly suspicious so he said ok, then acted like he was going to walk out then he turned around and asked for a business card and once she gave it to him, he politely said thank you and walked out. As soon as the secretary seen him leave, she rushed to the phone to make a phone call, Low watched her through the door the whole time. Once he seen she couldn't get a hold of whoever she was trying to contact, he figured he would wait till her shift was over so he could have a more personal conversation with the woman himself. After a couple of hours of waiting he finally saw the woman come out the building to lock up the office and his eyes followed her every step as she walked over to another building inside the complex, then into an apartment where she then shut the door behind her. Once he seen she was inside, he got out the car and walked up to the door and knocked.

Boom! Boom! Boom!

Who is it, she said as she called from the other side of the door.

He covered the peep hole so she wouldn't be able to see who was knocking at her door.

I'm here with your pizza!

I didn't order no damn pizza, so go the hell away!

He looked on the card from the office to make sure he spoke the woman's name correctly.

Keisha Smith, we need to talk,

Move your hand off my peep hole and talk about what?

He moved his hand to reveal his face,

We need to talk about the video tape of the murder, I know you know something, I seen how you was moving, I'm far from stupid.

Man how did you find out where I stay, we don't got shit to talk about, get out of here before I call the police.

Open the door, now I know you're not gone call the police.

She snatched the door open pushing a chrome .357 revolver in his face.

And what makes you think that? She said while showing a little aggression from his words.

Not affected by her actions, he moved in closer to close a little more space between them.

I think we can be of service to each other, I see you got some kids or kid, he said as he seen her little boy run from the back room, and I know shit can get hard out here in the streets, you know just trying to get by, but if you work with me I could be your way to a brand new start to a better

Her eyes showed interest in what he was saying, so he decided to push a little harder.

If you help me, I could give you $50,000 for the video tape and provide another $50,000 for you a new place to live, so they don't come looking for you, I know that you are protecting somebody.

The sound of the money sounded really good to her ears and put a million thoughts in her head, with that type of money life could change for her in a second, so many things was hitting her all at once, things have been hard for her but she didn't want to sell her girl out but at the same time, she has been the one first hand to see her struggling and never even asked once if she needed some help, for once she thought about being selfish, making her and her son her first priority.

Well how do I know, you aren't just bullshitting me? She said as she searched him over for the answer.

I got $50,000 for you in the car right now, that's how you will know, you show me the tape, we go get the rest, then, you and you baby can ride off into the sunset when all of this is through.

Let me see the money!

He left back out her door to go out to the car, he then went into his trunk and grabbed the duffle bag of money, then came back inside.

She still had the gun raised as he stepped into the apartment, watching his every move.

Hold on! Baby girl, take it easy, you gone have that gun on me the whole time?

I don't know you, you might think I got something to do with it.

Well do you?

No! I do not and if I did we wouldn't be talking at all; I would have been pulled the trigger.

He threw the duffle bag down in her direction.

Go ahead open it, and while you at it, do you mind if I have a seat, I'm a little tired I been running around all day.

She swatted down and opened the bag, once she looked inside, she could see that it was filled with hundred dollar bills, her eyes widened, she had never seen that much money before in her life especially all at once.

Damn you wasn't bullshitting me!

Well, I told you that, I just want that tape I know you are a single mom and I want to help you in the mist of you helping me.

Once she seen the money, she didn't give it another thought.

Ok, I'll help you!

After she put the money in her safe place, she kissed her baby, told him to watch TV, mommy would be back soon, then she locked the door behind her and they walked down to the management office. Once they were inside, she unlocked her desk drawer then pulled out a DVD and handed it to Low. Then motion for him to leave back out the door so she could lock it behind her.

Hold on! Don't move so fast Lil momma, I got to see what's on the DVD!

She fanned her hand showing a little attitude,

You want to do this here?

Yes, here and why do you care where we watch it, with all the money I'm paying you, you're not going to be working here tomorrow anyway.

Give it here!

She snatched the DVD back out of his hand and motioned for him to follow her to the back of the office, once they got inside, he could see it was the main control room. She put the

DVD inside the DVD player and pushed play, he instantly got sick to his stomach, he threw up in a nearby garbage can, he couldn't believe what his eyes were seeing, a part of him didn't want to believe what his eyes were seeing, he watched his cousin in his last minutes of his life, taking his last breath and the woman he grew to love in the last couple of days, was the one who take it from him.

A dude look we got to go, I kept my end of the deal, you want to keep watching it, then take it with you, but I don't want the police pulling up on us on some suspicious shit, thinking something wrong.

Did she tell you why she did this? he said with pain filled eyes.

No! she just wanted me to keep my mouth shut, she didn't give me any details.

She walked out the office, grabbing the trash to clean up so they don't find out she had returned back in the office after hours. As she walked out Low emptied the DVD player for his cousin video and the new one that was recording them from inside the office now and walked out behind her.

Once they got back to her house, he convinced her to get her son ready get in her car and follow him to go get the other money that he owed her, while they were riding she pulled up on the side of him and began to ask questions.

Hey roll down your window, she said as she motioned him with her hand.

He did as he were told, yeah, what's wrong,

Where are we going,

I got a Lil condo down by the riverfront, real nice overlooks the water I'm going to have you pull in the parking lot or come upstairs, whatever you would want to do, so you can get your money and be on your way.

O I know where you talking about, them condos are very nice.

Yeah, I paid a pretty penny to move into that place but it was well worth it.

I bet, ok, I'll follow you but I don't want to come inside, I'll just wait for you in the parking lot, just make sure you don't take long, I want to get me and my baby somewhere safe.

He assured her he wouldn't take long then they drove down by the riverfront, once he parked, he jumped out and disappeared into the building behind him for 10 minutes, when he reappeared he was carrying another duffle bag, instead of walking up to the driver side he approached the passenger side of her car, opening the door placing himself inside.

You were starting to worry me, I thought you might have played me, she said as she reached for the duffle bag he was holding.

Now why would I do that, without you, I would not have gotten this far, I needed this closure plus I am a man of my word.

Yeah you are, she said as smiled opening the duffle bag to check the money, once she looked inside, all she could see was a bunch of newspapers.

What is this, this isn't the money, she threw the bag back at him and went for her gun in the side of her car door.

A shot rang out, landing right square in her face entering one side of her jaw and exiting the other, stopping her reach for the gun, as the blood began to pour from her face, she screamed for help, she threw punch after punch, reaching for his gun to stop him from an attempt at getting off another shot but he overpowered her in every move.

Somebody help me, he's trying to kill me!

While they were fighting, the screams from her son in the back seat overpowered hers.

Mommy, as he cried, I want my momma, stop, crying, I want my momma!

Another shot rang out, this one landed in the side of the door, which made her want to fight harder and she began to scream louder.

Shut up bitch, I'm trying to hear myself think,

The second shot landed in her stomach and weakened her off of the impact, she began to beg for her life,

Please don't kill me, please my baby!

As she let go, he leaned back in the car, and watched her as she tried her best to fight for her life.

I told you I was a man of my word, I said that after our deal was done, that you and your son would be able to ride off into the sunset and I intend to let you do just that, I'm sorry!

He angled his gun at her head, letting the last shot hit her a little above her temple, throwing her brains out the window of the car, then he got out, went in her trunk, got the money and threw it in the back seat of his car, then he made sure he wiped everything down, put the car in drive and let it roll into the river, he sat and watched the car hit the water but decided not to leave until the babies cries couldn't be heard anymore, at that point he had turned off all his emotions, and knowing what he knew now only made him wonder did E-b know they were family from the start, and if so, then somebody put her on him. The only thing that bothered him when it came down to everything is why didn't she just take care of business, she had him right where she wanted him, so why didn't she make her move. At this point he didn't know what to think, but one thing he knew for sure was that he can't just let this go.

Myona:

When London and Myona walked into the prom, everyone greeted them with smiles and hugs. As if they were at a greet and meet, Myona started looking around and she could see from wall to wall that everybody was really enjoying their selves, instantly she could hear her grandmother's words echoing in her head (have a good time, nights like this only happen once in a lifetime) for once she decided to loosen up, let her hair down and have some fun, she danced to almost every song, she interacted with everyone who came her way. A lot of people was surprised to see her acting this way, because people were so use to her being alone not talking to anybody, they never knew she had a side to her, meanwhile, the whole party London was nowhere to be found and when she did come into view she was on the phone with somebody. Which was crazy to Myona because she was the reason she showed up in the first place, but instead of getting upset, she paid it no mind and continued having one of the best nights of her life, she had never had this much fun, out of nowhere they announced that they were Approaching the last 30 minutes, they told everyone to get that special someone on the dance floor and they broke out the slow songs, that's when she looked at the clock for the first time all night and noticed that it was I I :30 p.m. and she was supposed to be meeting Ace at 12:00, so she decided to skip the slow song and grabbed her things and headed to the door to walk out a little early so she could cool down, plus she left her phone in the car because she didn't want to carry it all night but now she needs it so she could call him to make sure he were still coming. As she walked out the building, she forgot to let London know that she was leaving, so she went back to open the door to the school and noticed it had locked behind her, instead of screaming at the top of her lungs for somebody to let her back inside, she just headed toward the car instead, she knew it would be pointless to try to scream, knowing no one would be able to hear because the music was extremely loud, it was so loud if they wanted to they could have a party in the parking lot. When she got to her car, she pulled out her keys and opened her car door, then out of nowhere somebody grabbed her from behind, forcing her into her car, pressing her head down between the seat and the middle arm rest, pulling her dress up over her waist, exposing her body to the public for whoever wanted to see, the harder she fought it felt like the more excited they got.

You like this shit, this what turn you on, this the shit you like baby, he whispered in her ear as he violently ripped off her panties, forcing them in her mouth and down her throat to stop her from screaming because it was breaking his concentration.

As she fought back as hard as she could, she screamed:

Somebody help me, please help, she said as she tried her best to shift her body in a way he wouldn't be able to go inside her, but none of her tricks worked, then out of nowhere he smacked her in the face, without pause he began choking her, one of her hands became free, she swung a blow catching him in the face, hoping that would get him off, but it didn't faze him, for the first time in her life she was scared, she knew she could fight with everything she had in her but still would not be able to match his strength, he overpowered her at every turn, he even at times laid his whole body weight on top of her to tire her out, forcing her legs open.

Please don't do this, stop please, she said as the closer he got to getting what he wanted, the more she felt powerless, the tears began to pour down her face.

He entered inside her, ripping through her walls, inflicting terrible pain, that shot all through her body, all she could do was scream in agony, helpless, thoughts of her mother started running through her mind, and at that very moment, she wondered was she too, about to die.

Ace:

As Ace rode through the school parking lot he called Meme phone over and over, only to get sent to the voicemail every time. Something felt stranger, and he couldn't place a finger on it but one thing for sure was he couldn't believe that she would stand him up, he kept a positive mind thinking maybe her phone just went dead, as he pulled into a parking spot to give her a little time to fry to call him, he remembered that she said the party lets out at 12:00 a.m. he knew in his heart it had not yet reached that time. He looked at his watch and noticed that it was only 11:47, as he rolled down the window to get some fresh air, he could hear, what sounded like screams for help, coming from somewhere in the parking lot. Once he cut the engine off to see if he could listen in a little better, he could hear the screams much clearer, instantly he could feel a strange feeling in the pit of his stomach that something was wrong, as he got out the car, he retrieved his gun from the glove department box, once outside he followed the screams until he walked up on a car that appeared to be two people having sex but the closer he got, the voice became more and more familiar, as he crept around the car to get a closer look, he could see the guy was choking Meme trying to stop her from screaming, all while fucking her violently halfway outside the car, an instant rage came over him, as he ran up behind him and hit him over the head repeatedly with the butt of the gun until he fell to his knees, releasing her in the process, not able to take the blows Ace had just passed down, it was hard for him to regain consciousness, not able to get back to his feet, grabbing at his head as the blood poured from his open wounds. Once he was able to get a clear sight, he seen a gun being pointed directly at his head. This was no longer a game, or a drew out fantasy, he began to beg for his life.

Hold up man! No don't shoot me, please don't kill me man!

As Meme got to her feet, she stumbled into Aces arms, As Ace wrapped his arm around her to let her know that she is safe now, he zeroed in back on him.

Take that motherfucking mask off motherfucker! Ace said watching his every move.

Ok! I'll take it off, just please don't kill me man!

Without hesitation, he snatched the mask off, revealing his face,

Frank! She screamed in disbelief, it was you, you the one who raped me, anger began to build inside her as she wiped her tears from her face.

Rape you no! I was just role playing, Frank said as he looked confused from her words and reactions.

You know this motherfucker baby?

Yeah he goes here to this school, she said as she turned her attention to Frank, you raped me and you talking about you was role playing, you think I wanted this, you think I wanted you to rape

Frank, seen by now that he had been played by London and now he knows his life depends squarely on the truth, so he started talking fast.

Look Myona, I swear to god, that's the god's honest truth, I would never rape you, London told me that you were into that type of stuff, so I went with it, because I like you so much, she told me you knew about it and everything.

You're a fuckin liar, she screamed at the top of her lungs, then snatched the gun out of Ace's hand and aimed it back at Frank's face.

Myona no! I'm telling you the truth!

My friend would never do something to me like that, she said as she pulled the trigger, sending bullet after bullet into his face at point blank range until the clip emptied, stuck in a state of shock, Ace's words snapped her back into reality. She fell to her knees, crying uncontrollably, overwhelm with a rush of emotions, she began to scream at the top of her lungs, Ace picked her up, trying his best to force her to her feet.

No baby no! we can't do this right now we have to go, he put her in the passenger seat of her car searched for her keys, found them then drove off as fast as he could, as he was pulling out the parking lot he noticed the prom was just now started to let out, as he looked at Meme, she were still crying, shaking uncontrollably, he became bothered, he couldn't find the words to comfort her at a time like this and that hurt his heart worse than anything, cause he so badly wanted to be the one she could run too, confused on what to do, he returned to the only thing he knows how, to try to calm her down, he pulled over and rolled up a joint, lit it and passed it to her.

What are you doing! I don't want that shit!

Listen! Meme I just really need you to calm down and this I know for sure can help, I know your head is in a bad space right now. But now it's a guy dead and we have to make sure we stay out of prison.

She took the joint out of his hand and puffed it a couple of times, then passed it back.

What do you mean, we, I'm the one who killed him they are going to come take me to jail and to be honest, I don't give a fuck, this motherfucker should have never raped me!

Once again Meme calm down! And believe me, you talking like your tough but in reality, you do not want to go to prison, I heard what it's like and I would rather die, then let them do that shit to me, I couldn't imagine being pent down.

He could tell that his very words were playing in the playground of her mind, taking a swing on the rides, of a beginning to an end.

Ok what should we do?

I need you to clean up, we have to go back.

Go back! Why in the fuck would we do that, I know the police is there by now.

Yeah, they might be but first of all I have to go back to get my car, if we leave it there, once the parking lot clears out, they are going to run my license plates and since I don't go to your school, they are for sure going to make me a person of interest.

And what is a person of interest?

That's the one they are going to suspect who did the crime.

Damn! Ok, she said as she looked in the mirror, trying her best to wipe away all the messed up makeup that's smeared all over her face.

Are you ok? I don't need you to break down if we come across some police or see some of your friends, you have to act normal, I know that's a little hard for you but for both of our safety, you have to keep your emotions in check.

She shook her head yeah as if she understood him, then she jumped out of the car, fixed her clothes, then walked to the other side of the car to jump in the driver seat, as he got out the car, he looked deep into her eyes to see if he could get a vibe from her, in truth, he seen nothing at all.

Are you sure you could do this?

Ace, watch out, I told you I got this,

When they pulled back up to the school parking lot, most of it was taped off, the police looked to be questioning a couple people about what happen, Meme pulled over to see what is it she should do next not able to figure it out on her own she decided to ask.

What should we do?

We are going to have to pull in, I can't leave the car here!

She looked around once more, ok, Ace give me the keys, you take my car and I'll go in and get yours.

Are you sure you can do this?

Ace give me the keys, I told you I got this, now hurry up we don't have much time.

Once he gave her the keys, he told her that he would meet her down the street at the shell gas station, then she jumped out the car and disappeared into the crowd. The car wasn't far in distance, she kept checking the alarm until she could catch it in her visual, wishing before she got out the car she would have just asked what kind of car was it, and since she didn't her actions also caught the attention of the Detectives on the scene, the closer she got to the car, she could hear a voice, sounding like they were calling to get her attention, she tried her best not to look back their way but the voice was getting closer and closer.

Excuse me, young lady, excuse me, I know you hear me talking to you.

When she turned around there were only a few feet that stood between her and the Detective.

Yeah, I heard you but I didn't know who you were, you could be somebody trying to attack me or something.

Yeah that would be smart with a million police in the parking lot, what's your name young lady?

Myona!

Ok, Myona what?

Myona Wright and you don't have to be so rude!

Ok, Myona Wright where are you coming from?

First, can you tell me why I'm being questioned in the first place? I'm just trying to get home before my grandmother starts getting worried about me and gets to looking for me, why are you guys here anyway? She said as she tried her best to pull the attention off of her as best as she could.

I'll answer your questions after you answer mines, now where are you coming from? and I'm not going to ask you again!

I been here at the prom all night,

Well if you been here, you would have known what was going on,

I left a little bit early to go grab me something to eat before the restaurant closed, then my friends drop me back off to get my car, is there anything else?

It depends on you, is there somebody who could vouch for you being here?

Can somebody vouch for me! Yeah how about the whole party, not to mention I'm dressed up as well.

Yeah I could see you dressed up but it doesn't look like it was to go to no prom, I'm actually surprised your family even let you leave the house like that.

His words had burned straight through her, she just dropped her head, usually she prided herself on how she dressed and just once, when she let her guard down, she ended up raped and looked down on by a cop like she was a hooker, she wondered from this point could things get any worse. Out of nowhere a girl who she had seen earlier in the party approach them crying, walking through she wasn't watching where she was going and ended up bumping right into the Detective.

I'm so sorry, sir, she said then she looked Myona's way and ran straight to her with open arms,

Myona o my God, somebody killed Frank!

What! When! How!

That's him under the white sheet, London was looking all over for you, she is really worried about you, she thought something had happened to you.

No! no! I'm fine, I told you guys I was hungry and going to get something to eat, o my God, what happen! How?

Somebody shot him, Myona and it was horrible, I can't believe they killed him like that, she said as she stepped closer, you could see his brains coming out of his head, o my God, I can't get that picture out of my head.

What! But how? I didn't see him at the party!

The Detective stepped in, yea he was found in a very suspicious way, that we are looking into.

And what way is that, Myona said as she watched his body movement to see if it would lead her to any answers.

I'm not at liberty to say, the Detective said as he started to walk away, then he turned back around.

Young lady I also need you to come with me,

Her heart felt like it was placed on a race track, running a hundred miles per hour,

What did I do? I didn't do nothing! Myona said as she began to back up.

Calm down it's just procedure, we just want to collect your DNA.

No, once again I did nothing wrong!

Myona it's ok! They did everybody at the party the same way, and we did nothing wrong so we got nothing to worry about, just give them what they want so you can go home, the girl said in a comforting tone.

Yes, please make this easy for the both of us, other than that I'm going to have to detain you and get a warrant for your DNA by a judge and trust me I will get it.

Scared from the outcome, but still feeling like she had no choice, she gave in and decided to give him her DNA, after they were through, she jumped in the car and met Ace at the gas station, as soon as she pulled up, he walked up to the driver side window, his face was covered with worry.

What happen? What took you so long?

I got stopped by a Detective,

What! Ace said as he took a step back and looked around.

Ace I didn't tell them nothing, but they wanted to collect my DNA!

For what? And I hope you told them no, did you tell them no?

I tried but he started talking about if I refused, he was going to detain me and get a court order from the judge.

Fuck! Damn what the fuck, why you of all people? I knew I should of went and got the car!

No then you would probably be in jail right now, that parking lot was crazy, and I'm gone be ok, he said it's procedure, they got everybody DNA who was at the prom tonight but other than that they don't have nothing on me.

Ace sat and thought for a second on why would they need her DNA?

Myona words broke him out of his thoughts, I just don't see why we couldn't just tell them the truth, that motherfucker raped me.

That gun isn't clean, we would have had to answer more questions than one!

What you mean by that?

The gun was used in another murder,

Why would you walk around, with a dirty gun Ace? I'm not in the streets and I know that!

I didn't think all this was going to happen!

So what are we going to do now? Myona said showing on her face, she was becoming more and more uneasy.

I want you to stay with me a couple of days.

But I can't go with you,

Meme listen to me, if they come for you and try to bring you in, then I'll tell them I shot him,

But you didn't shoot him, I did, why would you do that?

He couldn't answer her, he truly didn't know why he would take the rap for girl he truly didn't even know but he was willing too, he felt like in a crazy way he had to protect her, he turned around and started walking back to his car.

Ace where are you going?

He stopped in his tracks, turned around and said, I'm going home and I want you to come with me, but I am not going to force you, I'm going to leave the decision if you're coming or not all up to you.

What about my family? What am I supposed to tell them? I know they are going to be worried about me!

Believe me, they will be ok, it's only going to be for a couple of days, and you can message them and let them know you are doing ok in the process, just not tonight.

What will I do for clothes, I'm not going to stay in this for that long, what am I supposed to do!

Meme don't worry, I'm going to take care of everything.

After she put in a little thought, she agreed to go home with him, till things cooled off, she followed him all the way to his house, once they pulled up in the front of his home, another rush of emotions overpowered her, and she lashed out in anger, crying, beating the stirring wheel, she couldn't get the thoughts of what Frank did to her out of her head. One minute she was cool, the next minute her thoughts were all over the place, sending her into a complete melt down. She was in pain, even though she took his life, she felt her innocence could never be an even trade, her heart ached, pushing her past the point of not being able to breathe.

Ace pulled open the door, pulling her out of the car and trying his best to hold her close to calm her down as she fought him to get free. You could tell in her face she was experiencing real trauma from what she just went through and he knew it would take some time before she got any better but he didn't care, he was willing to help her in any way he could.

Meme baby calm down, I'm not going to hurt you, I just want to take care of you!

Even though he was holding her telling her it was going to be alright, and he felt like that was what she needed, reality was, she didn't know him and it scared the hell out of her, she was in a place in her mind that she didn't know who she should trust, a part of her felt safe but the other part of her wondered if he was just like Frank, she began to question herself, why am I here, what am I doing here, but the more she heard the comfort in his words, it began to calm her down and bring her back to a peaceful place. He let her go and looked her in her eyes, wiping her tears away.

Meme I know it's hard, but I need you to trust me I am not going to hurt you and I'm also going to make sure I do everything in my power to make sure nobody else will hurt you again either.

As her eyes stirred back at him, she could sense deep down he meant every word he was saying, when he was holding her tight, she could feel the racing in his heart, showing a true sign of love, just no words have been confessed. Once they entered the house all of her energy felt like it had left her body, she laid down on the couch and passed out, wanting to forget the whole night as if it never happened. Ace laid behind her, wrapping his arm around her holding her tight as he went to sleep as well.

Low:

As Low was driving home thinking about how he was going to handle facing E-b with all the information he just found out, a deep sadness overcame him, to him E-b wasn't just another girl, she was really special, his feelings had grown strong for her in a short period of time. As he began to play inside his thoughts about the special moments they shared, he wondered did she really care about him or was this all just a game to her. And if this was a game, then she had to be one of the best to have ever done it, because when he looked into her eyes, all he could see stirring back at him was love. Once he came to a stop light, he noticed that his phone was going off, somebody had sent him a text. Before pulling off he decided to read it and it read:

This is your Aunt J, I know you been getting my messages, I told you I need to see you and I don't mean later, I mean right now!

Damn, he knew she was mad at him and the truth is, he really was trying to avoid her, because he didn't have any information for her at the moment and he didn't want to let her down. But even now that he does have knowledge about who caused his cousin's death, he still doesn't know if he would want her to see the video, Julius was her only child, so he knew something like that would be hard to watch, but yet and still, he had to go see her, so he turned the car around and made his way to her house. Once he pulled up in the front of his auntie house, it felt like a great big weight fell on his shoulders, she had been watching from the window as the car pulled up, she rushed out on the porch and signaled for him to hurry up and come inside. As he stepped out the car, his feet felt like they had been placed in quick sand, dreading the conversation that was in front of him, he moved as slow as he possible could. Once he entered inside the house, his Aunt J embraced him with a hug and a kiss on his cheek, then they both sat down on the couch, giving him her full attention she lowered the sound to the television to make sure there would be no interruptions.

I did my research and I have something to show you, she said as she pulled Juices phone from her pocket. Then she moved in closer showing Low the phones call list, this is the last call that he made, do you recognize this number? I was going to call it back but I didn't want to do that without talking to you first.

Once he looked at the number, he knew right away that it was indeed E-b's number, he instantly became quit, not able to say a word.

His Aunt J quickly picked up on his vibe, sensing he knew something, so she decided push for couple of questions.

You know something don't you? Speak up! What is it that you are not telling me?

The sadness in his eyes told a story to a book she gave two fucks about reading, as she looked at him, begging him to explain his self, tears began to run down his face.

I know who did it, he said as he slightly dropped his head.

His Aunt J was excited by his words but threw off by his actions, not being able to embrace where he was coming from.

Ok! But now what's the problem, why you crying? They sole don't look like tears of joy to me!

He explained everything from the beginning to the end and after he was finish, it was clear to her that he was in love with the bitch who killed her son, his emotions had fell onto his sleeve.

And Aunt J it's something else I need to tell you!

What baby?

I have the videotape of the murder; I didn't want to tell you but I would be wrong to keep that from you!

You didn't want to tell me! Why because of some bitch, you were going to fry to keep this shit a secret? You would choose a bitch over your family?

No! I just know how hard it would be to see the tape, I would never choose anybody over my family, Aunt J you're like a mother to me!

I want to see it!

Are you sure, Aunt J? it was hard for me to watch.

I said I want to see the damn tape! The look in her eyes shown a total different person, a person that lost all peace in her soul, and would destroy whatever that came into her path.

He pulled it from his jacket pocket and handed it to her, then made his way to exit the room.

Where in the fuck do you think you're going, you going to sit your ass down right here and watch this video with me over and over again until you get it in your head, that killing this bitch who did this to my baby is not an option, it's a must, your cousin gave his life up for you, he admired you, he lost his fuckin life because of you! She said as she smacked him across the face, this mess is on you!

She turned the video on and as she watched, she instantly started to grab at her chest, her heart was not only broken into pieces but a strong pain had shot through her body, as she tried to stand up, she couldn't, the pain caused her to fall over, she began to get dizzy which caused her not to be able to keep her balance, her actions is what caught Low's attention.

Aunt J are you alright Aunt J! he called out to her.

Her facial expression was covered in pain, her eyes began to roll in the back of her head, her words began to leak out slowly, almost to a faint, like she had run for miles and was now well out of breath.

They killed my baby, why did you let them kill my baby? He never did nothing to nobody!

Scared she was losing consciousness he rushed to the phone and called the ambulance, it was obvious she was either having a heart attack or from what she had saw, her body had fell into a complete shock, he sat with her until the paramedic got there and once they placed her on the stretcher, he headed towards his car before being stopped in his tracks by a loud scream, as he turned to see where it was coming from, he noticed his Aunt J had somehow regain consciousness and was fighting the medic as they tried their best to help her, he ran over to see if he could calm her down.

Aunt J please calm down, please let them help you.

She pushed them off one by one, I don't want their help, I don't want to be here anymore, I just want to die, just let me go with my baby!

Aunt J stop it; you don't mean that!

I just want to die! I don't have a reason to live no more, that bitch took that reason from me, he was all I was living for, I'll kill that bitch, let me go, where she at, let me go, I'm going kill that bitch myself, and I don't care if they caught me, I don't care what they a do to me!

Aunt J calm down, he lowered himself next to her head so

he could speak to her in her ear, I got this, just trust me, I'm going to take care of it.

As he was lifting his body up, she with all her might, pulled him back down to her.

I want this shit to make the news, I want it to be real messy, an eye for an eye! Then she let him go and he stood up, assuring her that he heard her and it will be just that, the medic attempted to put the oxygen mask over her face but she motioned for them to wait, she wanted to make sure she could get her last words out.

I want it messy, you hear me! You owe me! You owe Julius, he paid with his life, you hear me!

They loaded her in the back of the ambulance and he watched as they drove her away.

It felt like his heart had fallen out of his chest, all he wanted to do was make E-b feel how he was feeling, his Aunt J was like a mother to him and once she said she had nothing to live for, it made him feel the same way, she is very important to him and not only did he lose her respect but he felt like he also lost her love as well. As he got into the car, his head began to spin, so many fucked up emotions were all attacking him all at once, crowding his thoughts, a deep stress came over him, making it hard to focus on what he should do next, the only thing that was clear to him was E-b had crossed a big line, now he had unfinished business to tend too.

Ace:

Ace sat up in his chair, watching Meme as she slept, admiring just how beautiful she truly is, he thought about everything that not only has happen last night but everything that has transpired in the last few days and things were starting to get more and more overwhelming ever since he got back into town, he had a feeling, the longer he stayed, the more bullshit were going to happen, the girl he is beginning to fall in love ended up having to kill a motherfucker because he raped her, now it's a chance Meme could get caught up in a murder case. He knew he couldn't let that happen, E-b killed a motherfucker because they were following them, and he had to kill a motherfucker in the bathroom of the club which also could have been a setup, made to look like a robbery which he will never know because he is also dead, he couldn't take being in Cincinnati so he knew he had to focus on his real reason for being here, putting out the truth about what happen between him and his dad, so he could close this chapter of his life forever, then he can head back home and when he leaves, he planned on also taking Meme with him, he wanted to take care of her, she was special to him and he wasn't willing to lose her for nothing in the world. After bathing in his thoughts, he got up from his chair and moved over to the desk and began to get started on his little research to see if he could find his grandmother last known address. It took him all but 5 minutes of looking around and he got it, he grabbed the journal, wrote down the address and headed for the door, making sure he was quiet, he knew she needed all the rest she could get, so he tried his best to move quiet so he made sure that he didn't wake her as he went out the door. Once he got in the car, he put the address in his GPS, it said he will make it to his destination in the next 30 minutes. As he drove, the closer he got, the more his thoughts began to play a big part with his nerves, he thought about once he knocked on the door and she answered, what he would say, how would he actually start the conversation, what would be her reaction to seeing him, would she be mad that he was even here or just happy to see him all together, after a while he pulled up to the curb, right in front of his grandmother's house. All his plans on how he would do things instantly went out the window. He was back to a blank slate, scared to get out of the car and approach the house. Confused on what he should do next, as he looked over to the passenger seat, he seen the journal laying there, he replayed all the times in his head of this day when he would finally get his moment to share his truth no matter how bad it is and he knew, he couldn't just get up and leave now. Once he blocked off his thoughts, his strength was able to return back to his legs. He got out the car, then walked up to the front door of the house, after he checked his surroundings, he got close but couldn't bring himself to knock, overpowered by his thoughts of the what if's, he got out a pen from his pocket and wrote a message on the journal stating:

My reasons, my truth, I'm sorry Aiden, then he rolled it up and placed it in the mailbox, then he knocked on the door, turned around and hurried back to his car, got in and drove off before anyone could come to the door to answer, as he rode away, he could see someone through his rearview mirror come outside, not able to make out who it might be, but he could notice they had come out to look around then they grabbed the journal from out the mailbox, not sticking around to be noticed, he turned off to the next street, feeling a big lightness in his spirit, now he could start working on his peace that he so longed for.

Jyel:

Jyel heard a knock at the door, so he rushed downstairs as fast as he could, hoping it was his sister, he had been worried about her all night, after the word spread about the murder that happened in the school parking lot, he had been calling her phone all night trying his best to get in touch with her but only finding her phone going straight to the voicemail, which is not like her, they always promised to keep open communication no matter what, deep inside he could feel something was wrong, he knew he wouldn't be able to rest until he knew for sure that she was ok, as he opened the door, no one were standing outside, all he could see was a car pulling away from the curb driving slowly away. Which was weird because this type of shit has never happened before, as he turned around ready to head back into the house, he seen a notebook sticking out of the mailbox. Once he grabbed it, his first instinct was to open it up to see what it is, the first thing that caught his eye was what was written on the front, which said:

My reason, my truth, I'm sorry Aiden,

He became curious on what that mean, he rolled it up and walked back into the house, as he was entering back in he was instantly greeted at the door by his grandmother.

Jyel, who was that at the door?

Nobody Grandma, he said as he slid the notebook behind his back and into his back pocket.

I know I heard somebody at the door now! Who was it?

Nobody Grandma, when I got to the door, nobody was there, but I did see a car pulling off from the front of the house real slow and they didn't stop when I came out, I just figured that they had the wrong house.

Her face twisted in a confused expression.

That doesn't sound right, what's going on around here, your sister hasn't come home and now strange cars is knocking on my door and pulling off, oh lord it's a lot going on tonight, have you talked to your sister yet at all?

No ma'am, every time I call her phone, it keeps going straight to the voicemail.

Ok, please let me know if you do end up talking to her, I'm really starting to get worried about her.

Ok I'll let you know, he said as he stormed up the stairs, he went into his room and shut the door behind him, once inside he pulled out the notebook he retrieved from the mailbox and began to start reading it from the beginning. Within just a few pages, he couldn't believe what he was reading, it appeared to be his dad's journal, sharing his deepest thoughts in detail about murders he committed when he was alive, he read for hours, caught up in every story, trying not to get choked up in all the mixed emotions, from all the pain his father inflicted on people's families, for his love of money he held no punches, through each story his imaginary image he built about his dad was slowly fading away. It talked about his brother Aiden and how his dad had drugged his mother in order to get custody, but it was those same drugs which ended up being the cause of her death. Right then he wondered if his brother knew all these horrible things and if he did was that the reason he left, or maybe his father killed him too, anxious to know more, he continued to read thinking if his dad actually had something to do with killing Aiden's mom, then it could be a possibility that he could have killed his mom also. He continued to read the journal to see if maybe he could find some type of answers to the questions he been dying to know, the deeper he got into the book, the more his heart was racing, with each sentence he got lost in time, at the same time he couldn't believe what he was reading, looking endlessly into his father's past he was at the point of not wanting to read anymore, then as he turned to the very next page, he locked eyes on a heading that was wrote in a different hand writing then the rest and it said:

The death of Lamar Wright and Myona Way, by Aiden Wright, his heart was no longer racing, it had fell all the way off the track, crashing into a wall of unspoken pain. Every detail broke his heart to the point his emotions became tied to a rope and was being pulled back and forth in a strong game of tug of war, on the other side was rage, there were no more questions on who killed his father and mother, because it was written with pride all over the pages, but what the book didn't explain was why. He sat out to find Aiden, swore nothing but revenge, he knew from this day moving forward that would be the only thing on his mind. A part of him understood him having hard feeling about his dad because of what he did to his mom, but there was no reason for Aiden to bring their mother into something that was between him and dad. She died from his father's mistake, he couldn't contain his thoughts, which only made more questions he needed answered, come into play, one of the main questions was, did he know about us? And if so, why didn't he care? Did he intend to make us feel the same pain he was feeling? He looked up at the clock and realize the morning had set in and Myona was still nowhere to be found, he went into her room, and placed the journal under her pillow and turned to walk out only to stop in his tracks thinking that his grandmother might check her room, trying to find clues on other places she might have went last night, so he decided to take it and place it under her bed instead, knowing that wouldn't be a place his grandmother would check because of her bad knee's she would never bend down that far. A part of him felt bad for not bringing the new found information to his grandmother but he knew it would break her heart and plus he knew she would only try to lecture him about God's forgiveness and that God would want him to forgive his brother and blah, blah, blah, he quickly pushed that thought out of his mind feeling like, she couldn't possibly know how he feels because she's not in his shoes, so how could she ever talk like that, her brother never killed her mother, the thoughts built more and more anger up in his heart, to the point his mind was made up, there will be no talking it out the day he sees his brother, just pure bloodshed, there will be no room for forgiveness, just a big pay back for all the pain he caused.

London:

London rolled over in the bed, her whole body was arching, a strong sickness had made it impossible to sleep any last night, she tossed and turned every hour on the hour, not to mention, when she was at the party, she felt strange the whole night, she tried to drink but the smell of the liquor only made her stomach turn, as she sat up in the bed, her body felt weak as she tried her best to make it to her feet, instantly she could feel everything that she had eaten in the last 24 hours, force its way up from the bottom of her stomach to the surface of her throat, exploding out of her mouth, covering any and everything that were in her path, as she made it to the toilet and began to pray to it faithfully, her mother came in the house and noticed all the mess she had made, following the trail all the way to the bathroom.

Bitch what the fuck is you doing? I hope you know you cleaning this shit up!

Momma, I don't feel too good, I been feeling like this since last night, I don't know what's wrong with me!

No shit dumb ass I could see that; the question is what the fuck was you out doing last night? Drinking, getting high, trying to be grown, doing shit you aren't supposed to be doing, you supposed to be going to school and getting a fuckin education, that's it that's all!

London mamboed under her breath, I am not doing nothing you aren't already did,

Excuse me, you little bitch, do you got something to say? Huh?

London tried her best to look away but it was too late to back down now, once London didn't say a word, her mother reached down and pulled her by her hair, smacking her across the face and snatching her to her feet.

Did I hear you say something smart? If so, say that shit to my face bitch, go head, speak the fuck up! Huh! I can't hear you, you got lips, how about you use them for something more than wrapping them around some Lil boy's dicks! Now tell me what you said!

Momma let me go, she said as she tried her best to fight from her mother's grip.

Not until you tell me what the fuck you said, come on, you bad!

I said nothing you wouldn't do momma damn!

Her mother swung her around by her hair causing her to fall to her knees, then she popped her in the mouth as hard as she could with a strong backhand, causing her to fall to her knees.

Don't you worry about what the fuck I do, you ungrateful, ass bitch! What I do, keep these bills paid and food on the table, you ain't talking that shit when you come in here soaking up my heat, eating up all my food out my motherfucking refrigerator, you don't be Judging what the fuck I do then, now all of a sudden you want to be Judge Judy, you running around here thinking you grown and you don't even know how to clean your pussy properly, after I use the bathroom after you, you leave that motherfucker smelling like the fish market, that's your problem, you worrying about everybody else when you need to be worrying about your damn self.

She let her go and proceeded to walk out the bathroom, then she turned around to look over her one more time, you make sure you watch your mouth, I am not gone tell you again, all of a sudden her facial expression looked like a light bulb went off in her head.

And I'm gone tell you another thing, if you come up pregnant out in the streets, trying to be grown, you on your own! Don't think I'm gone be taking care of no fuckin babies, I barely even want you around as it is, let alone you bringing another mouth to feed!

Her words had stuck like glue, tearing every bridge down of support she thought she had, as her mother walked out the room not looking back, London slid down the wall and cried, she tried her best to be strong, but she couldn't any longer, her mother's words over time has tore her down brick by brick, she has always felt like her mother didn't love her or want her around but she had never heard them words come out her mouth until today, once she picked herself up off the ground, she began to clean up her mess, thinking what would she do if she actually came up pregnant, where would she go, what would she do for money, as she were finishing up from cleaning up the mess she made, her mother walked back into the room.

What you about to do? Her mother said as she rolled her eyes.

After I finish up here, I was just going to go to my room and lay down, I'm still not feeling to good.

Not pleased with her answer, she stepped in closer,

O no you're not! You need to go outside or something!

Outside, momma I don't have nowhere to go!

I'm sorry, not my problem you have to go find you something to do, I have company coming over in a minute and I don't need you in my way while I'm getting this money, his eyes all on you, unless you gone help me!

She couldn't believe the words she just said, thinking maybe she didn't hear her cleanly, she asked, going to help you do what?

Once again her mother rolled her eyes before she gave her answer to her question,

Don't act like you don't know what's going on, you old enough to know what I'm trying to say, hell, you got a nice Lil shape on you now, and it wouldn't hurt if you could start pitching in on these bills around here.

Mom-na is you telling me, you want me to have sex for money?

Well yeah, why not? You running around here sucking and fucking these motherfuckers for free anyway, you might as well get some money for it!

Hurt and shocked, not able to get out a word, she ran pass her mother, leaving her where she stood as she ran out the house as fast as she could, once she was in the clear, she went to the store to see if she could find someone with a phone so she could call someone to come and get her, then out of nowhere it was like her mind had went blank, even when she found the phone, she had no clue who she could call, the only true friend she could talk too, she betrayed, set up last night to get raped, she hated herself for how horrible she became, passing on all the pain her mother gave her over the years, as she danced around in front of the store, feeling bad not only from the sickness that's been bothering her but also from what she done to Myona, stuck in a bind, she decided she would make up some excuse to why she was just now calling to check on her after all this time. She called Myona number at least 5 times and it went straight to the voicemail every time, then she called Myona's house phone to see if she would answer, thinking maybe she might have lost her phone last night, Myona's grandmother answered on the second ring.

Hello Myona baby is this you!

No Ms. Wright this is London, I'm guessing Myona not around, I been trying to reach her by phone but it's like it's off or something.

No London she is not, last time I checked she said she was going to be going to the prom with you and now your calling here telling me that she is not with you, o my God, what happen to my baby!

Grandma Vickie started to panic, realizing something could have happened to her.

London told her the last time she talked to her, they were at the prom but she left early because she wasn't feeling good, she asked her if Myona was the one who took her home and she stated no, she had gotten her own ride home.

Feeling like what she was saying sounded fishy, she asked where London was so she could come see her, so she could help her fill in the blanks about the whole night, London agreed to meet.

As London stood at the store pacing back and forth in the front, Myona's grandmother pulled up in her car, motioning for London to get in.

Hey London, she said greeting her as she entered the car,

How you doing Ms. Wright?

I'm ok, I wanted to meet up with you to see if you could give me a little more information on where you think I could find Myona.

I'm sorry Ms. Wright, I really don't know where she is, I been calling her phone but she isn't answering for me either.

You mean to tell me, you're her best friend and you telling me you don't know nothing, what type of friend are you?

London dropped her head and started crying,

Still angry but feeling a little bad for attacking her, she took a step back to reflect a little, to see if the girl can help in anyway.

London what's wrong baby, I'm just a little upset I didn't

mean to holla at you, talk to me, tell me what you know, is Myona hurt?

Ms. Wright I'm sorry, I'm a mess, it's just that it's a lot going on, and I haven't been feeling too good since last night, that's way I left the party early, I kept throwing up, I don't know what' s wrong with me, she said while not able to keep eye contact.

Grandma Vickie looked her over, trying to read her body language,

Did she take you home? She said trying her best to catch her in a lie,

No she didn't, I told you Ms. Wright I got a ride, I hope you believe me, I'm sorry about everything but I'm not lying!

Y'all came together, why didn't y'all leave together?

I didn't want to spoil the party for her, she looked like she was really having fun, so I told her to stay and I'll catch up with her later, Ms. Wright she is my best friend I would never want to see somebody hurt her, where is she, Ms. Wright you are really making me worried, is something wrong? Is she ok?

She decided to back down, seeing that she wasn't changing her story,

London I don't know, she didn't come home last night and I'm starting to really get worried, this isn't like my baby to go off and not check with me or nothing, I wouldn't know what to do if something happened to her!

I'm gone call a couple of people that we were at the party with to see if they have seen or heard from her, maybe they might know where she said she was going, but don't worry. I'm going to get on it and if I find out anything I will make sure I let you know.

Ok, Grandma Vickie said but not really wanting to let it go, she felt it was something the girl wasn't telling her, she had a bad feeling about her, she just hoped she was wrong.

After they hugged, London was about to step out of the car, she felt sick once again and began to throw up outside the car, after she were through, Grandma Vickie pulled her back in the car.

Baby you don't look to good, did you take something?

No, what you mean?

Did you drink or use drugs last night? And be honest, there isn't nothing I haven't seen, did, or heard, you could tell me what's up, it will be just between us.

Yeah, I have Ms. Wright in the past but not last night, I couldn't even stand the smell of liquor, just the smell, made me want to throw up!

Ah huh, baby I think I know what your problem is, just wait here, I'm going to go inside the store and get you something I think can help you figure out this problem, just don't leave!

Grandma Vickie got out the car, went into the store and found her a pregnancy test, a coke cola, and some plain crackers to give her something to help settle her stomach down a little bit. After she purchased the items, she got back into the car and handed the bag to her.

Once London looked inside the bag, her eyes got big and wide from what she was seeing.

A pregnancy test! Ms. Wright, you think I'm pregnant?

Some of the symptoms that you are experiencing line up with you being pregnant.

No Ms. Wright I can't be pregnant! It must just be something I ate, maybe I got food poisoning or something. Here take this back and get your money back, I don't want you to waste your money on this.

London take the test and use it, it won't hurt, I just want you to be sure if you are or not!

But I don't know how, what do I do, I never did this before, do I spit on it or something?

Heavens no baby 101, I'll help you, come on, they have a bathroom here in the store, let's ask them for permission to see if we can use it.

After she agreed to take the test, they got out the car, asked if they could use the bathroom, went inside where she showed her what to do, after waiting for a while the test results read positive.

The plus sign! What does that mean Ms. Wright, I'm not pregnant?

London baby, it means you are pregnant.

I'm pregnant! No, no, no, Ms. Wright that can't be, I can't be pregnant, my mother would kill me if she found out!

What are you going to do? Grandma Vickie asked with a concerned look in her eyes.

To tell you the truth I don't know what to do, I just have to think, everything is just moving too fast.

You're going to have to tell your mom what's going on baby, there isn't no way around that!

I can't, well at least not right now, I have to figure out what I'm going to do first.

You have to tell her, eventually you're going to start showing, if you want, I could go with you, so we can both sit down and talk to her, if that would make you a little comfortable, and I know she might not like it right away but it's her grandbaby, I'm sure she will come around.

London dropped her head and began to fall deep into her thoughts, wishing she were in this perfect world that Ms. Wright was describing but she wasn't and things was for sure to get worse before they would get better any time soon.

London pick your head up baby and believe me, things just seem hard right now, but it's going to be alright, I know because I been in the same exact sit you were sitting in before, this is just going to grow you into a woman a little faster, but you have to stand up right now what's done is done! Now do you know who the baby's father is?

Caught off guard by the question, she placed her head in her hands, trying to take her new found information in.

I take that as a no, that you don't! I tell you young girls you got to know who you lay down with, you playing a dangerous game just laying up with anybody!

Ms. Wright! I know who the father of my child is!

Good, that's a relief, have you talked to him yet.

NO!

Well yeah that was a stupid question, you did just find out, I'm sorry, I just want to help you out in any way possible that

I can, my emotions are running high, forgive me I really didn't mean it, I got a lot on my mind with Myona missing, so I am not the sharpest pencil in the pack right now, if you want you can call him off of my phone, but he really should know!

It's ok, you did enough Ms. Wright, I really appreciate your help, I'm going to have to take it from here, she said as she reached for the passenger side door to make her exit.

Baby wait, are you sure?

Yeah I'm sure, I'll be alright.

Ok, call me if you need me or if you hear anything from Myona ok!

Ok, I promise, I will.

As she got out the car, shut the door and watched her roll away, it felt like and even heavier weight landed upon her shoulders, one thing she knew for sure is that she couldn't hide her being pregnant forever, Ms. Wright was right, she had to tell somebody, knowing that if her mother founded out, she would kick her out the house, she decided to make that someone Ace, not wanting to wait until she got home, she went back into the store and begged the owner if she could use their phone one more time. After a while, they broke down and gave her the phone, telling her to hurry up and make it quick, she went to the other side of the store to try her best to get a little bit of privacy, after a couple of rings on the line, Ace answered:

Hello! Who is this?

Ace this me, MoMo, please don't hang up I really need to talk to you!

Man damn, showing disappointment in his voice, alright MO, what do the fuck do you want? You calling from strange numbers, acting crazy and shit damn girl, I told you what the deal is with us, we did our thang and that's it, I don't want no relationship with you, I thought I have been real clear on that, now I know I put all this good love all the way down on you but that don't mean you should be a stocker

Ace! I'm pregnant,

Pregnant! And! Why the fuck is you telling me for? I mean congrats, I'm happy for you!

Ace you were the last person I was with and you know we didn't use no protection!

Key words, last but sure not the first, hell and I don't mean ever, I mean first that day!

She started crying, every time he talked to her that way, she felt more and more worthless, like maybe everything her mom had said to her may be true, maybe nobody will ever love her, the way she loved or imagined love should be. Not giving her a change to react he continued to tear her down word by word.

I don't know why you crying, all you got to do is just dry your eyes and go call your real baby father if you could remember who that is, or you can line them all up and go down the line to test your luck on who the baby resembles the most but MoMo don't call me with this bullshit again, as a matter of fact, lose my number altogether, we don't have no reason to share another word, bye!

Before she could get another word in, Ace hung up the phone and when she tried to call back the phone went straight to voicemail, not finish with her words, she decided to leave him a message.

Beep:

I don't know who the fuck you think you are but you got me fucked up, that's the last time I'm going to let you or anybody else talk to me crazy, fuck you motherfucker, I just wanted you to know about you baby, and I know for sure the baby is yours, you don't know me, but yet you trying to paint a picture like I'm a whore and I'm not, you are so wrong about me Ace, I was just hoping you would be in your child's life, I never had a dad, it's important that my baby have a dad, it's not about us, now I'm not going to kiss your ass or chase you around to be in his or her life, but they're going to need their dad, you hear me! If you don't believe you're the dad, that's cool, I'll be willing to do a DNA test, look Ace just please don't do this to me, I don't want to do this alone, I don't have nobody else.

As she tried to continue the message stopped in mid-sentence,

If you would like to save this message, press one, if you would like to erase this message press two, if you would like to re-record this message, press three.

Not able to finish her message, getting more and more upset, she hung up and stormed out the store, shaming the door behind her. Nothing was going right in her life at the moment and as she thought about all her past wrongs she just couldn't put a finger on what is it that she did to deserve all the things that's been happening to her, she did everything she could to try to clear her head, she sat at the park and looked at the view overlooking the city, she tried to think of all the positive thoughts she could to lift herself up, telling herself that everything was going to be alright. But nothing worked and deep inside she had no sense of direction on where she was going in life and how she was going to get there, and that alone made her worry. That same worry began to overpower her to the point she started to consider committing suicide to end all her pain. The only thing that could get in her away from giving up is the life that she now knew was growing inside her, hoping she could be a better parent then the one parent she has, a part of her wished that she knew who her dad is, so he could save her from this madness she been raised up in. Tired from crying and overthinking, she broke down and made her way home. As she entered the house she didn't want to be heard, in fear that her mother might start more trouble and end up putting her out again, and in reality, she had nowhere to go. She moved as quietly as she could through the house, hoping she could just make it to her bedroom without bringing any attention to herself. Once she got inside her room, she stripped down to her panties and bra and got under the covers. As she laid there positioning herself to get some sleep, she could hear loud music blasting through the walls, along with her mother's moans, after she closed her eyes, falling into a decent sleep, it felt like not even 5 minutes later, her mother busted into her bedroom door, laughing and talking loud to her company as they followed behind her into the room. She reeked of liquor, barely able to stand up, the man tried his best to pull her by the waist back out of the room, but she resisted, moving closer to her daughter bed trying her best to make her presence known, though London knew she had entered the room, she acted as if she were still sound asleep hoping she would just leave the room, seeing that she was sleep but it only did the opposite, it made her more eager to show her she was there and not leaving any time soon.

London! London! Get the fuck up, I know you hear me, her mother screamed at the top of her lungs, making it impossible not to be heard not only in the room but through the hold neighborhood.

Her company tried their best to step in to stop her,

April baby come on, stop now, let the girl get some rest, and come on lets finish what we started, the man said as he continued to pull her in his direction, away from the bed.

As London adjusted her eyes to the bright light that her mother turned on when she entered the room, she noticed that her mother was almost completely naked, the only thing that were covered on her body was her Brest, her body looked like it had fought in a war, she could barely look at her, she now has the complete picture of her buried in her head, her face looks like she is ten years older than her age, real wore down and tired, anyone can tell the streets has had its way with her over the years. Not wanting her mother to cause any more of a scene, she responded to her call.

Huh! What is it momma?

Bitch don't what is it momma me! You think you can just sneak your ass back up in here and I wouldn't notice? Huh?

Momma I'm tired and had a long day, can we just talk about all this tomorrow?

London laid back down throwing the covers over her head, hoping that her mother would just go away, she didn't have the energy to fight, at least not tonight, but after watching London's actions, feeling disrespected, it turned her anger up to 1000 degrees, she got so mad, she ripped the sheets from off the bed, exposing everything under them.

Naw bitch we gone talk right now, so get the fuck up!

London tried her best to find anything in her reach to cover herself up.

Momma what are you doing? I don't have no clothes on, give me my covers back!

I am not giving you shit, and you don't need these sheets anyway you got work to do.

Irritated the man stepped in between them once again, trying to get her to move back towards the bedroom.

What are you doing April! I didn't pay for you to bullshit and fight with this Lil bitch all night, I'm ready to fuck and if you aren't gone give me what I want then you can just give me my money back and I could get the fuck on my way.

London got out of the bed and began to try to head for her clothes, her mother blocked her path.

Shut the fuck up Charles, you gone get your money's worth, I'm just tired damn can a bitch get a motherfucking break!

I didn't pay for no motherfucking breaks, you said all night and that's what the fuck I want!

As London stood up, trying to get pass her mother in search of her clothes, London's mother watched Charles's eyes cruise up and down London body, caught in a trance as he watched her every move, he groped himself.

Charles what the fuck are you doing?

What! What you mean? He said as he looked away as fast as he could.

You heard what I said motherfucker, you acting like you deaf now, I said what the fuck is you looking at?

I ain't looking at nothing! What the fuck is you talking about April, come on now, you know I only have eyes for you baby!

Naw you come on, and be honest, you like what you see? Huh? You think London got a nice body?

He paused before he answered,

Naw I ain't looking at her, so get that out your mind, I'm trying to finish up what we had going on, you tripping, why would you ask me something like that?

Bitch ass motherfucker, don't you lie to me, you sitting there with a hard dick, touching yourself, watching her every move, don't play with my intelligence, London come here!

No momma, I told you I'm not like that, London said as she was picking up on the vibe that was going on around the room.

No momma! No momma no! 101 bitch don't you no momma me, I said come here now! And don't make me say it again.

Momma please don't do this, I don't want to do this, momma please, London cried out, trying her best to make her plea.

As London backed up into the corner, trying to put space between her and her mother, her mother only moved in closer, cornering her off, then

Smack!

She backed handed her, striking her with a blow so powerful it instantly sent her to her knees.

Get the fuck up little girl! I'm done playing these fuckin games with you, now I told you, you're going to start pulling some weight around here, you owe me for all the work I put in over the years just so you could be comfortable and sleep safe at night, now it's time to wake up and smell the coffee, play time is over.

Just let me go, I would rather live on the streets, then be like you and lay up with man for money, degrading myself, just let me go!

Bitch you got a lot of nerve, bitch get up, stand up! Before I punch you in your face, you always looked at me with them eyes, that the judge or the prosecutor looked at me with, like I'm crazy for just trying to survive out here in these streets, the best way I know how, that always made me want to just pull your fuckin eyes out your fuckin head, let me ask you a question London, you think you better than me? You lived comfortable in my house and never missed a meal, all these years and this whole time, you been looking down on me. You always had it so much better than me, way different from the way I grew up, my mother started me off in the tricking business when I was at the sweet at of twelve, hell, right after I got my first period, she said once the cherry popped, businesses needed to be built and bills needed to be pay, and ever since my first John, I been working. I gave you the chance to live this so called American Dream because I didn't want you to grow up the way I did but I guess my momma was right, she told me when you were born that you weren't gone be nothing but another hoe and that I should break you in, earlier then I got broke but I told her she was wrong and that you were going to be somebody. But no! you want to run around town being a little slut, and everybody knows it, I hear about it all the time about all the different dudes you have fucked and in some of the craziest places you have done it, this pussy isn't free and neither is yours, so I feel like it's time for me to pass down the family tradition. Charles! Take your boxers off and lay down on the bed.

Charles out of nowhere became extremely excited from what he was hearing and rushed to the bed, doing exactly what he was told.

Come here and get on your knees, I'm gone teach you how to properly suck a dick!

London tried her best to fight pass her mother but the threat only became more intense the more she disobeyed her mother, she screamed out no momma as loud as she could, hoping someone would just bust in the room and save her.

London if I hear you tell me no one more time, we are going to fuckin have a problem, you are my child, you do what the fuck I tell you to do, and it isn't nothing a motherfucker can do about it, I brought you in this world, me! Nobody else! You my child, and God is my witness I will take you out, you remember the next time you get to calling for help.

The look in her mother's eyes, shot chills down her spine, her body had locked up in place, fear had set in, and she could not only put a foot in front of her to run a way, she also lost all thought on what she should even do next.

Her mother forced her in her direction, placing her next to Charles on her knees.

Now I want you to watch as I show you what you supposed to do, then you can go after me.

She got down on her knees and proceeded to suck Charles dick in front of London, giving him a real intense deep throat, so good it made his toes curl. Once she was done she motioned for London to step in and take her place, when she seen she wasn't moving fast enough, she jumped up and grabbed London by the hair, trying to pull her into position.

Charles stand up, she is acting like a naughty girl, so we are going to change things up a little bit, I got a way we can break her in real, good.

As he stood, he asked, what do you suggest baby? Showing a deep interest in following orders.

I want you to fuck her throat, till I tell you to stop, fuck the shit out of her throat real, good show her what it takes to really please a man,

It will be my pleasure, he said as he proceeded to place his dick inside her mouth, but when she didn't open up, her mother pulled her hair back then cocked back and punched her as hard as she could in her face.

Open your motherfucking mouth, bitch before I knock all your teeth down your throat, scared her mother would keep her word, she did what she was told. Charles stepped in closer, forcing his dick down her throat as he gripped the back of her head, he began to start humping her throat as hard as he could.

O yes, fuck, this feels so damn good, he moaned, lost in the pleasure from her throat, he spilled out demands, open up baby and you better not bite down on my dick! Or you're really gone be sorry. In a sick way, he found pleasure in the pain spilling from her eyes, she began to throw up because of the force he was placing in each stroke, fighting hard to breathe, her mother stood watch for a little while longer, before she felt like she had seen enough, then she turned around and started heading towards the door to leave the room. London tried her best to muster up the strength to pull away from his grip but once Charles released her hair, he placed his hands around her throat, in an aggressive manner to control her movement.

What the fuck is you doing bitch, I'm not done, he screamed in her face as she crawled back in the closest comer of the room. London begged her mother for help, hoping she would get this man off of her, which made Charles even more irritated as she began to cry. He rushed to her, hand raised ready to unleash his own blows over her face.

Charles calm the fuck down, I said break her in, not kill her, damn let her breathe and London it's time for you to grow up, I told you that, it's time for you to become a woman now, and besides you are in good hands, you can spend some good quality time with your daddy, you been asking to meet the motherfucker, now there you go! Lol be careful what you wish for!

Shut up bitch!

You shut up Charles and Charles, that money you gave me is for child support, nothing else because you haven't giving me shit for her in a while. Just so you know when your done you're going to still owe me some money and don't think you leaving without paying me, you hear me?

Charles stopped in his tracks to acknowledge her words, then continued about his business with London, as London's mother exited the room. He raped and beat her over and over again all through the night, and in the morning, he left her bruised body, laying on the on the bed motionless, barely holding on to life, as he walked out the room, he turned back to leave three hundred dollars on the dresser, after a while her mother came into the room to check on her, she walked over to the bed, quickly looked over her, then threw her a rag on the bed and told her to clean up, she informed her she will be having another customer coming through soon. At that very moment, all the light and love she were holding hold to in this world was lost, everything in her had turned to complete darkness, her mother sent man after man, one after the other into her room to climb on top of her to do their business and leave. Not able to move, all she could do is lay there and cry hoping and praying that the pain would stop.

Low:

After Low left his Aunt J house, still hurt from the sight of seeing her pulling away in the ambulance. He pulled up to his house with the full intentions of making E-b pay for the pain she has caused his family. He went straight to the house, before he entered inside, he pulled his Glock 9 from his waist and placed it behind his back as he walked in the house, he called out E-b's name to see if he could locate where she was in the house, he got no answer, his heart began to race as he slowly checked each room on guard not knowing, since he found out the information he did. He truly didn't know what her intentions were at this point, so just in case she really wanted to kill him he wanted to be ready. Once he got to his bedroom, he cracked the door and seen E-b laying on the bed leg's cocked wide open as another woman pleasured her with her tongue, once she noticed that he was watching, she motioned for Low to enter the room, he did as he was told, as he moved in closer, they stopped what they were doing and began to crawl from the bed onto the floor in a sexy seductive way that demanded his attention. As E-b crawled in front of him, he began to get overwhelmed with emotion, an emotion so strong, he began to start shaking, E-b and the other woman began to rip his clothes off of him, the whole time E-b maintained eye contact, she could tell from the look in his eyes that something was bothering him, choosing not to take much thought in his look, she continued on her mission to please him, she began by kissing him on the inside of his thigh all the way to the tip of his dick. Slowly working him to the back of her throat, as he grew harder and harder with each stroke, she became more and more turned on, making her actions as nasty as they could get. The other woman joined in with no hesitation, kissing him on the back of his neck, down to the lower end of his back, finally making it on her knees, with both hands she spread his legs as open as she could get them and from there she went to work with her tongue, going from his balls to his ass, then right back to his balls again, as he fell between pleasure and pain, in each passing second, it came with a different emotion, one second he thought about his cousin and how he needed to kill this bitch for what she did and in the next second he thought about how good she made him feel and how much he cares about her. Knowing he probably should be excited that two beautiful women are having their way with him, he couldn't and actually fell hard on his decisions on what he should do next. Tears began to fonn in his eyes, with the gun in his hand, a rush of anger pushed him to push the barrel of gun firmly to E-b's temple, finger on the trigger weakening to the voices playing in the playground of his mind, he searched for the fear in her eyes. To his surprise, she showed none, she treated his actions as of it was just a simple part in role play, she pulled the barrel from her head to her mouth, and started sucking on the barrel like it was just another dick she had to please, at the same time she placed soft words in his head. His heart called out to her, in ways that he has never seen before, and at that moment he just couldn't pull himself together to the point of taking her life, love was powerful, he had lost because love had won the race. He lowered the gun by to his side, inside he was a mess, the other woman joined E-b as they fought for his special juices, pumped straight from the source, one at a time he fucked they face, until he shot his hot and heavy load all over both of their faces. Without giving him any space to recoup, they restarted the party all over again. All night they had hot passionate sex all over the house, after they were finally through, they all passed out in the bed together, Low holding E-b tight and the other woman, found her place between them the best way that she could.

Ace:

After Ace got off the phone with MoMo, he tried his best to calm back down, He couldn't believe that she would even try to pin a baby on him, knowing in her heart, that she was the type that got around. Her name is known for sleeping with any and everybody, now usually he wouldn't get in the bed with somebody like her, getting drunk, being horny is the only reason he associated himself with her in the first place, if it got out in the streets that she could possibly be pregnant with his baby, it would put a big dent on his reputation and even ruin his changes with Meme all together and there was no way he was going to let that happen. As he walked into the house, he noticed that Meme was still sound asleep, so he decided to surprise her and wake her up to a fresh cooked breakfast, and just like he expected, the smell of fresh cooked bacon, took a tour through her nose, she sat up smiling with sleep filled eyes, looking as beautiful as ever. Every time he looked at her, his heart would jump out of place, as the time passes by, he would fall more and more in love with her and he didn't even know how he found himself in this type of mind state, she truly had chains connected to his soul. After they sat and ate their breakfast, they laid around and talked a little bit to fill each other out a little more, but her face remained in a state of worry, even as he tried his best to make her laugh from his corny jokes, no change had taken place and he was beginning to feel like nothing he could do or say could change that, so instead of him guessing what might be wrong with her, he decided to get straight to the point and find out what it is that's really bothering her.

Meme what's wrong baby? Ace asked as he stared into her eyes, looking for her to answer.

Well, I just can't stop thinking about what happen last night, I mean, everything just happened so fast, one minute I'm at the party having the best time of my life, then the next minute I'm in a parking lot being raped, then I committed a murder and now shit is all fucked up! Ace it keeps playing over and over in my head, no matter how hard I try, the crazy part is I don't regret what I did, he deserves everything he got for what he did to me!

As she spoke every word, she became real emotional and tears began to run down her face uncontrollably, Ace leaned in to console her, he wiped the tears from her face.

Meme you right, he did deserve to get everything he had coming to him, fuck that motherfucker! Running around in the dark, taking pussy, when it's a million other bitches out here that would have giving him the ass for free, I never could respect no shit like that!

His anger began to build the more he thought about it,

But baby for our oivvn good, we got to put all this shit behind us!

Ace tell me how in the fuck can I do that! I can't get that shit off my mind, I thought about it all night, even when I finally was able to fall asleep, I seen that motherfucker in my dreams.

You'll get out it, Ace said as he turned his back acting as if she were over reacting,

You speak like a pro or a man who has a lot of experience when it comes to dismissing pain committing and getting over murders!

I have my demons, but they are mine and mine alone.

And what's that supposed to mean? You talk like, one you don't care about my feelings and what I went through, and two, I'm supposed to be impressed by what you saying, you think I care of you building a collection of bodies of something?

No you wrong I do care about how you feeling but how long is you going to hold on to this, and what I meant about mines and mines alone is that I don't have to worry about nobody opening their big mouth, I'm not trying to go to prison for the rest of my life, what I did, I did alone, just so I won't have to worry about nobody else.

Is that a hint, for I might have to worry about you later, because you can't be worried about me, being the one to say anything, being that I'm the one who killed the motherfucker in the first place, and if so, you must think I'm stupid, go ahead just speak your mind, tell the truth, you think I'm going to be the one to tell on myself?

No! No! No! look I didn't mean it like that and I was with you when you did the shit so I'm just as guilt as you are! Baby I don't want us to fight, and I'm sorry if I came off wrong. I'm just not that good at expressing my emotions but I do mean well, I know that but I'm willing to take this one step at an if you let me ride this thing out with you, eventually we are going to have to put this all behind us.

He cracked a smile to try his best to lighten the mood a little bit.

Can we start over, I want us to try to have a good day and the best way to do that is to go out and have some fun, so what you think? I could call a couple of my friends and we can go out and celebrate your birthday the right way.

And tell me, what is the right way?

Maybe we can go and have a nice dinner, wine, and see a movie or something, whatever you want to watch.

That's nice for somebody in their 40's or 50's but boy I'm not old, I'm a young, fresh out the wrapper.

So what is it that you suggest we do then? Ms. New thing fresh out the wrapper,

How about we go throw a couple dollars on some strippers, I always wanted to do that, we can have some drinks and turn up a little bit!

Ok den, I didn't know you would be interested in anything like that, you being a good girl and all.

Your right I am a good girl, but damn Ace I am not a prude,

Alright well, I' gone call a couple of my friends so they could come out with us, of course if that's cool with you.

That's cool but I got to call my family, I have to let them know that I'm ok, I know they worried sick about me.

Ok baby, do your thang, Ace said as he walked out of the room to make a call to Low, he noticed that his phone had rang what he felt had to be 20 times before he finally answered, still sounding like he was half asleep.

Hello, who is this, Low said with irritation spilling out of his voice.

Bro, you know who this fuck this is, don't act like you don't have my number saved in your phone by now.

Ace what's up man,

Bro, I know you ain't still sleep it's like 2 o'clock in the evening, bro you can't get no money like that!

I know bro, I just had a rough night last night, so I was just laying here trying to get caught up on my rest, I didn't get much sleep last night.

You care to talk about it?

Naw man I'll be good, I fell a little off a little bit after I found out some new information about what happened to my cousin but I'm back on point, I can't stay down long in this world I got to get back up and keep it moving, I can't stay in that state of mind.

Sounds like to me, you need to come out and have a little fun with me and my girl tonight.

Damn you got a little girl friend now, what happen to the pimps up hoes down movement.

And when did I say such a thing?

You know, but Ace on some real shit, I don't know if I really feel like coming out partying and shit right now, I'm just trying to wrap my head around everything that's going on, I might just do my relaxation thing today, so I could get my mind right.

Low you aren't the only one who are going through some shit right now, I had a really rough night myself last night and I really need to step out and try to clear my head as well. Bro I need you with me tonight, it would really make me feel at ease, plus I got to holla at you about a couple of things, so what's up, can my right hand man come out and fuck with his partner or what!

Low dropped a long sigh and then he agreed he would meet up with him later, before he said his good byes and hung up the phone.

After getting off the phone with Low, he went back in the other room to let Meme know that everything was not only a go but he also thought of a nice little spot that they could go to, but quickly noticed that she was still on the phone so he decided to give her, her space.

Myona:

After Ace left the room, Myona jumped at the chance to call her grandmother and brother, she knew deep down in her heart, that they would probably be worried about her sick because she has never stayed out without checking in with her grandmother to let her know she was alright.

After the phone rang about two times, her grandmother quickly answered the phone.

Hello, Myona

Yes, Ma, am

O my God baby, you had me worried sick about you, where are you? Are you ok?

Yes, Grandma I'm ok I just had a little too many drinks last night, so I crashed at a friend house, there was no way I was going to be able to drive home.

I was worried, you know somebody got killed in the parking lot outside the school last night, then I didn't hear from you, that sent my mind all over the place, just a little while longer, I was going to head down to the police station to put out a missing person's report.

No! you don't have to do that, I'm ok, you don't have to worry,

I know that now, now that you called,

Sensing a real disease in Myona voice, she continued on with her questioning,

What's wrong, you don't sound like yourself and don't lie to me, you never lied to me before so you don't need to start now, now tell Grandma what's wrong.

It never mattered where she was in life, her grandmother could always tell when something was wrong, she could never lie to her even though every once in a while she would try, it never worked, she seen right through it every time, so she paused before she could speak her next words, which only put her grandmother, in an even more state of a panic with her silent approach.

Myona, what's going on?

Grandma I'm just waking up and I'm still a little hungover,

I just didn't want you worried so I made sure I made it my business to call you even before a tooth brush hit my tongue.

Yea ok, it's a lot of weird shit going on, I talked to your little friend London, when I asked her where you were, she acted like she didn't know, as if you magically disappeared into thin air, which is real fishy, being that y'all left here together, y'all is always joined at the hip, but somehow y'all end up in different places by the end of the night and she has no knowledge on where you could be. All this time y'all been friends y'all have never did something like that, this is a new one on me, and from the way I'm reading it, I'm just getting a bad feeling something ain't right about all this, her whole demeanor was off when I was with her earlier, she just put off a vibe like she knew more than she was leading on.

What you mean you was with her earlier! Why?

Worried about you, trying to see if I could find out some information about where you might be, and her energy was just completely off.

Grandma I just left the party last night, I was an uncomfortable drunk, to the point I could barely stand up, I figured I just talk to her later, but I didn't tell her where I was going or nothing, could it have just been that she didn't know anything and you scared the shit out of her from the way you were talking, you probably made her feel guilty about not knowing nothing, poor baby she probably been crying all day now I got to call her and let her know I'm ok as well.

Naw Myona listen to me, this was different baby, she put off a vibe as if she could care less where you were, and I just know she was hiding something, I could see it in her eyes, all I'm saying is watch that girl, sometimes we think people is our friend, but all along, they would do any and everything to be in our shoes, the sad part is you never know who is who until you or your shoes come up missing, I know that's your friend and you love her, and they say they love you, but the whole time, they only got their best interest at heart. They are the most dangerous to have around you, they hide their hate, behind a friendly disguise baby, I just need you to keep your eyes open, always remember people pray on love, love can get you killed, just please be careful.

Her grandmother words had cut her deep and she knew she meant well, but her thoughts and feelings she shared about her friend only made her question her reasons why even more, what did she see in her eyes to make her give off so bad of a judgment against her. She also thought about what Frank said before she killed him wondering could what he had said about London been üue, and if it was, then what could be her reason, for doing something so horrible to a friend she swears up and down she loves. she has never done anything to her but love her like a sister and had her back through everything that came her way. Her grandmother seen that she had placed a seed of thought in her mind, but yet she forced a change to the subject altogether.

Myona, is there anything that you need to tell me?

No, why do you keep saying that? if I had anything to tell you, you know I would have already!

Her grandmother got tired of beating around the bush and shot straight to the point.

Lil girl are you pregnant? Like your Lil friend London!

What! London is pregnant?

Yea, she pregnant, when I was with her earlier, she was throwing up and sweating like crazy, so I got her a little something to eat and had her take a pregnancy test, and it came up positive. Her tone change to a sweet and compassionate one, now we can make it through anything, you don't have to hide it from me.

Grandma stop, I am not pregnant! And if I was I wouldn't hide nothing like that from you.

Ok, I just want you to know, you can wait for all that, you got your whole life to be a mother, I want you to enjoy your life, go and explore the world your daddy would want that too, I know it.

Grandma I'm not pregnant, so you don't have to worry, ok!

Ok! Now when are you coming home?

I should be there by tomorrow; I'm going to finish having my little birthday turn up weekend then I'll be home.

She heard a long pause in her grandmother's conversation, which meant one of two things, she either didn't like what she heard or she ran out of words to say and Grandma never runs out of words to say, so it all came down to her not being happy with the answer that was given from the question that was asked.

Grandma, why the long pause, you were the one who told me to go out and have some fun remember?

Yeah, I said that, but I just got a bad feeling running over me baby, feeling that something is off, and it's something else I got to tell you,

O lord what now?

Your Grandma Renee is on her way back in town.

Grandma!

I had to call her baby, you had me worried to death, I didn't know what else to do.

Grandma you know how she gets, and I only went missing for a day, if you want to call that missing, and you called the army and the coastguard, damn Grandma!

First of all, watch your mouth, you ain't that grown that you can talk to me or in front of me crazy and hell yea I called out the big guns, hell I would have called the motherfucking president if I had too, you my baby and I love you.

I love you 2, Grandma is Jyel around?

Yea he in here somewhere, you want me to get him?

Yes, please,

After Grandma Vickie called Jyel and told him that his sister was on the phone, he damn near broke his neck to get to the phone.

Sis! Sis! Are you ok? He said half out of breath.

Yes, Jyel, I'm ok, I just had a little too much to drink last night so I couldn't make it home so I left with a friend.

Don't try to run that bullshit game on me, first of all you don't even drink and if you did you would not have let it get out of control, I know you, you are one of the biggest control freaks I have ever known, what you tell Grandma is one thing, but tell me the truth, you ain't on speaker phone, I understand if you trying to make sure you cover your ass, but sis this me, so you can tell me the truth, starting with where the fuck is you? You didn't come home, which had me worried, you don't never do shit like that, it's been a lot of shit going on since last night, strange cars coming around the house, dropping shit off at the door, sis I really got some shit to talk to you about, you're not going to believe this, I have to see you it's very important.

I'm chilling with my little friend right now, trying to have a good time, he supposed to take me out for my birthday but we can talk tomorrow I'll be home for sure by the morning.

Myona did you hear anything I just said? I told you this is important; this can't wait until tomorrow.

Just tell me what it's about then Jyel!

I don't want to talk to you about this over no phone.

From listening to her brother's deep concern pouring through his voice, it startled her, forcing her to be more concerned with what he had to say, she wondered if somebody was an eye witness to what happened last night and he was trying his best to warn her about it. It was a seriousness and a touch of panic in his voice, which she knows when he gets like that, she knew what he had to say, had to be very serious.

Ok! Ok! What are you doing tonight?

I don't have nothing planned, why what's up?

How about you come out with me tonight, have a little ftn, celebrate my birthday with me and my little friend I just met, I think you'll like him, and we can sit down and talk then.

He knew he really didn't want to go out and celebrate anything but he had to tell his sister about the journal, in his mind it posed a threat, they both could be in danger, he had to warn her to watch out for her surroundings, why else would he expose that he killed their mother and dad. So even though he didn't want to go, he had to, knowing tomorrow is never promised, he wouldn't be able to live with himself if something happened to her, knowing he had the chance to let her know what was going on, so he agreed to tag along anyway. After sharing a few more words, Myona told him the time and place they were going to meet, as she said her goodbyes her brother made sure before he hung up he told her that he loved her, then the phone clicked exposing the dial tone on his end.

After everybody got their proper rest, from a wild night, he got the girls up, and told them to get ready, he wanted to treat them to a night out on the town. E-b noticed the distance that Low had placed between them and it not only put her on guard but placed a bad feeling in the bottom of her gut, which made her wonder should she make a clean exit or was she just paranoid, looking too much into things, she knew she also always got like that when a man would get to close to her. The first chance she got, she slipped off and called Ace, it took him a while to answer but once he did, she could tell he was around somebody he couldn't talk around, but besides that he was very dismissive about the conversation as a whole, her thoughts was all over the place.

Ace! This is serious, I think he knows something, last night, while we were in the middle of a threesome, he had this look in his eyes that spoke of disgust, I didn't know if I should finish the job or go for my gun, not to mention, while I was sucking his dick this motherfucker put a gun to my head, I thought he was going to kill me right there,

Damn!

Yea, I couldn't sleep at all last night, this motherfucker was up all night, walking around the bed, acting real creepy, looking out the window, like he was expecting someone to come to the house or something, I don't know if he called somebody on me or he thought I might have called somebody on him, just real weird shit Ace!

You gave that man a threesome already, damn you must really like him.

Ace motherfucker I'm done, my job here is done, you hear me, I'm not about to stick around here any fuckin longer, I got the feeling something bad is going to happen, I'm damn near just ready to kill his ass before he kills me!

E-b chill, have you been doing any coke?

Yea and! That don't have shit to do with this vibe this motherfucker putting off, it's so bad, whatever video that's playing in his head, he can't disguise it, he can't fake it, how he is feeling right now, he is wearing that shit on his sleeve. And when it gets like that Ace,

Like what E-b?

Like I got to make a choice, my life or his, believe me, I never think twice, the only reason I didn't kill his ass after we was done fuckin was because of you, which you need to cut all ties as well, because if he finds out, one, we are connected in any way, he gone instantly get suspicious, how long you think we could hold this bullshit up, you know the streets talk, and two, if he finds out that me and you are involved in his cousin murder, both of our lives are going to be in danger. You think I want to sit around and wait for a motherfucker to sneak me out of the blue, you must be the one getting high, how much of that shit is you putting in your nose.

Once again, calm down, and where the hell are you anyway?

I'm still at his house,

And you talking like this, you tripping, he could be laying around a comer listening to your every word, damn think E-b, what if he hears you, look I told him I want him to come out to the club and celebrate my little lady friend birthday, did he mention anything about that to you?

Yea, he wanted me and my friend to get dressed up real nice, talking about it's a night we ain't never gone forget.

Ace laughed as she shared her feelings about what she thinks Low plot is, thinking that she had a strong imagination.

Look we are going to have some drinks and have a good time and then I'm going to pull you out of the whole situation baby, so just relax, your job with him is done. I know you think I'm not hearing anything you're saying but I am, baby I love you and I hope you know that.

I love you 2, I wouldn't do know crazy shit like this for anybody else.

I know, alright baby, get off the phone and get ready for tonight, I'll see you later on.

Ok later.

Low:

As Low walked into the room, he saw E-b quickly rush off of the phone.

Hey baby, is everything alright, you seem a little jumpy, Low said as he watched her body language.

Yea, everything good, I just had to call my mom to check on my baby, to see if they needed anything before we headed out for the night.

Well, are they cool? Because if not, we can go over there and get them anything they need before we go out to the club tonight, it wouldn't be nothing to just swing by there, plus I would love to meet your mom and the baby anyway

E-b stepped in and wrapped her arms around his waist, aww how sweet, you really care about me huh, you ready to play step daddy, she said as she passionately kissed him on his lips.

Yea, I'm serious about you, I really want to be a part of your life in any way that I can and that means, taking on the full package as step dad, the baby needs a strong father figure in their life. I been running the streets all my life, I think it would be nice to settle down and built a family of my own, and, I think it isn't a better person to start that with than you.

Those words touched her heart the moment he said them, to the point it almost brought her to tears.

Low you're a real sweetheart and I'm glad I met you, but the answer to your question, is yea they good and no they don't need anything, my momma told me he misses me, screaming momma every 5 minutes but other than that, he doesn't need nothing, I'll be home soon so he could go without me for a little longer. As far as you meeting them right now, I'm really not comfortable with that just yet.

Why baby? He said as he moved in closer, gripping her waist, pulling her into him, is it something that I did?

No, you been perfect, it's just a little too soon to me, I just been having some bad run-ins with guys, not knowing what they want and I just can't have people running in and out of his life, I want to make sure what we have is real.

You think I'm gone hurt you? Is that what you think?

No! well I hope you're not going to hurt me, but the truth is, I really don't know if you will.

Baby all I could say is you're going to have to let me prove it to you, believe it or not, E-b I love you baby.

Low how do you love me? When you don't even know me!

He pulled her by her hair gently, and kissed her on the lips.

She loved his kisses, from the first one he laid on her, her knees always got weak,

Let's just say the feeling you give me, I have never felt before, I mean I have never felt like this about no other woman in my life. You are truly special to me and I don't want to lose you, out of your fear in not believing in our future together so just calm down and let love take its place.

Damn he always knows the right words to say to keep my heart off balance, she thought as she became more and more confused on what she truly should do next, she battled with herself back and forth, one side of her knew staying with him would be dangerous, especially if he found out the truth about her, that love he says he has for her would turn into pure hate, but on the other side of things there is always that 1 % chance that he would never find out and they would live happily ever after, she knew her ending the relationship quick would be the better choice, because the longer she stayed, the harder it would be for her to leave. So she broke the embrace between them, then turned around and walked away.

E-b! E-b! he called out to her to get her attention.

When she turned back around, she began to wipe the tears away that was pouring down her face, her feelings had taken a ride on a roller coaster, that didn't plan on stopping anytime soon, no matter how much she wished it would stop, it just kept rolling, with no sight of an end or an exit point.

Baby why are you crying?

To tell you the truth, I don't know, I have always been the one to be tough in the relationships I have been in, right now I don't know what's going on with me.

Why do you feel like you have to be tough with me at all?

I always just had to be, and if I didn't, a man would just fry his best to chew me up and spit me out, they will say anything to get in your head, they tell you how much they love you, and they need you and once they get what they want, then they dumb you, use you up and throw you to the curb.

Ok I could clearly tell your scared of building new relationships and I don't want to push you into things, so we can just take things slow baby, one day at a time, to your pace, we don't have to rush nothing at all, I really want to get to know you, whenever you ready to let me meet your family, I'm down, ok!

She thanked him with a kiss on the lips and then headed to the bathroom to take a shower, Low watched her walk away, as he tried his best to keep his composure.

London:

Once London got a chance, she made her escape from her mother's house, determined to never return again. She made up her mind that she would rather live homeless on the streets, then let all types of different men have their way with her. Over all, she felt lost, she thought how could her mother do this to her, she realized that she didn't have anybody to talk too, but Myona, she knew deep down that she was the only true friend she had and yet she betrayed her all because of the jealousy that she had towards her. After walking the streets for a while, she became so hungry and tired, that she could barely stand up, she had not eaten in a couple of days, her mom would continue to push for her to keep going, no matter how much she begged for her to stop, she just kept sending men into her room, one after the other, greed played its part and crazy part about everything is her mother didn't share a dime of the money she was making off of her, so when she decided to leave, she left with nothing. She used her and she would have continued to do so, if her choice would have been to stay. London seen a sign, that read: The Drop Inn Center, it was a local shelter that all the homeless people go to get out on the streets especially on the really cold nights, she knew about the place for a long time, she just thought that she would never be the one to ever need help in this way. They asked for her name and age at the door, once she was signed in, they connected her with a social worker who could better help her in whatever she needed, the social worker was very nice to her, she made sure that she got London something to eat, she was able to take a shower, and she even provided her with some new clothes to wear.in a relaxed state She ended up taking a nap, after a while, she was woke up by a different person claiming to be a social worker as well, but this one was from job and family services, they told her to get all her things and come with them, the other social worker who she dealt with the first time quickly assured her that everything would be ok, trusting her judgment because she had not lead her in the wrong direction so far, she decided to trust her and take her word that everything was going to be ok, not knowing what it is they wanted, she followed them, not putting up a fight, on the drive downtown to their office, they began to ask questions, for some of the questions she didn't have an answer for.

London how long has it been since you ran away from home?

That question alone threw her off guard,

The more the social worker spoke she stared at her through the rearview mirror while driving, there was another social worker in the passenger sit but they acted more like an assistant, letting the other do all the talking while they wrote everything down in there notes every time London would speak.

What do you mean ran away, I didn't run away, I been living in the streets taking care of myself for a while now!

No you have not, and yes you did run away, and how we know this is because we had a talk with your mother.

You talked to my mother! How? My mother is dead, that would be impossible, there is no way you could have did that, I been living on the streets, no family, no nothing!

London I was hoping that you would be honest with us, sweetheart, that's the only way that we could help you.

I am being honest, I don't know where you getting your information but I'm good from here, I don't need no help, so if you could just pull over right over there, I'll get out on the corner at the store.

Well London we are not going to be able to do that for many reasons.

And why the fuck not!

London began to get really angry with them to the point she went into an instant fight or flight mode, looking for ways to escape.

One of the reasons are your are not 18 years old yet.

Yea and so!

That means legally, we are not allowed to just drop you off anywhere, unless we have permission from your legal guardian to do so, plus your mother filed a missing child report with the police station, so the whole city is out looking for you right now as we speak, that's why we know so much about you.

I told you my mother is dead, you got me mistaken with somebody else.

The social worker's assistant who was sitting in the passenger seat the whole time taking notes, sat up in his seat and turned around so he would be facing London, and as he looked her directly in her eyes, he pulled out of his notes a piece of paper that contained her picture on it and all her personal information, without saying a word, he handed it to her.

As she read everything placed on the paper, she became very speechless to what she should say next.

Now do you think we are lying to you? Your mother's name is April Johnson and you Father is listed as Charles Carter, you attend William Howard Taft High school, you're in the 1 1 th grade, but you are at risk of failing due to your grades, we know this because we came to the school and had a meeting with your teachers to get a feel of who we are dealing with as a person, and

London I would also like to ask you a question and I want you to be very honest with us.

She nodded as she waited for the question to be asked,

How long how you been prostituting for money?

I don't prostitute for money, who the fuck told you something like that?

Your mom told us that you been an out of control teen for a while now, that you barely want to come home, you don't do good in school because you're not able to focus on anything that doesn't have to do with sex, drugs, or money. She has told us that she has caught you in her house with countless men, some your age but most much older, she is in fear that if you don't turn your life around, that somebody might take your life in the streets, and I'm here to tell you, she is not wrong for feeling that way, I have seen a lot of girls get killed your age, the streets are nothing to play with.

She is lying! Everything she is saying is not true, she is lying, she made all that stuff up, just to hide the real truth on what's going on!

London I also want to let you know we also talked to your teachers and they also had a lot to say as well, plus some of the students, spoke about you, now all is not bad, some of the teachers at the school say that you are a great student but they would love to see you apply yourself a lot more, but just like your mom said, they also say you have a hard time staying focus in class, the students from your class expressed you have a reputation going around the school for having sex with a lot of different guys, see London we don't just take someone's word for it, we do our own investigation, to make sure we could get you the best help we possibly can. The road you been going down is not good, you could end up pregnant or even worse there are a lot of deadly diseases out there in the world that could change your life within seconds, we really just want the best for you, believe it or not.

London, couldn't believe what she was hearing, somehow her mother was able to turn everything around and make her the bad guy, everything her mother did to her, she made it look like it was London's life choice, smart move, she made it look like she cared about London but everything she told these people was to gain favor with them, just in case if she tried to go to the police to tell them what her mother did, she could cover her own ass. She was lost and didn't know what to do next, no matter what she says, they weren't going to believe her. Those thoughts began to overpower her, she cried to the point she had lost control, it was too much for her to bear, the last couple of days was some of the worst days she had ever experienced in her life, she never felt more alone and trapped then she was feeling right now. Once they seen her instantly break down in the back seat, they tried their best to calm her down, but nothing they did would work, the harder they fried the more she fought back and screamed at the top of her lungs like she was going through a psychotic break.

Let me go! No! Let me go!

She began to lay down in the back seat, kicking the window as hard as she could,

London please calm down; we are just trying to help you!

You don't want to help me, you believe everything that bitch is telling you, and I don't care if you believe me or not, but I'm not going back there, I would rather die before I let you take me back there.

Her words had cut through their heart like a knife, whatever she had went through in that house, she was willing to die before she encountered it again. The rage she had in her eyes spoke on many levels.

What did she do to you to make you not want to go home? You say you would rather die, it can't be that bad that you would rather die than be there, is it?

I would rather die than let my mom send all types if men into my room all hours of the night to rape me, over and over again, so many in the last couple of days, I lost count, I don't know, don't ask me how many it was, I don't know! I should know, she screamed as loud as she could, making sure they heard every word. She had snapped, Before the social worker could say another word, she increased the pressure to her kicks to the window, until the glass shattered into pieces. Before the social workers could pull the car over to make a complete stop, London opened the car door and jumped out the car while it was still in motion, falling hard but was able to jump back to her feet and run as fast as she could, both of the social workers chased behind her but was not able to keep up, and ended up losing her in the process. Once London seen that they were no longer behind her, she ran to the only place she felt like she would be safe, Myona's house, once she got to the front door, she noticed that Myona's car was nowhere in sight, she knocked on the door as hard as she could, after a couple of minutes she heard somebody on the other side of the door asking, who is it? In an angry tone, she quickly stated who she was and asked if Myona was home, in hopes that she was because she couldn't stand to get turned away, especially at a time like this, as the door flew open, Grandma Vickie had a surprise look in her eyes.

London, o my God girl, get in this house, Grandma Vickie said as she pulled her into the house by her arm, she quickly looked around to see if anybody was watching before she shut the door. Once inside, she looked London over from head to toe, noticing all the bruises she had on her face and arms, she knew something was terribly wrong with her.

Girl do you know you are all over the news, they put out an amber alert talking about you ran away from home, girl go ahead and sit down so I could call your mother and tell her that you alright!

No! she quickly said standing back up to her feet as if she was ready to make a fast motion towards the door.

Why not, she been calling me, worried sick about you, when I talked to her, I told her I haven't seen you since the other day, but I told her if I see you I would give her a call, I know how it feels to be worried about your baby, hoping they ain't somewhere dead in the street, but from the looks of thangs, somethings going on, now tell me what's up.

No, ain't nothing going on, I'll call her, you don't have to do that, I was really just hoping that Myona would have made it home by now, I really just need to talk to her.

Grandma Vickie seen that look in her eyes over a thousand times before when Myona or Jyel was in way over their heads in trouble and didn't want to talk about it with her, she wondered if she had run away from home because her mother didn't take the news well to her being pregnant, which would be common for a child to do because she had to do the same thing when she were younger with her first child, her mother threated her to get the baby aborted and she didn't want that, so she decided to run, so in a way she could relate to her in so many ways but she also had the feeling that wasn't it, this look also held on to something much more serious.

She sat down next to her and wrapped her arm around her to comfort her,

London, tell me what's going on, did you end up telling your mom that you were pregnant and you guys got into a big fight?

No I didn't tell her I was pregnant and no we didn't get into a fight, what makes you think any of these things happen, trust me Ms, Vickie I'm ok, I just want to talk to my best friend, did you talk to her, is she home?

If you ok, then why are you here, why was you just beating down my door like you were on the run from a vicious mob, threatening to take you away, and not to mention girl I am far from stupid, you jumpy as hell, the last time I saw you, you didn't have all them damn bruises on your face, now I ain't gone say it again, what the fuck is going on little girl?

While she was talking, she so happened to glance at the TV and notice that London's mother was on the News with a camera crew pleading for people to help, she stopped in her tracks, found the remote control and turned the volume up so they could hear what were being said to the media.

See look at this shit, this don't look like a situation that's cool to me, if y'all was cool, she

As they both tuned in to what was being said, London couldn't believe the role her mother was playing.

London's Mom April on the News:

London baby if you could hear me, if you somewhere watching this, come home baby, I'm worried about you baby, whatever you feel I did wrong, we can fix it, I hope you know I love you, I know you probably are scared out there, feeling alone, but you are not alone, I'm here for you baby, you hear me, we in this together.

News Reporter:

Ms. Johnson why would your daughter want to run away from home in the first place?

I think she thinks that I'm disappointed in her, for some of the decisions she has made in life and I'm not, baby I'm not disappointed in you, nobody is perfect we all make mistakes, we just are going to have to work on doing better moving forward baby come home.

News Reporter:

It sounds like to me that you are a good mom and she comes from a loving and caring home, has she ever did anything like this before?

Yes, she has run away from home countless times, but never for this long, it seems like the older that she is becoming, the more she doesn't want to listen to me anymore, I just wish her dad was more active in her life, all I tried to ever do was be there for her the best way I could, it's so hard to be a single mom out here! I just want the best for her, she told me she was pregnant and I admit I was upset and might have said some things I knew I was going to regret later, I was just really upset at the moment, I didn't want her to go through what I went through at an early age, like I did, I just couldn't hold back after she admitted she didn't know who the baby's father was, I became outraged, I wished I would've just sat down and had a talk with her I didn't want her to run away,

News Reporter:

Ma'am when we talked to you earlier you stated that your daughter could be possibly selling her body for money, can you tell us when you think all this started? And do you think that was the result and reason her pregnancy?

News Reporter 2:

Was she molested when she was younger? Could this be the reason she been acting out this way?

As soon as she heard the second reporter make her comment, she snapped her neck, and went straight to giving her a piece of her mind.

Molested! No she has not been molested, who do the fuck you think I am to let somebody come into my home and molest my daughter and I not do nothing about it, I do everything in my power as a mom to keep that girl safe, I love my baby and I would die before I let somebody hurt her, you hear me, if I even got word somebody touched her, I would proudly live out the rest of my days from a prison cell, I love my baby, baby if you could hear me, please baby come home, I'm sorry!

She began to wail as loud as she could, laying in the persons arms that were the closest to her, as they wrapped their arms around her to console her, she broke down even more, losing her footing as if her knees had buckled from underneath her, it took three people to hold her up. Grandma Vickie couldn't take watching any more, she pointed the remote and turned the TV off, she could not believe that London's mom would go on TV and paint a picture of her own daughter in this way, for the whole world to see, was it was real or fake, she didn't know, but one thing that she could point out for sure is that it was very messy for a black mother, this made her want to question London to see if what her mother was saying was true, she been dealing with kids all her life so she would be able to tell if she were lying as soon as the words flowed out of her mouth.

London, when did you start selling your body for money?

My mother lied! I have never sold my body for money, my mom is just saying those things to cover her tracks!

Cover her tracks from what? She went on TV and painted a picture like you are completely out of control, like you have never had no home training and I know that can't be true because I have watched you with a close eye over the years, now I do think you are a little fast but I can't see you selling your body for money, but why would she say those horrible things about you?

She broke down and told Grandma Vickie everything that happen to her after they last seen each other, from the rapes and beatings she had to endure before she made her escape to the shelter she tried to stay in and then her encounter with child protective services, Grandma Vickie could tell as London was speaking that the last couple of days, had placed a toll on her, she had bags under her eyes, it was no secret she was in desperate need of sleep so instead of her making a comment on what she told her, she just decided to let her stay for a while to catch up on her rest, she told her at least until they could figure something out as far as finding her a safe place to stay, she knew in her heart, no matter what, she wasn't going to send her back to that house to let her get abused again, she knew she had to help her, even if she had to move her into her house and take care of her, herself. After she convinced London that she would be safe there, she was sent upstairs to Myona's room to lay down, until she could cook her something to eat. London did as she were told, as she entered into Myona's room, she looked all around, admiring everything in its place, she had been in this room over a hundreds of times, but it was only this time it truly felt like home, all her life, she wished she could be in Myona's shoes, she has always had the nicest things, and all she had to do was keep her grades up and she would get anything she want, after looking around she went over and sat on the bed, tired from a long day, she laid back and rested her head on the pillow, her thoughts played in her head like she was watching them in a movie theater, up close and vivid, she tried to force them out of her head but it became harder to do with each passing minute, so bad it was like that all she could focus on were the vision she was having, seeing the different men on top of her, the faces they made as they pleasured there self, made her want to throw up, she didn't know what to do to make them stop they just kept playing over and over, like she was reliving the moments every five minutes, to the point she even thought about killing herself just to make the visions stop, in fear of closing her eyes, thinking someone might come into the room, her eyes were drawn to the night stand, where she noticed a picture of Myona and her brother Jyel standing in a picture with a man, everyone were smiling, Myona and Jyel were little babies, they both were stuck to the man legs, one on each side. As she picked the picture up to get a closer look at the man in the picture, she took a notice to him instantly from a picture that Ace had in his house on his mantle over the fireplace, at first she thought damn I might be tripping but everything in the picture was the same as the other one, only thing that was different was the roles was reversed Ace was in the picture and Myona and Jyel was missing. London turned the picture over to see was there anything written on the back, and once she seen the words

Daddy loves you, always have and always will, it was like her heart had fell in her stomach, Ace is Myona and Jyel big brother, she couldn't believe the information she had just found out, she knew she had to tell Ms. Vickie so she jumped to her feet and ran downstairs as fast she could to find her, yelling out her name as loud as she could like a crazy person, she replied from the kitchen.

Girl what the hell is wrong with you, why in the hell is you yelling all through this house, have you lost your mind?

She handed Grandma Vickie the picture, that she got from Myona' s night stand in her room,

Who is this man? Is this really Myona and Jyel father, or a friend of the family or something?

Yes, it's their dad, and my first grand baby, Lamar Wright, he has been dead for 10 years now, why, do you think you know him or something?

Know him no, but when I was over this guy house named Ace, this same guy was in the picture with him.

I don't know anybody by the name Ace, but it's possible they could of knew each other, Lamar was a very popular guy, he knew a lot of people.

No! the picture was taken in the same place as this one,

Grandma Vickie looked closely at the picture trying her best to grasp where the picture might have been taken, not seeing anything familiar, she quickly dismissed what London was saying as a big misunderstanding.

It's probably ain't no big deal London, probably just somebody he knew,

No I think it's a little more than that, when I read the back it said daddy loves you, always have and always will, just like this picture.

Grandma Vickie stopped in her tracks and turned around to face her,

How does this Ace guy look?

He's mixed, nice curly hair, looks like he could be this guy twin, let's just say if they were in the room together they would be hard to tell apart, besides one is light skin and the other one is dark,

Ace ain't that old either, I would say he is about 23 years old.

Grandma Vickie couldn't believe what she was hearing,

Mixed how? Mixed with what? What do you mean when you say he's mixed? Grandma Vickie pressed for answers as she moved in closer to London, anxious about what she might say next, even though she already knew the answer, it was just a big pill to swallow, nobody has seen him in years, she had to be sure, she didn't want to get her hopes up for nothing.

He's mixed, like black and white mixed, so I'm guessing that his mother is white, being that this is his dad,

Grandma Vickie paced the room,

That sounds like my grandson Aiden,

Aiden! London said as she looked more into the picture with disbelief to what Ms. Vickie was saying,

Yes, his name is Aiden it's not Ace, that's Myona and Jyel big brother, where did you see him at again?

His apartment,

Does he stay close to here; what part of town does he stay in?

Yea, his apartment is in Westwood, but I remember us going to another place like out in

Beechmont but I can 't remember where that place is, but I do know how to get to the apartment in Westwood though,

How long have you been dating him?

Me and him been messing around for a little while now,

Girl speak English, what do you mean y'all been messing around, I haven't seen him in years every since his father got killed, I need to see him, this is very important to me!

Ms. Vickie he is my child's father,

What! So Aiden is your child's father, you're having his baby?

Yes, ma'am, but I don't think he wants to be in the baby's life, because when I told him I was pregnant, he acted like he didn't want nothing to do with me or the baby, he told me don't call him and then he blocked me.

I need you to show me where he stays, right now I need to pay my great grandson little a visit, Ok I have to ride with you because I have to show you I can't just tell you, I'm more of a visual person when it comes to directions,

While London was still in mid conversation, she rushed to the back room and grabbed her jacket and car keys, then she raced to the door ready to go,

London come on, show me where this apartment is!

London followed her close behind as they got into the car and began to drive to Aiden's apartment, Grandma Vickie began to fill her in on the family history, which almost brought her to tears, she never knew what Myona had been through and all the tough times she has faced in her life, from her mother and father getting killed, to their Grandma Renee, Lamar's mother losing her mind to the point they almost didn't have anybody. They could have easily been in the same boat as her if it wasn't for their grandmother, Ms. Vickie and all this happened when she was just a little girl, she felt selfish, she never saw her pain, she just looked at her as a spoiled kid, who didn't know what it felt like to struggle, because she has always had everything she ever wanted. When it came to Ace, she was a little embarrassed to find out she is having a baby by a person she didn't even know their real name, but the love she had for him she couldn't shake at all, and once she found out what he been through in life, it made her understand him even more, shit she felt like, if she was in his shoes, she would probably push people away herself, no matter what, she wanted him to know that she is there for him and would do anything it takes to build a family with him, that she loves him and truly has his back, as crazy as it sounds, she made up her mind she didn't want nobody else, that she was going to fight for this relationship, but another part of her wondered was she being stupid chasing after a dream, Aiden is a product of his past, she wondered was that the main reason he treated her so bad and if so, was he ever going to change. She found reason after reason to defend her love for him in her mind. Maybe it's because he never got taught how to love, maybe he just needs someone to show him that they love him for him for him to be able to give that same love back. Never that maybe he is incapable of love, only thoughts build around a future with him, in her mind she truly couldn't picture life without him. In some ways, she felt they were alike, when it came to love, and not knowing how to properly show it, all her life, the only way she knew how to show she cared about somebody was through sex, when it came to Ace, everything wrapped around a different feeling, something she has never truly felt before, she knew deep down inside her soul this had to be the real thing, she has fallen in love with him, and there won't be nothing that's going to get in their way from them being together. What hurt's her the most, is he might not feel the same way about her, her only choice from here on out was to make him see, that they belong together, that they are truly meant for each other and in time, he'll see it too, as Grandma Vickie pushed her turn after turn for her to tell her more directions on where they are headed next, London's eyes was stuck in a strong daze, as she watched every car passing by.

London! Grandma Vickie called out loud to pull her back into the world, she can tell that her mind had fell far, far away from where they were sitting.

Yes, ma' am

Baby listen to me, I know you going through a lot right now with your mom doing all this messed up stuff to you, but believe me, everything is going to get better.

London shrugged her shoulders, showing no interest in her words,

London, come on now, you can talk to me, I been in a bad place many of times, and one thing I know for sure, if it doesn't kill you, it's only going to make you stronger, and another thing is it's not good to hold things in, it could only destroy you later down the road, you could end up dealing with bad trust issues, abandonment issues and the list goes on and on!

What am I supposed to say! I don't even know what I'm supposed to say!

Just tell me how you feel baby! Let's just start there!

At this point, I don't know how I feel, my life is all over the place, I'm homeless not because my mom kicked me out, but because I had to leave because my mom let random men ride me like I was a ride in an amusement park, I'm pregnant and my child's father hates me!

No, he doesn't, he just doesn't understand the things that you have been through in your life, now and days, it's so easy for people to judge the outside of things without stepping inside to check the facts.

He really hurt my feelings, the last time we talked on the phone, he called me all types of hoes and told me, that the baby I'm having is not his, Ms. Vickie, I'm not even 18 years old yet, I can't do this alone, if Aiden is not going to be here with me to help me raise this baby, I don't know if I really want to have this baby, I don't know where I'm going to be tomorrow, I can't even take care of myself right now, how the hell am I going to take care of a baby?

London, I know you going through a hard time, and it's looking like you can't see any light down the tunnel, but you are not alone, rather you see it or not, you are family, I'm not going to let you be homeless or go hungry, so you can get that out your mind right now, if I could help you in any way that I could, than that's what I'm going to do, plus I be damn if I let you get rid of my great, great grand baby over one little life struggle, just trust me, we gone be ok!

London hugged Grandma Vickie as soon as the car pulled up on the curve, outside Aiden's apartment, she put the car in park, jumped out and started to head inside, when she noticed that London wasn't behind her, she turned back around and headed to the car to see what was the hold up.

London what are you doing? Come on now, I need your help up here!

Ms. Vickie I told you the apartment number and everything, I don't want to go in there, I would rather just sit in the car until you get done with the family business, I don't want to take away from the special moment y'all are going to have from not seeing each other in years, plus I don't know if I could face him right now, I just been through so much today, I need to sit here and get my head together for a minute.

Girl get the fuck out of this car! Now you're not about to avoid each other, y'all are having a baby together, so y'all are stuck dealing with each other for the next 18 years weather you like it or not!

London, didn't want to fight with Ms. Vickie so she just did as she was told, as she got out of the car and started to head inside the building she noticed that Ms. Vickie had went inside the trunk and grabbed something and placed it in her purse, what, she couldn't tell from where she was standing but she seen her hun•y up and place something in her purse and that caught her attention more than anything!

Is something wrong Ms. Vickie, she asked as she saw her look around before entering the building.

Yea, everything is ok, come on let's get inside.

Once they got to the door, Grandma Vickie knocked on the door for like 5 minutes, calling his name in hopes he would answer the door, but no one answered.

Ms. Vickie no one's home, let's just go, maybe we can swing back and catch him when he is home a little later.

She paid London words no attention as she went into her purse and pulled out a flat head screwdriver, and jammed it inside the door in an attempt to pop the lock, it popped open on the first try.

Wooh, Ms. Vickie! What are you doing? We can't just go breaking into his apartment, we can get in some serious trouble if we get caught doing this!

Naw we good, I have a great lawyer, who eat these type of situations up, besides nobody is going to believe that an almost 80-year-old woman who has had a great record all her life has all of a sustain turned to a cat burglar, overnight, plus I 'm not leaving until I find out if this is my grand baby or not.

That's just it, what if it is not him who you are looking for?

That's a chance that I'm willing to take, and don't worry if something goes wrong, I'll tell them I forced you to come with me, but I have to do this, I haven't seen this boy in 10 years, up until last week when he called me, I thought he was dead, now he is just popping up all of a sustain, I just got the feeling that something suspicious is going on.

Suspicious like what? London said as her face showed strong signs of worry.

I think he is running from something, and I wish I just knew what it is, I have so many questions that I need answered, hell where has he been all these years, who did he stay with all this time?

She went around the apartment searching room after room, looking through his things, searching for any kind of clue she could find that this was really his apartment, then she came across a photograph of him with a couple of guys, standing in what look like a bar setting, posing like the pictures were taken in prison. The sight of him almost made her heart jump out of her chest, he looked just like his father, it was like looking in the mirroring image of Lamar, the only way to tell them apart was Aiden's curly hair and real light skin, not wasting any time, she took the picture and placed it in her purse, then she took out a piece of paper and began to write him a note, telling him who she was and that she really needed to see him, also she put down her address and phone number just in case he needed to get in contact with her in any way, P.S. Granny Love you, always have and always will,   at the bottom, she also placed a hundred dollars next to the note as a peace offering for the door she broke, then she turned around and walked out the door once her mission had become complete,

Aiden:

As Ace was getting out of the shower he became startled from the loud noise his phone was making, when he came back to Cincinnati he made sure he placed cameras all around every piece of property he owed in the city, one of the reasons was so he could keep an close eye on everything he had all at once and the other reason was for his protection, he paid a pretty penny for the air tight surveillance system, they were set up to where if someone would break in, they wouldn't notice that there was an alarm going off because mainly it was set on silent, leaving the burglar to believe they was getting away with something that they really wasn't, leaving them caught red handed in the act, the notification, poured loud sounds all through the house, before he could make it to the phone to cut it off, Meme entered into the room looking around trying to find out where the loud noise was coming from, you could tell from her actions, the noise and curiosity was driving her crazy.

Ace! What the hell is that noise? Is something wrong? Is somebody trying to break in or something?

Meme chill out it's nothing but my alarm, that I set, to make sure I take care of some business today I been putting off for a while, Ace watched her body language as his words lead to anything but the truth.

Her eyes stared him down, from top to bottom, checking to see if she could place his energy in any category she could find, to see if she could displace him in anyway and Ace noticed it.

What's wrong, why are you making that face for, you know I have seen that look many times in the face of other people and I have to say it makes me real uncomfortable.

What business do you need to take care of where you would have to set an alarm, that sounds like we are at school running a fire drill?

Damn you nosey, how are we going to get to know each other if we don't start first on our trust, I told you I'm willing to do whatever it takes and for however long it takes baby as long as you're willing to work on it.

Yeah, yeah, yeah, I hear you, you always got something slick to say, she said cutting him off not willing to hear any more of what he had to say, as she walked back out of the room he watched her take every step, he admired her toughest, it always made him smile. Once he seen that she was gone, he rushed to look inside his phone, so he could playback the surveillance cameras from his apartment on the Westside, the note flashed across the phone showed him that whoever broke into his apartment came in through the front door, once he pressed play on the video, he saw the front door fly open as if it him been kicked in, then an old lady entered inside, which threw him off because that was far from what he had expected, he would have never thought that he would get robbed by an old woman, if he called the police, they probably would just laugh at him if he told them he was be burglarized by a senior citizen, he watched her as she moved through the house, not taking anything but just basically looking around like she was lost or something. Then he noticed that she had someone else was with her, he quickly zoomed in on the persons face, and he could instantly tell that the person who was with the old lady was indeed MoMo, which was also crazy, he wondered if it had something to do with how he responded to what she told him earlier, and he has had crazy girls do all types of stuff to get his attention but nothing to the extreme like this, he imagine her telling her grandmother what had happen and she became gangster like in the movies for her baby, those thoughts made him laugh. He thought In truth there was no way in hell that could be the reason they was there, no revenge over a few words was that deep to end up in jail for, it had to be more to the story. Every possible thought crossed his mind until he became completely mentally exhausted, as he watched them Rome through the house, they didn't tear anything up or move anything out of place, so the question became, what is it are their looking for? What is it that they want? The more he watched the more he became anxious, ready to jump up and run to his apartment to see if he could catch them in the act, then the old woman picked up his picture, he had placed amongst others on his dresser, after she took a long look at the picture she held the picture close to her heart. That part seemed weird to him, so he zoomed in on the older woman's face to see if he could recognize her in any way, not getting the satisfaction from the videos resolution, he snapped a screenshot photo to be able to pull her features in just a little closer, the sight of the old woman made him draw a flash back to his dad's funeral, then it became real clear to him that the old woman he was staring at, was his grandmother, Vickie Wright, his picture was clear on the last time he saw her, she was sitting with two kids, as he stood in the distance, unnoticed, those was moments no matter how hard he tried to get out of his mind, he was never able to erase them altogether, that's one of the things that still haunt him to this day, the other is the visions he still has of his father laying in a casket, it became to be too much at times for him to bear, playing over and over in his head, in odd places, always at the wrong times, after a few minutes of having his eyes focused in a locked in stare mainly from disbelief, he was sure that it was her, he could tell that she had aged over the 10 years, but he could tell her face from anywhere, he remembered how they use to spend a lot of time together when he was a kid, mainly when his dad had to make important runs, his dad felt was too dangerous for him to ride along, that's when he would take him over his Grandma Vickie house so she could keep an eye on him. As he lost track on where he was in the world, placing the video on repeat, watching her and MoMo move through the house, it dawned on him that the whole thought of them being together was odd, he wondered how they were connected, his mind began to drift for a second, and the more unpleasant thoughts began to enter his head, the more his body began to heat up, than out of nowhere he became dizzy, to the point he had to sit down before he were going to faint, the thoughts ofMoMo possibly being his family member started to become too much for him, he remember a long time ago May-so telling him that he had a brother and a sister but he never believe any of that, he didn't believe that his father would hold that type of information from him, despite what happen between them, he felt like they was at least that close, up to the point where his dad was holding back the secret of what he did to his mom in a journal, they were best friends.

Without even being aware of anything going on around him, he screamed No, as he thought, what is the chance of MoMo actually being his sister, he blamed himself for not checking up on what May-so had told him, for staying away for so long, and for many other things, to tell the truth were out of his control, but yet and still, the thoughts made him sick to his stomach, knowing it was possible he had been engaging in sex with his sister, just didn't sit right with him, he also thought about how he has been treating her, made him feel even worse, he tried his best to get back on track by placing all those bad thoughts back to the far part of his brain, where he found them in the first place, as he rationalize the situation, he wasn't able to bounce back as fast as he usually would, as he sat on the bed, stuck in his thoughts on what is it he think he should do next, he wanted to call his grandmother to clear everything up, but didn't have a clue about what he would say if she answered, when he delivered the journal over to her house, his one and only mission was to make sure he showed the reasons of him leaving in the first place, he only thought about telling his part of the story, relieving himself with the truth, he only wanted to show her the reasons for his pain, he never thought or even cared about anybody else pain, he never thought of the reply to his actions, it's only now that he sees that he does have a selfish part in his heart, because he placed it in his next thought to not answer when they call, before they catch up with him, he planned to just leave and never look back, never, that's the only way he wouldn't have to see them knowing in his heart once he leave again it would be for good. He wanted to get up and leave today but he couldn't, the time he has spent with Meme was very special to him and if he was planning on leaving, he wanted to at least see if she would be willing to go with him. Before he could pull his self together and go back into the other room, Meme walked back into the room ready to make a joke of his corny lover boy ways, when she noticed he had a real serious concerned look on his face, which gave her the feeling that something very weird was going on and that he might be hiding something, so instead of questioning him to see what it is that is really bothering him, she decided to come at the situation a little different and do a little investigation of her own.

Hey baby, do you know what time we are going out tonight?

He looked up, seeing that she had beat him to the punch, when it comes to sharing in each other space, he stood up to greet her, forcing a fake smile on his face.

I should be ready to head out in probably about an hour or so, are you going to be ready by then is the question? You know how you women are, you take hours and hours to put on make-up and squeeze into them little pretty dresses, with a man, all we do is throw something on and go, it doesn't take us long at all.

No you are not just going to just throw something on, and the answer is yes, I can be ready by then, but I'm kind of getting the vibe, you're not feeling up to going out tonight, and if that is so, then we can just go out another time. I want to have fun; I don't want you all out in the club distracted!

No baby I am good, I told you we were going to go out and celebrate your birthday and that's what we are going to do, I feel like we both need this night out, just to relax and have fun, clear our minds of all the bullshit we been going through for the last couple of days, baby I need a drink no ice and maybe a back massage to loosen me up a little bit.

Yea I could use a back massage as well, are you going to set us up an appointment with the spa?

That would be nice and very well needed it.

We don't need to go to no spa, I can massage your back for free, and I promise I could do a great job.

I bet you could, but as far as us going out tonight you are right, we do need a night to relax, with everything that's been going on, I'm surprised I haven't lost my mind already, I really just want to put what happen the other night behind me and move forward, but I would be lying if I didn't say it bothers me, to see that look on your face, come on Ace, it's obvious that something is bothering you!

Why do you keep thinking something is wrong with me, baby I'm ok, I been in my thoughts about a lot of things that's been going on in my life but it isn't nothing that I can't handle!

That's what you say, but it's written all over your face, now are you going to tell me what's going on or not?

He wanted to open up about everything that's been going on between him and his family, but his heart wouldn't let him, so he quickly dismissed it altogether, deciding to throw a little white lie together to get her off his back for a while, at least until he finds out if he could truly trust her with not just his heart but with also the deep dark secrets of his past as well. Ace became very good with his words, so good, they soften her heart, causing her to back off a little but he still was not out of the dog house, even a blind man could see, she still didn't fully trust him, the words of her father echoed in her head as he quoted the bible:

Micah 7:5 put no trust in a neighbor, have no confidence in a friend, and close your mouth to the one who is in your embrace.

So she acted as if she were going into the other room to get ready but once she turned the corner she waited until he returned back into the bathroom to finish getting ready before she decided to go through his phone, as soon as the screen came on, she could see that he had last been viewing what looked to be surveillance cameras, which only made her more curious, wondering has he been watching her the whole time since she has been there, or was they cameras to somewhere else, and if so, then where, she tired her best to get inside the app but it required a password, so after a few tries, she went back out of the app and started her search in other areas of the phone, nothing caught her eye until she looked inside of his photo gallery, instantly becoming uneasy once she saw a still photo of her grandmother Vickie, a real close up photo of her, how did he get it? And what was he planning on doing with it. As she continued on in her search, she heard the toilet flush, she knew she didn't have too much time left, he would be coming out the bathroom pretty soon, so she placed his phone back in the same spot that she got it and quickly exited the room before he came out and seen what she was doing, once she got far on the other side of the house, she hurried up and called her brother, he answered on the second ring, what's up sis?

Jyel I need you to do me a favor!

Damn girl what now, I hope it has nothing to do with me going back to the house, because I left there a couple of hours ago and I wasn't planning on going back there until after I leave the party with you tonight, unless I get lucky then I am not going back to the house at all!

I really need you to go pick something up from the house and bring it with you tonight,

Sis anything you need from the house, I'm sure you can just go buy it at the mall, damn you got all that money, isn't no reason for you to still act like you broke, lord knows you been saving your lunch money since the first grade.

Jyel I really need your help, this is important, I mean like cool beans!

He paused as soon as he heard cool beans, when they were kids, they made those words as a means to be a code word for help, if they were ever in some kind of trouble, one or the other would drop everything and come to the other rescue, they swore that whoever would make the call, the other would be there for them no matter what. So he asked her what is it that she needed for him to do, she gave him some directions to her hiding place she had in the basement of her grandmother's house, she wanted him to go and retrieve something for her and bring it to her, her directions made him grow even more curious to what she wanted him to retrieve from the basement, before he could push her into telling him anything else, she quickly told him that she loved him and hung up the phone. Once off the line, he felt weird about the whole situation, he tried his best to call back two more times but he got no answer. That only made him move his feet faster in order to get the job she so badly needed done. As he rushed into the house, he tried his best to keep a strong awareness on his surroundings, doing his best not to make a scene, the last thing he needed was his grandmother shaking him down for information he himself didn't know all the answers too, once he got down in the basement, he searched the very exact spot that Myona had informed him to search, he reached in under the stairs and pulled out a small black Nike shoe box, once he looked inside, it was something heavy inside, he couldn't tell just yet what it was because it was wrapped in an all-black t-shirt, he sat the box on the floor so he could give whatever it was in the t-shirt his full attention, as he unwrapped the shirt, he couldn't believe his eyes, a chrome Glock 19 fully loaded with one in the chamber fell into his hands, right at that moment, he knew whatever his sister was involved in, had to be serious, if she would go as far as using the code word and have him pick up a gun, her life just might be in danger. He began to get more and more worried with each passing minute, feeling like he had no more time to waste, he stuffed the gun in his pants and returned the shoe box back to its original place, as he began to go back upstairs, trying his best to still remain unnoticed by his grandmother, he noticed the house was to quiet, there was no way his grandmother was home, he hurried out the door of the house, frying his best to get as far as he could before his grandmother returned, his thoughts began to be all over the place, the only thing he had on his mind that made sense was getting to his sister.

Ace & Meme:

As Ace rode in the car on their way to the bar, he thought about making a detour to take Meme to a nice restaurant, but as he glanced over at her, he could tell that it was something that was truly bothering her, so he decided to scratch the surface to see what it was that was on her mind.

Is there something wrong baby? Something we might need to sort out before we get this night started? Because baby I could tell something is wrong, but we promised each other that we were going to have a good time tonight, have a couple of drinks, clear our minds, remember?

And we will, it's just with everything going on, I think I'll feel a little bit better if I could have some family around.

Yeah ok, I could understand that, but didn't you invite somebody to come out with you tonight and celebrate your birthday? Did they decide they didn't want to come or something?

I invited my brother, and he said he was going to come but,

But what baby?

I'm just a little worried he might not make it tonight!

Why wouldn't he make it, you said that he was coming, is he the type to tell you he coming or going to do something but don't?

No he's not like that, if he says, he is coming, then he will be there, the problem is I know he don't have a ride, do you mind, just swinging by and picking him up before he gets to the club, it will take a lot of weight off my shoulders, because I would know for sure he would be there to share this special moment with me.

Damn baby! Why didn't you tell me all that, before we got in route, I would have made a plan to go get him, before we made it way over here on the other side of town.

You don't even know what part of town he's on and you already trying to shut me down, why even ask me what's bothering me if you are not willing to hear me out anyway?

Stop! Meme I'm not shutting you down! I just wanted to spend a little personal time with you before everybody and everything began to pulling you left and right. I was going to surprise you by taking you out to a very nice restaurant, where we could have some dinner, open up a little more with each other, I really like our talks. But to ease your mind, this is what I'm going to do so we don't have to stop our plans in the process.

I'm listening! She said as she turned around in her sit to face him.

How about I call my homeboy Low and tell him to swing by and pick your brother up on the way to meet us at the strip club, that way we can kill two birds with one stone.

Her face shown a strong sign of disagreement but after he begged her a little longer, convincing her everything will be fine, she broke down and went with Ace's plan, she didn't care how her brother got there, as long as he was with her by the end of the night. After giving Ace her brothers number, he made the call to Low, he answered after a couple of rings.

Before responding, Low looking at the phone, took in a deep breath then said, Jyel this is Low,

Low! Man who is this? How you know my name?

Listen man, I'm a friend of your sisters!

Yes, so, what do you want?

Your sister wanted me to swing by and pick you up on the way to the club her and Ace had to make a run so I gave them my word I would come get you to make sure you make it to her little birthday celebration.

Why wouldn't she just come get me herself, I don't know you, you could be on some real creep shit!

Low began to lose his cool with him, more and more as the conversation went on,

Look I'm just doing them a favor, if you don't want the ride then suit yourself, I'm not going to kiss your ass to give you a ride, ain't nobody offered me no gas money or babysitting fee for your ass, I'll just tell them if they want you at her party that bad, then they should come get you they self!

Alright, man, my bad you can come get me,

Are you sure? I don't want you uncomfortable or anything, plus the bus is still running,

Yeah I'm sure, I just didn't know if you really know my sister or not, I can't just jump in the car with anybody, it's too much shit gong on these days.

Man think, how else could I have gotten the number?

I don't know, maybe I'm tripping, look I'm in Westwood over by the plaza,

He described to Low where he would be standing when he pulled into the parking lot, he also described what he was wearing so he wouldn't miss him if he passed by. Low assured him he was close and that he will be there no later than ten minutes.

Once Low pulled up beside him, seeing if the guy he was looking at, fit the description, Jyel approached the car real slow, looking inside to see who all was in the car, he saw an older man who looked to be in his 40's and two women, whom none ended up being his sister but to him, nothing screamed out at him as if he was really in some type of danger, so he got in the car with no hesitation, once one of the woman asked him if Jyel was his name, as he sat in the car Low got a real good look at his face, it was then that he realized why the name sounded so familiar, it was the boy he seen on the news the other day, Lamar Wright son, the little junior Detective, to be sure if it was him, he began to slowly ask questions, nothing to serious, but just enough for him to get a positive ID, plus he wanted to make sure that the little guy was comfortable, he seemed like he was already on guard, he didn't want to run him away.

So Jyel how you doing today brother, it seems like you been having a bad day, you snapped on me when I was just trying to make sure you were straight, Low said as he watched him through his rearview mirror.

My bad man, I know we got off to a rough start, it's just a lot going on for me today, so when somebody call your phone, who you don't know, talking about picking you up, you got to make sure you ain't just walking into some bullshit!

Look it ain't my business what's going on with you, but at least tell us if we in any type of danger, because I could go grab my strap, I don't want nobody pulling up on us, shooting at us and we naked out here, do you got some type of beef with somebody that I should know about?

Low checked his body language, to see how he would react to his words altogether,

What! Naw we good, I don't roll like that, I stay out the way, ain't no beef, Jyel said as he stared off out the window, not making any eye contact at all.

Ok cool, Low said as he watched his reaction in his rearview mirror, he knew something was off with the kid, and by him not knowing his angle, it made him put his guard up as well. Jyel jumped as the lady in the passenger sit, placed her hand on his leg, trying her best to grab all his attention in her direction.

Relax baby you in good hands, my name is Candy, how are you doing handsome?

He stuttered his name out as she pressed in closer to him to whisper a little something in his ear,

You are very handsome and I would be lying if I didn't say I wasn't feeling you,

Jyel said thank you as he backed up a little to put some space between them.

Candy seeing his shyness, made her smile and want him even more, she quickly turned to Low and E-b and thanked them for Jyel, he was a birthday gift wrapped just for her.

E-b shook her head in disbelief to how her friend was acting, sense the young boy enter the car,

Girl you better leave that little boy alone, before you catch a case, E-b said as she laughed, tears rolled down her face, he looks scare out of his mind!

Girl stop! This gone be my little boyfriend for the night!

Low brushed off what she said as if he never even heard a word she said,

Tonight Jyel we gone have some fun, fuck what she talking about, we are going to go throw some dollars on some strippers, have a couple of drinks, and over all just have a great time.

Jyel seen that the ladies were clowning him about his age, so he denied that he was a young guy and tried his best to make an excuse for the reasons why he won't be able to go to the bar with them, trying his best not to stick out, but they all seen through what he was trying to do especially Low, so he assured him that he would take care of everything, Low knew from his smooth baby face, that he wasn't the legal age to do anything, not even buy a pack of smokes from the local comer store. As they pulled up to the strip club, Low could tell that Jyel had a real nervous look in his eyes, as everyone was getting out the car, Jyel made sure he stuck back a little to buy himself some time on what he should do next, lost about where he was going to hide the gun before he went inside, Low noticed once they all started walking towards the club that he had stayed back so he told the ladies to go on ahead of him he would catch up, while he checked on Jyel to see if he were good. As he walked up to the car, he looked inside and seen that Jyel was in the middle of texting somebody on his phone.

What's up little bro, what's going on, I told you I got you, you don't want to come in or something?

Yeah I want too, but I told you I don't have my ID, so I know they are not going to let me in, I been here a few times and they always turned me away!

Listen little bro, I know you're under age, hell, we all do, that's something you can't hide.

How you figure that?

Bro anybody can tell that, even a blind man can see that, but look, like I said, you in good hands, they might have turned you around before, but that was because you weren't with me, I'm the man in this spot, we walking straight through to the V.I.P!

Is that right?

If you don't believe, you will see, my name got some respect on it, not just in this club but around this whole city, and it's been that way for a long time, so come on, don't trip I got you, everything is on me.

Jyel got out of the car and started walking with Low to the front of the entrance, but before they could get through the door, Low stopped once again and pulled Jyel to the side of the building.

Jyel, one more thing,

Yeah, what's up?

Do you have your gun on you? Low leaned in and made sure he talked in a whisper to make sure nobody else heard him that was walking by

No, what would make you think that?

You just putting off a real nervous vibe to me, so I just wanted to know if you do, because if so, it isn't no big deal or nothing, we in this together, I'll hold it for you until we safely make it in the club and then I'll hand it back to you. I know they aren't going to pat me down, but you on the other hand, your new, so they might be on you, but you said you don't have it on you so cool let's go!

Low took a few more steps closer to the door, than Jyel called out his name in a low tone, Low turned around once again to see what was wrong.

Ok what's up Jyel, is we to be able to go in here or is you gone play around out here all night, what's wrong now?

I do have a gun on me!

Low stepped in closer, to close the space between them so nobody walking pass would see him hand off the gun to him.

Give it to me, I'm going to carry it in for you.

Jyel reached into his waistband and pulled out the all chrome Glock 19 and handed it over to Low, who then turned around so he could put it in his waist, then he turned and walked inside the building, as soon as he got inside, the bouncers greeted him as if he was a superstar, he walked right off to the side, handing off a couple of hundred to the bouncer as he skipped right pass the metal detector, Jyel on the other hand had a much different experience, he almost didn't make it through the line at all, the first thing they did was damn near strip search him at the front entrance, then after he made it through the metal detector, they wanted to search him once more to see if they had missed anything, in the meantime, Low had slipped out of sight, as if he forgot Jyel was even with him at all, right as they was about to kick him out of the bar for not having an ID, Low popped back out from around the corner and told the bouncer that the young boy was with him, which stopped the bouncer in his tracks, he instantly released his grip from Jyel's arm, letting him walk on by him into the club, as they walked through the strip club, Jyel was so amazed at all the half-naked woman, twerking all over the place, it became really hard for Jyel to keep his focus to anything that Low was saying along the way. Once they sat down with the girls at their table by the stage, Low signaled for the waitress to bring a bottle to their table and a couple of dancers to sit in Jyel's lap, he didn't waste no time trying to get the party started, Low went into his pocket and pulled out a stack of money and began to pass it out between Jyel and the ladies to keep them occupied, while he go and talk to the owner real quick about some business, after they fanned him off, he got up and headed to the back of the club, once upstairs, he went straight into the owners office without even knocking, as he walked through the door, the man glanced in his direction, then back to the large set of cameras, he had set up in the room, exhaling a deep breath,

Low why are you here?

What Bam! A man can't come out and have a little fun tonight without it being some kind of problem with you, I thought you would be happy to see me, considering I spend a shit load of money in this place every time I come.

He turned away from the cameras to face Low, then he motioned for him to have a seat, in one of his chairs, directly in front of his desk.

You most definitely can come out and have the time of your motherfucking life, the question is why, here? And why do you got that young ass little boy with you? placing one of the biggest targets I have ever seen on my back!

I'm doing a favor for a friend, keeping an eye on the Lil young buck until we meet up a little later, I might as well show him a good time in the process.

Doing a friend, a favor huh, you must really think I'm stupid as hell don't you, like I don't know who the fuck that Lil motherfucker is, that little motherfucker was all over the news a couple of days ago, and you bring him up in here for what, to do an undercover sting, to get my business closed down!

Bam get the fuck out of here, don't you ever put no police shit on my name, he in here with me, not on no police shit, the motherfucker didn't even ask to come here, I told you I'm keeping an eye on him until I meet up with one of my guys, this is business, now you telling me, you are going to stand in front of my business now!

Really man, out of all the places you could have come too to do business in the city, you bring a junior Detective to my place, come on Low, and to put the icing on the cake, they also said something about how he is Lamar Wright kid, I hated that piece of shit with a passion growing up, if his daddy was still alive, I would make it my business to kill that motherfucker myself

Yeah, yeah, whatever Bam, you ain't gone kill shit or let nothing die!

Yeah whatever you say motherfucker, I bet, nobody better not test me, I know that, they would most definitely find the fuck out the hard way!

As Low laughed at every word he was saying, he could also tell that Bam was getting real upset, one of the bouncers, entered the room just as they were finishing up their conversation.

Damn Low, why you ain't tell me you were going to be up here in the office with Bam, I been looking all over the place for you, I was beginning to think you left!

Low stood up out of his seat and started walking towards him,

Did you take care of that business for me?

Yeah I switched the real bullets out with blanks just like you asked, but I'm still puzzled on why! The bouncer said as he reached into his pants and handed Low back the chrome Glock 19 he had handed him when he came through the entrance to the club, without giving him an answer, Low safely tucked the gun into his pants, then passed the guy a couple more hundred for his troubles, and made his way out the door of the office and back down the stairs so he could rejoin the party he had left unattended.

Bam:

As soon as Bam seen that Low was gone, he got right on the phone to call his boy Boone, Boone had told him if he ended up seeing Low, no matter the place, to call him immediately, Boone answered the phone with no hesitation,

What's up Bam, what you need? I'm kind of entertaining a lady friend at the moment!

Even though Boone was on the phone, it didn't stop his lady friend from doing her job of keeping his dick nice and hard, as she deep throated his dick, trying her best to make it disappear in the process, she didn't move at the chance to be quit, instead she made sure her love making could be heard for the whole building to hear, making it no secret what was happening on

Boone's end of the line, even Bam got turned on from the sounds she was making on the phone, to the point he almost completely lost his train of thought, Boone's voice brought him back to the conversation altogether.

Bam what's good?

Damn, o ok, yeah,

Bam focus!

You told me to call you if Low popped up in the spot,

And, come on Bam, this shit getting good over here, spit it out!

And he here in the club right now, and you're not going to believe who he is with!

Who! Boone said as he pushed the girls head off the tip of his dick, and stood up so he could indeed get more focused

He in here with Lamar Wright kid,

What! Lamar Wright has kids? I never knew that!

You mean to tell me; you didn't see that shit all over the news the other day.

Once Boone told him no, he brought him up to date from the beginning to the end about the little junior Detective, while Bam was still talking, Boone made sure he looked the story up on his local news feed from his home computer.

What the fuck is Low into? He been on some real weird shit lately, why would he be hanging out with that boy?

I don't know beats me!

Well look Bam, I want you to make sure that Low is real

comfortable, give him the best service the place has to offer, I need you to keep him occupied for a while till I get there.

Cool, I could do that but Boone, I don't need no bullshit up in here, I just wanted to make sure that I do right by you, you know, you and Blue Chip always take care of me, I love y'all guys man.

Love you too Bam, and Bam don't tell him that I'm coming, he been ducking me for a while, and it's just important that I talk to him, so just make sure you just keep this between you and me, not even Blue Chip could know about this, ok!

Ok! Bam said, once he hung up the phone, he called the waitress up to his office and pointed out

Low on the camera,

I want you to give them the platinum package, keep it coming all night long and it's on me, they won't have to pay for nothing, tell the girls, it's out of my money, so they could get as nasty as they want, just send me the bill, but tell them don't front, the eye in the sky is watching everything.

Low:

Once Low returned to the party, he seen that the party had gained momentum even more then it had before, Ass and tits was all over Jyel, it was like he was having a live threesome for the whole club to see, it was evident, he was no longer the shy guy in the room, he had now become the life of the party, once the DJ put on a slow song, he pulled Jyel away from the crowd, so he could talk to him, one on one, once Jyel got up from his seat, Low could tell that all that liquor that he had been drinking was starting to take a strong effect on his operational skills, he could barely stand, his head was rolling from left to right, and the whole time that Low was trying to talk to him, he placed all his weight on the wall closest to him, which gave him the impression that at any moment that he might just throw up.

Jyel, what's up Lil bro is you good?

Hell yeah, I'm having the time of my life, I can't remember the last time I had fun like this!

He stopped and looked around as if he was in some kind of deep thought,

Damn come to think about it, I have never had fun like this before, man thanks bro I owe you one.

Look I been holding your gun for you, I was wondering if you could handle it, if I give it back to you right now.

What! Jyel said as he felt his waist in search for the gun, stumbling in the hallway trying to keep his balance at the same time, how did you get my gun? I never gave you my gun!

You gave it to me, to get it in the club remember? Look never mind, the question is, do you want me to just hold on to it for you or not? I could tell you really feeling good right now from all that drinking you doing, I don't want you to do nothing stupid.

Give me my gun, I got this!

As low was handing it to him, he snatched it out of his hand and checked the chamber to see if it was still one in the head of the gun, then he stuffed it in his waist band.

Lil homie you sure you good?

Yeah I'm good bro, I'm Lamar Wright son, ain't nobody fucking with me, Motherfucker's know what it is,

Low's eyes lit up as the young dude confirm that he was indeed Lamar Wright child, he decided to push a little more information out of him before they rejoined the crowd.

Jyel, the girl that's planning on meeting you here tonight, is she really your sister?

Yeah she is my sister, who just goes around saying their brother and sister and they really ain't, unless they on some weird shit,

Naw, I have had friends, I have called my sister, but it was only to hide the fact we were fucking altogether and if that's the case, I ain't mad at you, play on playa,

Hell Naw, watch your mouth bro, that's my real blood sister, we got the same mother and father, you weird as fuck for saying shit like that bro, I wouldn't do no shit like that!

My bad, let's forget I even went there, let's just go back to the party and have some fun.

Once they got back to the table, he ordered more drinks and then he noticed that when it was time to pay, the waitress would just drop the drinks off at the table, then would quickly turn around and leave, at first he felt like maybe he was getting away without paying because the club was packed with a lot of people, so it was a chance that the waitress could really just be distracted by everything that was going on, but then on his very next round of drinks, he decided to test his theory, before the girl could even get the drinks on the table, he forced the money onto the serving tray, she declined,

No it's ok, everything is on the house sir you can keep your money,

Who is paying the bill then, Low asked as he took a quick scan around the room to see if anybody was watching, the only eyes he seen glued to him at the moment, was E-b. as he stared away in back in the direction of the waitress, he told her, she could just keep the money for a tip then instead, she waived him off once again.

The owner told us to give you anything you want, and to take no tips, the bill is on him,

Low told the girl to tell him that he said thank you and then he sat back in his seat and pondered on what the girl just told him about Bam's request to pay for everything. He wondered, what was it that made him change his mind, knowing that just a short hour ago, he didn't like the idea that they were in his club in the first place, to now, he has started passing out special treatment, like he was a well-known celebrity, at that point, Low felt like something had to be up, Bam's actions instantly put him on guard for anything that might be coming his way. As E-b continued to watch him from a distance, she could see by his overall body language that his mood had changed, so she left from Candy side, who was still busy working her body to the beat of the song, and made her way over to Low's side of the room, cleared his space, then sat on his lap.

Is everything ok baby, I was watching you from over there and it just seems like your whole vibe got threw off, is it something that the waitress said?

He looked her over and turned his head, not saying a word, as if he didn't even hear a word that she said, E-b gently grabbed his face and pulled it back in her direction and leaned in and planted a passionate kiss on his lips.

Baby I love you, and I want you to know, that from now on, we in this together, just in this little time we been together, you have stolen my heart, and the truth is I don't want to live another day without you my life, I just wished that I would have,

She stopped talking, catching herself from saying the wrong thing, as Low looked her in her eyes, he could tell that it was something, she was holding on too, that she wanted to release and even though he had a great idea on what it was, he acted unfazed by her words, and instead decided to see if she would spit it out, by repeating her last sentence, pushing for her to give him an answer.

What! You just wish you would have what E-b!

She dropped her head, and said, would have met you sooner!

A strong anger had built up in his chest, he just wanted to get away from her, tired of being tossed to and from, with mixed emotions about her, he tried to move her from his lap without making a scene, knowing the truth about what she did to his cousin had his heart tied up, playing hostage, all for the four letter word, love, he tried over and over to make any excuse he could to justify what she did, maybe this or maybe that, but wasn't able to come up with anything worth holding on too, overwhelmed with so much emotion and crowded thoughts, he took her face into his hands, picked her head up, and waited patiently until they both could lock eyes and said,

Yeah I wish we could have too,

The look in his eyes sent a chill down E-b's spine, a part of her mind told her to get up and get the hell out of there, but her heart had a strong hold on her, drawing her closer in to the side of staying, she was held bound by the love she has for him, lost on what it is that she feels she should frilly do next. Just as Low released his grip from E-b's face, he scanned the room once again, just in time to see that one of Blue Chips men from his crew, had just entered the club and started walking by their table, but before he could get close in their direction, Low leaned in close to E-b a gave her a heart stopping kiss, E-b's heart started beating a thousand seconds per minute, lost in the moment, mainly because she had never been kissed this way before, his actions only placed more mixed signals in her mind, once they released from there kiss, he looked off to the side, seeing that the guy had already made his way pass, he embraced E-b in a tight hug and whispered in her ear,

Baby let's get out of here,

She replied, but what about your friend, wasn't you supposed to be meeting him here?

Yeah, but I'm getting a little tired of waiting around in here, I'll just call him and tell him, it's been a change of plans, everybody could just meet up at my house.

As they both stood up, they motioned for the others to get their attention, then they all headed towards the door.

At first Jyel was headed towards the exit with them, then all of a sustain he turned back around and started heading back toward the party, Low grabbed his arm and tried his best to pull him back in his direction, without causing too much attention to what they were doing,

Get the fuck off of me! Jyel shouted as he snatched his arm away from Low's firm grip,

Look Lil bro, we need to step outside for a minute to regroup,

Regroup! Fuck that! I don't need to regroup, I'm good,

Bro we came in here together, it's best we leave here together, I'm just trying to watch you're back the best way I could, I could see you a little drunk and you need some fresh air, so just step out here with us for a little while.

Jyel stumbled around, trying his best to keep his balance,

Look man, I came here to meet my sister and I ain't leaving here until I do, so no I ain't going nowhere, if you want to leave, then by all means motherfucker, leave.

Low motioned for Candy to go get him, hoping she could be the one to get him under control, as he headed out the door, taking E-b with him.

Once Candy reached him, she shifted his body weight so he could land on the closest wall to

Bitch what is you doing? Get the fuck off of me!

Baby chill out, there isn't no need to get upset, nobody said we was leaving, we just getting a little air for a minute.

I'm going to tell you, like I just told him, I don't need no fucking air, I am good!

Baby calm down, I'm not trying to fight you, we all came out to have a good time, let's just continue to do that, but all I'm asking from you is for us to have a little alone time, that's all,

She stepped in closer to him, closing the space between them, pressing her body tightly up against his, letting her hands wildly explore his body, she nipped on his ear and moans began to escape him the more pressure she placed on him, she slowly began sliding her hand down the front of his pants, once she got inside, she took hold of his now rock hard dick, each time she stroked it back and forth, it caused him to inhale and exhale large breaths at a high rate, almost as if he was running a race, as she slowly pulled her hand from his pants, she decided to take things up a notch by licking and sucking all over her fingers, showing him that she was in deep need to witness his taste, first hand, after she took a quick taste, she spit into her hand and placed it back down his pants, stroking him once again, than began to whisper in his ear,

Baby I want you, baby why you teasing me, I want to taste you so bad, and damn my pussy is so wet, do you want to see?

After he shook his head yes, she took him by the hand and guided it right under her skirt, letting him run free and wild like a kids, first time at a neighborhood playground, who hasn't been outside in mouths, the strength in his hard penis, showed that she had him right where she wanted him, locked in for the night, she knew for sure she wasn't going home alone tonight, at the moment, she knew he was completely under her spell, he would follow her to the moon and back with no question, as they walked out of the building and into the parking lot, Jyel eyes began to Rome around the area, trying his best to find a quick spot they could sneak off too, so they could finish what they had started in the club, but every direction he tried to pull her in, she would pull away, showing that she had a direction of her own, getting frustrated, he let out a large sigh, when she went for the car door that Low and

E-b was already sitting in, feeling that he might have been tricked into coming outside, he began to back paddle back towards the club, noticing his grip was loosening from her, she quickly turned around to see what the problem was,

Jyel where are you going?

I'm going back in the club, you just played the fuck out of me, just so I could come outside for this so called fresh air, y'all kept talking about, fuck all that, I told you I was cool, so I'm going back inside, I thought we was gone fuck, that's the only reason I came out here!

She pulled him in closer to her, making sure that he didn't get away from her grip,

Baby relax, I told you, I got you, now get in the car!

It took a minute to force him to get inside, but once they both got in the car, Candy didn't waste any time on backing up her word, she instantly began to try to loosen his belt, so she could get his pants down, her juices began to overflow to the thought of forcing as much as she could of him down her throat, Jyel moved her hand, not sure where any of this was going,

Stop! What the fuck is you doing? You frying to fuck me in front of them, what! The fuck is wrong with you, did this motherfucker put you up to this, if so, that's some weird ass shit, I don't get down like that!

No baby I told you I want to taste you,

Ok, but here though?

I thought you was a man!

I am a man,

Then stop acting like a little boy, I don't care if they watch, now lay back!

She finally was able to get his pants down just enough to get his dick out, then she aggressively licked him up and down, once she got to the top, her tongue rolled around the tip of his bell head until she could feel him throb in her hand and pulsate in her mouth, as he forced her head into his lap, it only made her get turned on even more, as he leaned back, almost as if he was in a position to run, she felt the control swaying heavier to her side, which only made her want to take even more advantage of the moment, she got to work deep throating as much of him as she could, each time swallowing more and more of him trying her best to make him disappear, as if she was performing a magic trick, meantime Low was busy in his phone trying his best to ignore everything that was going on behind him, E-b on the other hand, could not help but watch as the sounds filled her ears, she became aroused, even though she wasn't into joining in the action they had created, it still did not stop her from the thoughts of performing some acts of her own, as Low looked through his Miss calls list on his phone, he seen that he also had quite a few voicemails left on his phone as well. E-b, leaning into Low's direction, kissing him on his neck, then down to his chest, not in the mood, Low stopped her in her tracks from going any farther, then shifted in the opposite direction, telling her he had to make an important call, as he made his exit, opened the car door and stepped outside the car, he pressed one to listen to the first voicemail message left on his phone, one by one, most of them was just from a couple of guys he knew, who was either looking for him because they haven't seen him around in a while, so they was checking on him to see if he was ok or they needed to meet up with him because the streets was drying up, so they was in a desperate need to re-up, still feeling that he had not came across nothing that was much of importance, he deleted message after message clearing his list, until he came across a unfamiliar voice, the guy spoke very fast, so he had to play the message over to make sure he could hear what the guy had to say a little better. Once he became tuned in a little better, the guy said he was from the hospital and that he needed him to call, it's very urgent that he speak with him, as the doctor spoke the phone number over the message, he replayed it over and over again until he knew it was placed firmly into his memory, his heart was racing, in every thought, he questioned what the call might be about, he didn't waste any time trying to get the doctor on the line, once the doctor answered the call, he went through a few questions to verify if

Low was the one emergency contact he should be talking too, then he delivered the News:

Mr. Latrell Smith, I'm sorry to inform you that your Aunt Jackie Carter didn't make it,

Those words coming from the doctors' mouth, was a devastating blow, words that he definitely didn't expect to hear, it hit him so hard, he had to grab a hold of the closest thing to him, because he was beginning to lose all the strength in his legs.

Doc what do you mean she didn't make it? I just talked to her, when they were putting her in the back of the ambulance, she was just fine, what the hell happen! He screamed at the top of his lungs into the phone, causing the onlookers, to stop and put a nosey ear into his conversation.

On the way to the hospital, your Aunt Jackie went into a strong state of shock, Mr. Smith, she died from heart failure.

Heart failure, what! How?

We did everything that we could but we just couldn't bring her back, I'm really sorry for your lost, when you get the chance, we are going to need you to come in and fill out some release forms for her body, ok

Low hung up without giving him any response, confused and distraught as he headed back to the car, once inside, his emotions began to build beyond his control, tears slowly began to run down his cheek, noticing E-b watching him from a distance, he turned his face trying quickly to wipe them away, hoping it went without notice.

Damn bro, you crying up there! You good, what the fuck is going on tonight!

Low tried his best to ignore his words but the harder he tried, the more Jyel talked,

Bro only bitches cry, that ain't the type of shit a man would do, suck that shit up, whatever it is,

Jyel said, as he laughed pulling his pants up, adjusting himself for the conversation.

Did you cry? When your mommy and daddy died!

What! Huh, what you say motherfucker?

You heard me! I said, did you cry, when your mommy and daddy died, or should I say was brutally murdered!

Man watch your motherfucking mouth, you speaking on shit you know nothing about!

O believe me, I know a whole lot more then you think I do, sitting around me talking like you some motherfucking gangsta or something, and that ain't you, you just a little punk ass bitch, who daddy is probably rolling around in his grave, knowing he gave his life to the streets, but his baby boy, on the other hand is a silver spoon, scooping, junior Detective, that don't know shit about laying their life on the line, you just the type to get the police on the line.

Offended by his words, Jyel didn't waste any time, reaching inside his pants and pulling out the Glock 19 from his waist, aiming it at the back of Low's head, ready off safety, in case he has to blast,

O so you going to shoot me now, unlike you, I ain't afraid to die, so go right ahead, do your thang, I don't got shit to lose!

Baby calm down put the gun away before somebody really gets hurt, come on now, just put the gun away, face showing real panic, Candy tried her best to deescalate the situation as best as she could.

Naw fuck this motherfucker, you think shit sweet, I could show you just how much I am my daddies son, since you want to see so bad!

Jyel swung the gun at Low's head as hard as he could, landing an unbelievable blow to the back of his head almost knocking him unconscious, but he was able to quickly shake it off and laugh at Jyel as if what he did didn't faze him at all.

O you think I'm playing dude? You think this shit funny, how about I blow your Lil bitch head off, would you still think this shit is a fucking game huh Low?

Jyel pressed the barrel to the back ofE-b's head causing her whole body to freeze up in the process, Low looked over at her, seeing the fear in her eyes, then back at Jyel through the review mirror, as he leaned back in his seat, he slowly went for his gun he had stashed in the side of the driver side door, Jyel just continued to taunt him,

Say something now big man, talk that shit now!

Lil bro, what do you want me to say? Huh? Please stop, no, please don't shoot, you know I couldn't stand your dad, back in the days, but I always respected him and felt like he was a real piece of shit as well at the same time, yeah the motherfucker was a real live slime ball but as time went by, I also grew to understand him, and where he was coming from on a lot of things!

Man, fuck what the fuck you talking about, I know you are about to hand me them keys to this car and shut the fuck up, before I shut you up, speaking on my dad like you knew him all your life, that type of shit makes me jealous, what's the next thing you going to tell me, your my long lost big brother, y'all shared valuable memories, large amounts of quality time together, where he held your hand and taught you the ropes to the streets, get the fuck out of here, if you say one more word about him, all those good ole memories you got stored in your head about him, I'm going to leave them all on that front dash board up there, starting with hers, yeah I'm willing to put some type of example into place.

To tell you the truth Jyel, I don't think you got it in you to pull the trigger, as a matter of fact fuck it,

By now Low had the gun in his hand as he was talking, once he was on his last word, he took his gun and aimed it at E-b's head, drawing confusion but wasting no time, in one smooth motion, he squeezed the trigger, sending E-b's brains all over the faces of everybody in the car, Jyel turned his gun in Low's direction and began to start shooting, and at the same time, he pulled Candy in his direction, to use her for a human shield, it didn't take long for Jyel to notice, as he continued to shoot, there were sound, but no bullets exiting the gun, Low laughed at him as if he was at a comedy show, enjoying one of his favorite entertainers, Jyel reached for the car door trying his best to make his escape, but as his door was on the verge of opening, Low made sure before he tried to get away, he threw some shots of his own, one landed in Jyel shoulder, then his side, his leg and the last one ricocheted off the door, catching him in the face, the impact knocked the wind out of him, but his adrenaline made him jump back up from his fall and run as fast as he could, to put some kind of distance between him and Low's gun. As Low jumped out of the car, the only thing that was on his mind, was finishing the job, but before he could bend the corner of the car to get another shot off, Candy jumped in his way, screaming and crying, begging for her life, her actions gave Jyel just enough time that he needed to get away, which made Low even more furious, instead of doing what any smart person in their right mind would do, which is try their best to escape, instead she got in the way, so because she froze up, he turned around and aimed the gun at her firing every shot he had left in his gun, ceasing her screams, her body folded up like a lawn chair, from there he wasted no time, as he made his way to the passenger side of the vehicle, he opening the door and pulled E-b's lifeless body from out of the car, then he immediately ran to the other side, stepped over Candy body, got I the car and drove away still in pursuit to find Jyel, As he pulled down each street, he seen that Jyel was nowhere to be found, he didn't want to give up, so he spent the block a couple more times, in hopes he can find him laying somewhere along the way, he hoped in his heart he had died from all the shots, he took, the thought alone, put one of the brightest smiles on his face, from a distance, he could hear the police sirens, making its way in his direction, he decided to leave before they arrived, he hit the expressway and disappeared from the area without farther notice.

Jyel:

After running as fast as he could, to get away from Low, he continued to look back once or twice to make sure that Low wasn't behind him, seeing that he were scot free, he ducked into an ally just in time to see Low's car slowly roll past in search of him, Jyel's eyes locked onto him, he wanted to get up and start running again, but his breath began to shorten and the weight in his steps began to be too much for him to handle, it was as if, out of nowhere he had gained a thousand pounds, before he knew it, he fell against the wall trying his best to catch his breath, his heart pounded, at what it felt like to be a hundred miles per hour, as he held his wounds, trying his best to stop himself from bleeding the best that he can, it was at that moment, he watched the blood pour out of him, he began to worry if he would make it through this situation, his eyes slowly began to fade in and out, he could feel himself slipping in and out of consciousness, he fought hard to stay awake, an image, came from out of nowhere, standing over him, mumbling something, he couldn't quite make it out, so he tried shaking his head to get his eyes back in focus, one more time, to get a clearer picture, he seen that the person who was standing over him, was indeed the old man he saved from being robbed a couple weeks ago.

I got you kid, just stay with me, stay strong kid, I am not going to let you die, come on now, I got you, just stay with me!

Jyel was no longer able to speak, the pain was too much for him to bear, he passed out.

Ace & Meme:

As Ace and Meme ate dinner, they laughed at each other jokes, and each gave up just a little information about each other's past, but not enough to lower their guards, they had in place not just for each other but for the world. Neither one of them has ever been comfortable sharing anything that had to do with feeling or something from their past, but as the conversation went on they began to loosen things up just a little bit, as Meme watched him, she began to fall deeply into her thoughts about Ace, to her, he became hard to figure out, usually everything with guys was just right in the open, you knew what they wanted as soon as they opened their mouth, but not with Ace, he was so different from the rest, he made her for the first time in her life, feel like a queen, he showed her no matter who was watching that she was the most important person in the room, he kept good eye contact, there was a strong sense of understanding in his words, he was a real gentlemen, it showed in his actions and even though he tried his best to hide it, she can still tell that he was very over protective with something he badly wants or loves, but at the same time, he is very distance when it comes to business, whenever he would get a phone call, he would answer it and walk away as fast as he could, she hated the secretive type, all types of thoughts would play around in her mind, she would read his whole body language, every time he would do it, just earlier, when she walked into the room, he looked real suspicious, those types of situations only made her question deep down in her heart, if she could really trust him or not.

The feelings she was feeling was truly hard for her to sort out, all she knew, was the longer she stayed around him, the more it became a good outweighing the bad situation, and that her heart was the one leading the race, it was clear, that she was surely falling in love with him by the minute, but before she could fully commit to her feelings for him, she had something she needed to get off her chest, she still suspicious on why he would have her grandmother picture in his phone, not wanting to beat around the brush any more, she leaned in and kissed him in mid conversation, as a way to grab his full attention, as she pulled back.

Well ok, he said as he tried his best to straighten himself up from the passionate kiss she just laid on his lips. I thought the good night kisses usually came last, at the end of the night!

Yeah, they do, but I couldn't help myself, your lips, just kept calling me, Meme said as she smiled at him in a sexy and flirtatious way.

It's something I do want to talk to you about, that's been kind of bothering me a little bit all night, and I wanted to make sure I had your undivided attention!

Of course you do baby, what's wrong? Ace said as his eyes followed hers.

Before she could even speak, her attention was pulled towards the TV that hovered over the bar, Breaking News flashed big across the screen, shooting at Sneaky Peaks, leaves two dead, they both glanced at each other then they both ran to the TV over the bar, as they rushed to the bartender, they told him to turn the volume up on the TV so they could hear it better.

News Reporter:

There was a double murder in the parking lot of Sneaky peaks, witnesses say they heard an argument between two men inside of a car, then shortly after, shots were fired and two people ended up fatally shot in the process, there is no information on have the two women were connected to the situation, but officers are still trying their best to put all the pieces to the puzzle together.

News Reporter 2:

Sharon is there anything that you can tell us about the victims?

News Reporter:

Well Bill, since the officers been on the scene we have been able to identify one of the victims as 32-year-old Ebony Ford and the other victim as 28-year-old Candice Jackson, police are still looking for the suspect of the car that the two men that were arguing in before this incident took place.

New Reporter 2:

Sharon do you know if anyone else might have gotten hurt?

News Reporter:

The police are scanning the area to see if they could find any clues or anything that would help to solve this case, but as of right now, they have been no other reports of other people injured at this time.

News Reporter 2:

Thank you Sharon, now if you have any information on what happen tonight, please call crime stoppers at 513 352-4052.

The bartender changed the channel,

O my God, this is breaking news on every channel, the bartender said as he tried his best to turn the channel onto something different.

Wait, wait, wait, Meme said, as she signaled for the bartender to stop changing channels, turn that back to channel 9 I want to hear what that girl was saying.

The bartender did exactly what he was told,

A witness stood outside from Sneaky Peaks describing to the reporter what she encountered in real time, a deep sadness filled her eyes, nonstop she wiped tears away from her now puffy eyes as she tried hard to speak,

Witness:

O my God, what happened to them people is horrible!

News Reporter:

Ma'am where were you, when the gun fire erupted?

Witness:

I was headed inside the club, and the shots grabbed my attention immediately, my first thought was to duck and get out of there, so I ducked behind a dumper and as I looked around to see where the shots could be coming from,

She instantly began to start shaking, you can see in her eyes in each word she spoke she was reliving the event, in her mind,

That's when I saw some guy jump out his car, like he was getting ready to run after somebody and the woman stepped in front of him, and, and,

News Reporter:

Its ok, you don't have to say no more if you don't want too!

Witness:

The man just shot the woman down, like she wasn't nothing, then he went to the other side of the vehicle and pulled the other woman out of the passenger seat, then he jumped in the car and just drove off and left them there, like they were nothing, I tried to help them, but it was too late, o my God, it was just so much blood,

As the reporter looked the woman in the face, he could tell she was going into shock, so he tried to change the subject, making sure he didn't lose her in the process.

News Reporter:

That is truly horrible, did you end up getting a good look at his face?

Witness:

No I was too far away to get a good look at his face, O my God, this is just horrible, she said as she broke down and started crying uncontrollably.

As Meme looked at Ace, she caught him staring out into

space, with a strong look of worry, painted deeply across his face.

Hey baby, what's wrong? She said in a soft tone, as she leaned in closer to him, placing a hand on his lap, to show her concern, his face looked as if he was fighting back his emotions, so before they could break free altogether, he turned his head, as a few tears rowed down his face.

I knew one of the girls, who got killed tonight, she was a really good friend of mine.

By the way you acting, I got the feeling that she was so much more than a friend!

Yeah I admit, I loved her, look I'm sorry but I don't think I could go out tonight.

Hold on, wait, I could of swore I heard you tell your friend over the phone, that we were going to meet him at Sneaky Peaks!

Yeah we were supposed to meet them there, but he didn't call me, and tell me he made it there yet, so I doubt they even made it.

Well, could you call him and see if my brother is with him, if he ok, something!

Ace assured her that he would call his friend, he just needed to go to the restroom first to relieve himself, but in reality, he knew that if she knew that the girl who got killed tonight was with the guy he sent to pick up her brother, she would panic and for the moment, he just needed a minute to figure out his next move, and in the process, he needed her calm to do it, while he was in the bathroom, he decided to call him to see ifhe would answer, and if he did answer, what is it that he would say? It only took the phone a couple of rings on his end before he answered, in a cool and calm tone,

Yo, what's up Ace, where you at?

We just now leaving the restaurant, we were about to start heading your way right now.

Cool, cool, I'm waiting on you brother, but I think we should change up the location for tonight,

Ace pulled the phone from his ear in disbelief, how cool and calm, Low's demeanor is, he acted as if nothing never happened, without being obvious, he tried to pry a little farther.

Why? What's good? Is something wrong?

Naw, everything is good, I just drove by there a little while ago and it just looked a little dead out there, we would be wasting our time, going there!

That's crazy! That place is always pretty packed on a Saturday!

Yeah, that surprised me too, but hey we can't cry over spoiled milk, so I figured we meet up at that new spot by the river, I think it's called, Club blue flame!

I know where you talking about, that's the new spot they just opened up, it's the one under the bridge in that big warehouse by the river front.

Yeah, that's it, so you gone meet us there?

Yeah, just give me a minute, I'll be there,

Ok, hurry up, don't have me waiting too long, we trying to get this party started, and it would be rude to start without you and the birthday girl, brother we gone turn up tonight, we gone throw her a birthday party she ain't gone never forget, and then just like that, Low hung up the phone.

As Ace came out of the bathroom, he saw Meme, nothing short of losing her cool in the corner by the door.

Ace damn what took you so long to come out of the bathroom, taking a shit don't even take that long, I was beginning to believe you made your escape out the bathroom window or something!

Girl quit playing!

Did you call your friend to check and see if everything cool with my brother, I keep calling his phone and it just keeps going to voicemail, and I'm really starting to get worried, that's just not like him to just cut off his phone!

Calm down, I just got off the phone with them and everything is fine, he just had a couple of drinks, I asked him was he ok and he said yeah, him and my friend are having the time of his life right now, but he also told me to tell you he love you and his phone is dead, he will see you when we meet up tonight, but I told my friend, he was going to have to either take him home or drop him off at my house, it just depends on what you want me to do,

Ace what do you mean, that he had a couple of drinks, is your friend crazy, he is only sixteen, plus he doesn't need to be drinking.

Meme relax, he is in good hands, we are going to meet up with them in a little bit, just let the boy have some flin for once in his life, let's just pay our bill and get out of here!

She acted as if everything was cool, but deep down in her heart, she had a feeling that something was ten•ibly wrong, so as Ace went to pay the bill, she continued to try to get in touch with her brother, fry after try and was still unable to get an answer, at the moment, she knew by him being with a stranger, he would never just cut his phone off like that, knowing that she would be trying to reach him, once they were back inside the car, Ace attention became strongly thrown off, and he instantly fell ill all of a sudden. He talked about how bad the food from the restaurant made his stomach hurt, he apologized over and over again for ruining the night and offered to take her home, if that would be something that she would like, she declined his offer of going home, a part of her didn't want to go home right away and she definitely didn't entertain the thought of leaving without her brother, but she also couldn't help to feel curious about his actions, so once she got back to his house, she laid down a couple of excuses of her own, not even letting the car cut off, she comforted him on his way out of the car.

Ace I want you to go in the house and lay down and rest until I get back,

Where are you going baby? I know you're not going home I could of took you home you didn't even have to drive all the way out here!

I have to go check in with my granny, I have been gone for a few days now and she isn't answering her phone, I need to see if she is alright, but I promise to come right back afterwards, and take good care of you, I'll be you're in home private nurse, ok baby!

Ace said ok and before he got out of the car, he handed her

a spare key, leaned in and gave her a kiss, then made his exit out of car, before she pulled off, she checked her phone, one more time to see if she might had missed her brother call, there were still no call, but she noticed she had a text message from him that she had not noticed before, she pressed the button to open it, it read:

Sis I wish you would hurry up and meet me, this guy is giving me some weird vibes, I don't know what it is about him or how to explain it, I keep trying to stall him out, but he just keeps pushing for me to go in the club, this dude might have something up his sleeve, if something happens to happen to me, just know that I love you and it's something you really need to see, I left a journal under your bed, since you been gone, sis it's been a whole lot going on, the journal I found it outside the house but I think our brother Aiden left it intending for Grandma to find it, luckily I did instead, Myona it's some very deep and dark things, wrote in there, things about mom and dad, things that you would not believe, sis please hurry, damn he is coming, I got to go! After reading her brothers text message, she couldn't believe what she just read, her heart began to beat extremely fast, her palms became very sweaty and her mind was racing at a hundred miles per hour, as she drove home, all she could think about was what was in that journal her brother had told her about, once she pulled up to the front of the house, she could barely focus on parking the car, so she just pulled in the best she could, jumped out of the car and ran into the house, as soon as the door flew open, to her surprise, London were there laying on the living room couch watching TV, she jumped up to her feet as soon as she seen Myona enter into the house.

O my God Myona, where have you been, you had me wreaking my brain wondering if something happened to you.

London ran in for a hug, and when she did, her embrace felt off, nothing about her words felt genuine to her, it was at that moment, Frank's dying words played right in the back of her mind.

(London told me to do it)

Instead of wearing her emotions on her sleeve, she decided to keep her composure and let everything play out, her grandmother, always told her, what's done in the dark, will always come to the light. So if what Frank said was true, in time it will show.

London, what are you doing here and why do you have all those bruises on your face?

Myona it's a long story, a lot has happened in these last couple of days and I will tell you about it, but it's so much more important things I have to tell you about right now.

In mid conversation, Myona started to get more and more impatient, she didn't want to get any more distracted then she had become as soon as she walked in the door, so before London could get into any farther details, she dismissed the conversation altogether.

London, that's cool, you could tell me, whatever you need to tell me, but it's gone have to wait, I had a long weekend and I just want to take me a shower, and relax and regroup for a second.

London took a step back, and said ok, as she stepped to the side and let her pass.

Myona quickly moved pass her and headed up the stairs, straight to her bedroom, in search for the journal her brother said he left under the pillow, once she located it, she went into the bathroom and started her bath water, closed the door, and sat on the toilet, glancing through the pages, until she could no longer read any more, it had begun to become too much for her to bear, she could not stop the tears from pouring from her eyes. For a long time, she fantasized, what it would be like the day she would actually get the chance to meet her big brother, how happy she would be for them to all reunite and finally get to know each other, with the circumstances of their parent's death, they had so much in common, it was hard growing up without a mom or dad, now the truth is out, and it cut deep to her soul, all she could think about, is how could he do this to them, yeah, he lost his mom but he had no right to take hers. Yeah, from the way it was wrote, her dad made a mistake, giving his mother those drugs, but it still gives him no reason to play God, the more her thoughts replayed, the angrier she got, so angry she began to tear and kick and punch into the walls, trying to release herself from the pain she was feeling, the noise alerted London and her grandmother Vickie downstairs, they ran to her as fast as they could to see what was wrong.

Myona! What's going on in there? Are you alright?

Once they got no answer, they both beat at the bathroom door, anxiously, almost to the point of knocking the door down.

Not much time had passed before Myona finally responded,

I'm ok!

What was that noise up here, open the door!

I fell! but I'm alright, I'll be out in a minute,

Ok, baby when you come out, it's something we need to talk

to you about, so as soon as you get finished in there, come downstairs baby.

Once Myona promised she would come downstairs, they left the door, still overwhelmed with emotion, she decided to jump into the bath tub, to try to relax for a minute, to get her head back in the right place, but it would not be an easy task with all the information she just uncovered. With any little energy she had left, a part of her just wanted to crawl in her bed into a ball and cry, as she sat in the tub, she read what her brother had did to her mother, at least a hundred times, it sent chills up her spine, each and every time, he wrote in detail how it felt to be inside her, that each spoke moved him closer to being in the presents of God, each word was as if it had jumped off the paper and played a life of its own, in her mind, giving her a clear vision into her mother's pain, as hate began to fill every inch of her heart, she still tried her best to leave some kind of room for understanding, as she got up from the tub, frying her best to pull herself together, in a slow pace, she dried off and lotion up, once she were completely done, she opened the door to the bathroom, only to see London standing on the other side of the door. There was a chance she would no longer be able to hold back anything she was feeling at the moment.

London! Why are you standing by the door, I told you I would talk to you when I was ready, damn! Can I have some space please!

Myona, I know you going through some things, but we are friends and have always been able to talk about any and everything, I could tell something is really bothering you, can you just tell me what's wrong!

Are we? Myona said as she took two steps closer to London,

to close in the space between them, her eyes cut deep into her soul

Are we what? London said, as she took one step back, sensing trouble was approaching,

Are we really friends?

Yes, we are really friends, why would you say something like that?

Did you tell Frank to rape me? Myona checked her body Language to see if she would show signs of her telling a lie, she always knew when she was lying, before London answered the question, she dropped her head.

What! No! who told you that? London said, but not able to keep eye contact the whole time,

It was Frank's last words before he died, (London told me to do it!) is exactly what he said, can you believe that?

I didn't tell him to do that, Frank! so hold on, you had something to do with Franks Murder?

That motherfucker raped me! so yea, he had to go!

Is that why, you haven't been home, this whole time? Where have you been?

It doesn't matter where I been,

Myona sifted the conversation, changing the subject on the spot,

But what's up, what's so important that you and Grandma got to talk to me about? that would have y'all stalking the bathroom door

The way she sifted the conversation so fast, it kind of scared her to what Myona just might do next, she had never witnessed indifference in Myona's actions like this before, not knowing what to do next, she shut down, didn't say another word, she just turned and began to walk out of the room.

So what! Now you don't have nothing to say! I guess it wasn't that damn important huh! Bitch just go ahead and get the fuck out of here!

Irritated by her words, London spent right back around on her hills.

You ain't the only one, shit has happened too, in the last few days, I got rape too!

A rage shot through Myona, causing her blood to boil,

Damn you want to be me like me so bad, you would even chase the spot light in a tragic situation, you more pathetic than I thought you were.

Bitch if I wasn't pregnant, I would break your fucking face,

Bitch fuck that baby, try your luck!

Hey! Hey! Hey! What the hell is going on in here?

Grandma why do you got this no good bitch in our house?

Why are you calling her that? I thought this girl was your friend!

This bitch isn't my friend, this bitch ain't nothing but a snake!

Calm down Myona! are you guys fighting because London is having your brothers baby?

What! She having my brothers baby, damn, besides you

running around sucking and fucking the whole city, you had to lay up and give Jyel that nasty ass pussy too, I'm disappointed in him, I thought he would of knew better than that!

Myona calm down now, you are going too far, Grandma Vickie said as she stepped between them before they could start throwing any blows at each other.

No it's ok, Ms. Vickie, I get the point I'll leave, I don't stay no place that I am not wanted, but before I go, I'm gone clear the air, no I did not have somebody rape you, regardless of what you think, and no I did not fuck your little brother Jyel, I'm pregnant by your brother Aiden.

As soon as Myona heard his name, it was like someone had punched her in the stomach and knocked all the wind out of her, she instantly grabbed at her chest, the room had lost all its air and began to spin, she tried her best to find a place to sit down, it was clear to her at that moment, she was having a panic attack. Grandma Vickie rushed to her side, to catch her from falling.

Sit down baby, breathe, come on now, just breathe baby!

O my God, what's wrong with her, should I call the ambulance?

No! baby, just go get me a rag and some ice, she will be ok, she is just having a panic attack, she hasn't had one in a while, she used to have them almost every night after her mother died,

She ran to do exactly as she was told, when she came back, Myona was laying down still trying her best to catch her breath,

Are you sure she will be ok?

Yes, she is going to be just fine,

Once Myona was able to get her breathing back under control, she drew attention back to what

London last said,

London where did you see my brother Aiden, when, how, nobody has even seen him or heard from him in years, how do you even know what he looks like? Hell, I don't even know what he looks like!

It's really a long story,

That I'm willing to listen to, so spit it out!

Ok, when I was in your room, I saw a picture with you and Jyel with your dad and it got my attention because when I was over Ace's house, I am not going to lie, I was a little nosey, looking around and he had a picture with him and the same guy, in the same place, on his mantle over the fire place.

But how do you know it's actually my brother, my father knew a lot of people before he died, it could just be some old friend of his,

On the back of the picture it was signed, daddy love you always have and always will, just like yours, I doubt he tell everybody the same thing!

Myona paced the room, as everything London was telling her were setting in, then out of nowhere she stopped in her tracks, hold on, wait a minute, what was the name you just called

Aiden?

When I met him, he didn't go by the name Aiden, he called himself Ace,

As soon as Myona heard Ace's name, it felt like her heart had fell into her stomach, she did all she could, not to throw up, she asked London to describe him and describe him is exactly what she did, all her details were laid in the right place, she had been with her brother the whole time,

As London continued to talk, Myona got dressed,

London seen what she was doing and tried her best to slow her down, so she could figure out why she was moving so fast, but Myona were not willing to share any of her details, the more

London talked, the faster she would move.

Myona talk to me, where are you going?

London didn't you say you had somewhere to be?

Myona, do you know who Ace is? Have you seen him?

Now why in the hell would you think that? Didn't I just tell you I didn't even know what he looks like!

London, followed her every move not backing down,

Because as soon as I said his name, I could see it in your eyes, you know something, they lite up, it was like a bright light went off in your head, you just flat out started acting weird, just tell me what's going on, have you met him and didn't know it was him?

London can you do me a favor and just stay out of my way? damn just give me some space!

After she got fully dressed, she grabbed her car keys and

headed for the door, London tried one last attempt to try to stop her from leaving but Grandma Vickie blocked her path.

London just let her go! Let her cool off, she just upset right now, Grandma Vickie said as she first embraced London in a hug, then she turned and walked out of the room behind Myona, once Myona got to the bottom of the stairs, she turned to face her grandmother as she came behind her down the stairs.

Grandma, you don't have to follow me, honestly I'm ok!

I know you are and even though I have seen that look in your fathers' eyes before, I'm not going to try to stop you, you are grown, it's time for you to make your own decisions in life, whether they are good or bad, I just need you to know, that I'm here for you, if you ever need me for anything, I just need you to promise me, you won't go off again without at least letting me know that you are ok.

Myona promised, then embraced her grandmother in a tight hug, almost draining all the air out of her body,

Baby, now you starting to worry me, you hugging me, like I'm not going to ever see you again!

No Grandma, it isn't anything like that, I just love you so much, I'm not going anywhere, and I want you to know, if I never told you, I appreciate everything that you have done for me and Jyel, we wouldn't have made it without you.

O no baby, yes you would have made it, you are a Wright, if you look up our name in the dictionary, right next to our name, it would say, strong, the break down would be, solid as a rock!

Myona laughed, then embraced her in a hug one more time before she turned and walked out of the door.

London:

In the meantime, once Myona had left the room, London rushed into the bathroom to investigate, why it had taken Myona so long to come out, once she went in to look around, nothing right away seemed to be out of place, until she picked up a used bath towel, laying on the bathroom toilet, a notebook fell on the floor, still open to the bookmark that was put in place, once she picked it up, she could tell that it was some kind of journal. One that could not have been

Myona's because she had never seen it before. What caught her attention the most, were the title that were wrote in bold print at the top of the page.

How it feels to make sweet love to revenge, the author of the writing, Aiden Wright, after scanning through a few pages, it was clear why she got the reaction she did from Myona, through the pages, it spoke of pain, she knew at that moment she was in love with a monster, Myona brother would be the last person, Myona would welcome home with open arms, let alone her best friend having a baby with him as well. Before her thoughts could build any farther, she ran downstairs to see if she could catch Myona before she left, as she ran to the top of the stairs, she seen Ms. Vickie standing inside the door way, waving Myona goodbye,

Ms. Vickie, Ms. Vickie, don't let Myona leave,

Grandma Vickie turned in her direction,

Baby it's going to be okay, she just need to get some air, she will be back, she just need to calm down for a while,

London ran down the stairs, ignoring her words, as she ran pass her, and looked out the door to see if she could catch her, herself, but it was too late, she was gone, nowhere in sight as far as the eyes could see.

No! Ms. Vickie, can you call her, act like you need her to come back to the house for something important, I know she won't answer for me if I call,

London just tell me what's wrong! And what is that book you got in your hand?

I think she knows who Aiden is and might be going to find him!

Okay! That's a good thing, right? there brothers and sisters, what's so wrong about them finding each other and catching up?

London handed Ms. Vickie the journal, leading her through page after page to unbelieve truths of their family's secrets, showing her why she felt the way that she did and once Grandma Vickie took everything in, she couldn't believe her eyes, then instantly a deep sadness fell into her heart, she became not only lost for words, but placed into a blank thought on what It is, that she should do next. As Ms. Vickie continued to read, London paced the floor back and forth, calling

Myona's phone in hopes that she would answer, but only getting the voicemail in the process, it was more than obvious that her worry had turned to an uncontrollable panic. Her voice cried out in distress,

Ms. Vickie o my God, what if she kills him or something, what do we do?

Grandma Vickie moved past her on her way to sit down on her living room sofa, she moved in a real calm manner, her look was almost as if she were unbothered by the situation altogether.

Baby, all we could do is wait, we got to put this in God's hands, he is in control, at this point, there is nothing we could do, but hope and pray, that none of this turns out for the worse.

And just like that, Grandma Vickie turned her direction back to the pages, shaking her head as she continued to embrace everything from beginning to the end, so many regrets made a way in her mind about all the things she wished she could do differently to change this situation, but quickly realized, that she can't stop any and everything from happening, her thoughts caused her to mumble her feelings out loud,

Lord please help her to forgive this boy Lord, yes lord, it's in your hands now, let your will be done lord, lord let your will be done!

Low:

As Low waited for Ace and the girl to pull up to the place they were supposed to be meeting, he began to get more and more impatient, he called Ace's phone a couple of times, but the phone just continued to go to voicemail, after a while, his intuition began to weigh on him heavy, so he went on and checked his local news feed using the internet from his phone to see if he could find any information about the shooting at Sneaky Peaks earlier tonight, it didn't take long before he not only seen a lot of information about the shooting but also people giving brief descriptions of him as well, with a full identification of his car and license plate, it would be only a matter of time before they would find out his address and come and start asking questions, so without hesitation, he got into his car and drove away, as he headed home, more than a few thoughts, forced its way into his mind, one being Ace, he wondered if that were the reason he didn't answer the phone, was the call he made to his phone a test the whole time to see if he would speak up about the shooting, altogether, if so, he knew there would be a war, which he had no problem with, but the problem was, not only was the guy a moving target and he wouldn't even know where to start to get the guy, not to mention, he had more problems than one, Blue Chip would also be on his tail as well, and deep down he didn't know if he could cover all angles, his pride pushed him to fight, his heart told him to leave, and his mind were frozen solid, because of the open flood gates of emotion that flowed uncontrollably inside of him, he was unable to move forward, because of his pain, which was in a constant replay in his mind, he wondered, what lengths he would have to take to be set free. After a long drive to his house, he pulled into his back driveway to hide the car as best as he could from the main street, he rushed into the house, went straight into his safe and grabbed all the money he had stashed for a rainy day, he wanted to stay and badly fight but reality set in and he realized there were nothing to stick around and fight for. His mom passed away a long time ago, his cousin and his Aunt J, was all he had left, and now they are gone as well, he went outside and stashed his clothes, money, and the couple of brinks of heroin he had left from Ace into the backseat of his other car, then he went back into the house to find a couple of things that he could use that would help him destroy the evidence in the car he had to get rid of before the police got a hold of it, and build a for sure case that would place him up under the jail, as he opened the car, he could smell the blood and gun powder in the air, once he sat down in the car, a strong rush of emotions came over him causing a delay in his speed to pull away from the house, he reflected on just how much the streets had placed a toll on his life, he had lost so much over the years, and put every inch of his life on the line, to become successful, not as a productive business man in the community, but as a simple street thug turned to a drug kingpin, a chasing after the wind, just for a couple of bucks, it didn't take long for him to realize, that the worth he placed on money, didn't really hold as much weight that he thought it would, yeah over the years, he gained everything he could ever want and need but the down side of things, is he has nobody to share it with, everything in his life came with a price, nothing was free, the cost of his friends and family lives, an even the life of the one and only woman he loved besides his mom and aunt J, as he looked over at the passenger seat, a deep regret brought him to tears, he ran his fingers through the blood that were splashed all over the window and that's when he realized that what he did was irreversible, there was no way she was ever coming back, he buried his head into the steering wheel, and that's when he heard a loud click from a gun, he quickly raised his head and looked behind him, only to be staring directly down the barrel of a nickel plated 45, all chrome with an extended clip, Boone stood behind the aim,

Damn Boone, your kind of rude motherfucker, sitting behind me this whole time without even bothering to speak, I thought we had more respect for each other than to intrude on another's man 's personal moments,

Low turned his head back around and stared back at Boone through his rearview mirror, and with no shame, began to start wiping the almost dried up tears from his face, as he continued.

Catching a brother in one of his most private moments, I don't care what nobody told you, but I was told, when you're a man, a man is not supposed to see you cry, especially in front of another man!

You know what Low,

What Boone?

I'm more disappointed in you than anything!

Why? Because I didn't run to meet Blue Chip when y'all wanted me too, or because I am not going to bow down and kiss his ass like the rest of you, motherfucker's do, Fuck Blue Chip! My cousin Juice dead, my Aunt J just died, and I killed the one and only bitch I have ever loved, being loyal to the same game that hasn't ever been loyal to me, everything I love is gone because of me, bruh do you think I'm worried about Blue Chip!

Once he was finish talking, Boone shook his head, then mugged Low in the back of the head with the barrel of the gun.

You forgot to add Baby Yee to your unlucky list of death, the crazy thing about it, is I bet not one of them tears you were shedding was for Baby Yee, and I bet you thought I wasn't gone find out, did you!

Boone you can't believe everything that you hear, the streets always put a hundred on ten! Don't be the type who live for the extras, find out the facts!

Come on now Low, you know I know better than to listen to anybody throwing around information to get a response out of anybody ready to jump on it, I did my research, at first, I was trying to get in contact with you for Blue Chip but once I seen it in your face that you were hiding something, I had to go out and seek the truth, and once I found it, it made this visit just a little more personal for me than usual.

And what's the truth?

That you sent Baby Yee on that mission to kill your boy Ace, but somehow he ended up dead in the process, then you and Ace become partners and I know that's true because that's been the word all around town, everybody knows since you hooked up with him, you been selling the drugs for the low, he is dead and gone, and you didn't bother to even come to his funeral, just to get a little richer, you really a fucked up individual!

What makes you think I was the one to send Baby Yee on a mission to do anything?

Are you serious Low? I told you I did my research; you think I'm stupid? I saw the text messages between you and Baby Yee and not to mention the video tape from inside the bar that night, First your boy Ace, went to the bathroom, then Baby Yee slides in right behind him, then out of nowhere, you coming running in like superman to save the day, but for the wrong person of course, a couple minutes later, you and Ace come walking out of the bathroom like nothing never happened, it's kind of fucked up, you would cross someone that were so close to us, someone you said that you love, just for a financial gain!

Low didn't know what to say, he just leaned back in his seat and closed his eyes.

So what now Low? You don't have nothing to say?

What is it to say Boone? It seems like you got it all put together, your minds all made up on what you want to do, what you want to hear, you right, well you right Boone! I fucked up and no matter what, I got to take whatever that comes with it, in this world or the next!

My question is why did you do it? Why call him over to kill somebody for you and then he ended up being killed in the process, was Baby Yee the target all along? Did Ace want him dead and you took the hit for him?

No he wasn't the target! I truly loved Baby Yee, I just got a little too greedy, I tried to call Baby Yee off before he got in there but I guess I was too late, and I couldn't let him take out my one and only ticket out of this hell hole I been laying in all these years,

SO!

So what motherfucker!

So he became part of the game, I wish I could take it all back, but I can't so fuck it, I made my choice and now you got to make yours, and if you looking for me to beg for my life, it isn't going to happen, I would rather die like a man on my feet, than a bitch on my knees, so go right on ahead and pop that bitch, change my physical to spirit, I'm tired of living anyway.

Boone opened the door and stepped outside of the car and disappeared into the woods without saying another word to Low, as Low opened his eyes after a few moments of silence, he looked around only to see that he didn't see Boone nowhere in sight, he took in a deep breath feeling as if he had cheated death one more time, and the crazy part is he didn't know how, he leaned back in his seat again to try his best to collect his thoughts from what just took place, heart still in a little bit of a panic, he closed his eyes again in hopes he could calm down, take in deep breaths from the nights wind, deep in his heart, he knew he was done with the streets, E-b was the first woman to make him even consider the thought of slowing down and starting a family and even though she is now gone, he still wanted to try with the one chance he may have left, he realized that life is to short and he damn sole was going to give it a try, then suddenly he heard a noise, he quickly opened his eyes, only to see Boone standing over him by the driver side door, before Low could even speak a word, Boone swung a hammer at Low's head with all the power and force he had in his body, the impact was so strong, it knocked Low's eye back into his skull, as Low grabbed for his eye, screaming from the unbearable pain he were experiencing, Boone continued to deliver blow after blow until the screams from Low stopped altogether, then he grabbed the gasoline can Low had just minutes earlier placed in the passenger seat, and without hesitation, he began to throw it all over him, inside and outside the car, then he lit a match and threw in inside the car, took a couple steps back and watched him bum, as the flames built up all around him, Low began to gain consciousness, within seconds his entire body was consumed by the flames, he was being burned alive. The smell of Low's human flesh in a sick way gave him a sense of peace. Boone smiled and laughed as Low begged for help,

No motherfucker, can't nobody help you now, it's just me and you, I got a front row seat to the Low can burn in hell show, and it's gone be our little secret and unlike you, won't nobody find out, burn motherfucker, Lol, you deserve to bum for what you did to Baby Yee!

The hatred he carried in his eyes was enough to kill a million men, once the car became invisible from the flames, there were no chance of Low recovering, he knew his job was done.

Ace & Meme:

As Meme pulled into Ace's driveway, she tried her best to keep all her feeling in check, as she walked into the house, she yelled out his name to let him know that she had finally made it back, the sound of her voice made Ace come running down the stairs to greed her with one of the biggest and brightest smiles she had ever seen him smile before,

Hi baby, you look like you really happy to see me,

I am, but I were beginning to think that you weren't coming back tonight, you been gone for a long time, was everything ok at home?

I told you I had to go home and check on the family, I couldn't just run in and back out, I had to chill with them for a minute, let them know I'm ok, I just didn't think I was going to be gone for this long, but if it helps, I did miss you, she said as she stepped in and gave him a kiss right square on the lips and embraced him with a very tight hug.

Her aggressiveness caused him to stutter a little bit with his words,

I, I, I missed you too!

Good, even though I know it's kind of late, I was hoping we could sit down and talk a little bit,

Talk about what?

Not much, just a little bit about our backgrounds, nothing to deep right away, so you don't have to worry, she said as she grabbed his hand and lead him into the living room and sat with him on the couch, he gave her his full attention.

Nothing to deep huh, well, ok what is it that you want to know?

Well for starters, is your real name Ace?

He laughed at her question, before he gave her an answer.

No! my real name is not Ace, it's Aiden,

What's your last name?

Damn woman! You acting like you the police now! Do you want my birthday and social security number too?

Ace! Quit playing, how could I ever take you home to meet my family, if I don't even know your real name, that would only make me look stupid, and I'm far from stupid, my family raised me way better than that!

O this must really be getting serious, if you thinking about taking me home to meet your family, you must really like me huh?

She leaned in closer and gave him another kiss, I do like you, the question is, do you like me?

Yes, I do, a whole lot, more than words could even describe.

Then knowing each other's names is the first step.

Ace leaned back in his chair as he pondered what he should do, every since he been back in town he has never disclosed his name to anybody, but he wanted to start their relationship off on a good page so he let out a sigh, then told her his name,

My last name is Holtmann, I'm Aiden Holtmann!

As soon as she heard his name, she paused in thought, damn, that's why they weren't able to find him over the years when they searched for him because he was using his mother's maiden name this whole time, the pause threw Ace offa little bit as well, he could tell the wheels in her mind were turning as he looked at her and he wanted to know why.

Damn did I say something wrong? Your eyes lit up as soon as I told you my name, you heard that name from somewhere before or something?

She started laughing to try her best to soften the mood,

What's so funny?

I just wouldn't think you would have a name like Aiden Holtmann, with a name like that, nobody wouldn't even know, you had any black in your blood let alone your body! With a name like that, it's white family written all over it.

O so it's like that huh, my grandmother on my mother side named me Aiden, but I see, I get it!

What!

You racist!

No I am not!

They both laughed and talked a little more about how they grew up, some of the things they been through as kids, some of the places they lived at growing up, once she acknowledged that Ace were getting choked up on his words, she quickly changed the subject altogether.

Ace you are such a gentleman, you have a beautiful woman that's been sitting around you this whole time and you never not once made one pass at me, I'm not use to that type of behavior when it comes to a guy, I usually have to beat the guys off of me with a stick because they can't control themselves when I'm around.

Well, I'm not going to lie, usually, I am one of those types of guys, I'm not always this well manner when it comes to the ladies but everything is just so different with you, it's hard to explain it.

Well, at least try!

I mean, everything about you is just screaming out you are special, you are so much more than a quick night of passion, your image exposes a queen and I just want to treat you like the queen that you are.

Their eyes locked into a deep gaze, as they both let the words shared between them resonate, Meme leaned in and kissed Ace on the lips passionately, then out of nowhere she stopped and stood up.

Ace tonight, I want to play everything by my rules.

By your rules, we playing some kind of game, what do you mean? Ace said as he stared back at her, with confusion in his eyes.

Well, you said you wanted to treat me like the queen that I am, now is your chance.

Good then I want you to be my personal servant for the night, all night long.

He got in character as he spoke in a foreign tone as if they were in an imaginary castle.

Whatever you wish is my command, my queen!

I want you to come right here in front of me and get on your knees.

Once he did as he were told, she slowly undressed in front of him, pleasing his eyes with an amateur strip tease, then she placed both of her hands on the back of his head, threw one leg over his shoulder and began to straddle his face.

Open your mouth, eat this pussy, tell me how good I taste! She said as she moved her hips in a continuous motion.

As he licked and sucked her clique like it was a way to survive in the jungle, she guided his head to all her sweet spots, the tension became so strong her juices began to explode all over his face and down his neck and chest, he tried his best to back up just for a second just so he could have some room to breathe, the excitement began to become a little too much for him to bear, he jumped outside of his instruction, when he stood up and quickly began to snatch his clothes off of him, exposing himself to her in the nude.

She mudded him in the face and stepped back,

What are you doing? I didn't tell you to take your clothes!

He stopped what he was doing with a facial expression of confusion painted all over his face, his manhood stood strong and at attention, ready to jump into action, but yet he was still at a complete lost for words. He just stood there as she chastised him with her words.

It's my birthday, tonight it's all about me, you do as I say, you understand me!

He nodded in agreement as she grabbed him by the hand and lead him into the bedroom once inside, they began to slowly start kissing and caressing each other all over, the heat in the room, turned up really fast between them, she pushed him down on the bed and climbed on top of him, arch in her back, gripping the head board, as she eased her way down, he spreaded her cheeks and entered inside her, once in motion she cocked her hand back as far as it could go and she slapped him hard across his face. He was thrown off guard and didn't know what he should do next.

Fuck me, and I want you to choke me, pull my hair, no shy shit, I like it rough!

As he proceeded to follow direction, he reached up and grabbed her by the throat, she moaned and began to grind her hips as hard as she could, yelling at him to fuck her harder, no matter how hard he tried to push, it was never enough for her, once it seemed like he wasn't following her commands in any way, she would cock her hand back again and deliver an even harder blow then the last.

I told you to fuck me harder!

Before she could swing at him again, he rolled her over on her back so he could get some leverage and be the one in control, he grabbed her arms and pinned them into place, she still tried her best to fight back with everything she had inside her, going as far as biting him when she got the chance, anger began to build up inside him, he began to fuck her violently, throwing her all around the room, not sparing her in any way.

This how you want it, huh? You want it rough, how about nasty, you like it nasty too?

He stopped right in his tracks and hawk spit in her face, then he snatched her off of the bed by her hair, forcing her to her knees.

You had your turn to be in control, now it's my turn!

He gripped the back of her head with both hands and began to cram his dick to the back of her throat as hard as he could, as far as it would go, the force was so strong, it caused her to vomit all over him, as sick as the visual was, he became more and more turned on by her pain, the look in his eyes were far from kind and loving, he had changed, she pulled the breast from the darkness, the one he tried his best to hide from the world, he was exposed, brought back to a part of the light he ran from for so many years ago. Her eyes stared up at him, as he stared back, his thoughts began to drain him more and more, he fell into a weakness that made him want her even more, he was lost in his love for her. Once he pulled himself from her mouth, to give her the little bit of room she didn't give him to breathe, she moaned, licking her lips like he was the best she ever tasted, his knees got weak.

Now are you gone fuck me the way I want to be fucked?

And which way is that? Her aggression made him tune in to her actions even more.

I want you to slap me, choke me, and pull my hair, and fuck me as hard as you could, I want you to make me cum.

Every word that spilled from her mouth, only made him aroused even more, as he rough housed her all around the room, giving her everything she asked for and more, her juices exploded all over him, over and over again to the point his stomach was covered, it began to drip down his legs. The more he looked into her eyes, he began to get weak inside of her, not able to take any more, he relieved his load all inside of her, he instantly became drained, not able to move, he laid on top of her, trying his best to get his composure together before he stood up and walked away.

OMG! That was so damn good, damn where you been at all my life Ace said as he shyly admitted before he rolled off the top of her, before he cleared himself from her space he made sure he kissed her on the lips one more time.

She smiled as his reaction, then sat up on the bed and watched his every more.

Yeah, tell me about it, it feels like we have known each other for years, I just feel so comfortable with you and not to mention I love how you make me feel when I'm with you, and you drive me crazy when your inside me, just a few days ago I was a virgin.

No I would never have believed that baby, damn you are a natural freak, you turn me on in everything you do!

You just make sure you don't try to go to sleep, I'm definitely are going to want to go another round or two or three, she said as she laughed, watching his reaction.

He laughed with her as he got up not saying another word, he headed to the bathroom and closed the door, once he was inside and she heard him turn the water on to the shower, immediately she jumped up out of the bed and started to look around the room to see what she could find, as she opened the night stand by the bed she stumbled across a loaded 9 M.M hand gun, after hearing the water cut off in the bathroom, she quickly jumped back into the bed and waited for him to return, as he stepped out the door to the bathroom his smile quickly turned to a frown once he seen her pointing a loaded gun right in his direction.

Meme what are you doing? Put the gun down, I don't play like that!

She ignored his request and matched it with a question,

Why did you do it? She said as she hopped off the bed and moved in closer to him to close off the space between them. She gripped the pistol as tight as she could the closer she got, there were no mystery when it came to her anger, he could easily see in her face by the grit in her teeth.

Baby what is you talking about? Everything was just cool, I just went to take a shower, what did

You think when your mom died, that you were the only one hurting, huh, the only one living with pain, pain that we watched Dad put in a cup and drink every day and night, one after the other, until he couldn't fucking stand up! You think that the day your mother died were the day that shit just changed for you! Well brother, I'm here to tell you, you were not alone, because of your next moves, because of the shit you did, our shit changed too, how could you rape and murder our mom, and leave her there for us to find her the next morning, I still have visions of her dancing around in my head.

Girl you tripping, I think you got the wrong guy! Put the fucking gun down, now you starting to make me mad.

POW! A shot flew pass his face, exploding into the wall behind him, then another shot followed immediately after, this one landed in his shoulder, the shot instantly knocked him off his feet sending him to his knees, as he tried his best to stand and make his getaway, she delivered another shot into his leg, crippling him in the process, making it impossible for him to stand, he crawled through the house, not willing to give up on getting away just yet.

Stop! He cried out, don't shoot me again! who are you? what

do you want? I got money in my safe the code is 0612 you can have it all just let me go!

What do I want! Well I'm going to get to that in a minute, and let me tell you, it's not what you think I want, I could tell you that. Before I get down to business I am going to answer a couple of questions for you, ok you ready? Now the first question you asked is, who am I? I'm the one and only daughter of Lamar Wright, that woman you killed was my mother! I could have sworn that I just made that clear to you a couple of minutes ago but maybe you didn't hear me so I figured I break it down for you again!

After hearing his father's name, he rolled over on his back to engage in eye contact with the girl who identified herself as his sister, he was confused, he looked deep into her face, and that when he could finally see his Dad features standing out in her, his defenses began to shut down, the only words he could get to come out his mouth were,

I'm sorry!

Yeah you are! You sorry as fuck, that's the only type of sorry you must be claiming you are, you sole aren't sorry for what you did. How I know? I read the journal, you were bragging big time, talking about when you were fucking her each stroke brought you closer to God, how close was he to you when you were fucking me? Huh! You sick as fuck! On my ride over here I was going to just kill you on site, but then a part of me wanted to taste death, I wanted to feel that connection with my mother in her last moments, I wanted you to beat me and choke me within inches of my life, with the power of knowing that I'm the one in control, I know she were scared, you took that control away from her!

Look what your mother took from me! If your whore of a mother and Dad wouldn't have been messing around, my mom and him would still be together, my mom would still be here! Your mom broke up our family, messed up our happy home!

If that's what you think, you are a lot dumber than I thought! What Dad did to your mom was truly fucked up but it was an accident, he never meant to hurt her, he was just trying to dirty up her name so he could get custody of you! If your little family was in a happy place, why did it have to come to that? But what I could say is when your mom died, even with the news you found out, you didn't have to kill him, he was already killing himself from the guilt he was feeling every day. You were there, why you think he was drinking himself into a coma like he was? Once you found out the information that you did, you didn't even give him a chance to tell his side.

Give him a chance for what! He was the reason my mom is dead and that's all I needed to know, sis, Meme, Myona Wright, whoever the fuck you are! Now that you got you some dick, felt your little weird ass connection with your mom, what's next? We going to build on our little family relationship, maybe have a family reunion, or maybe keep this little love thing we got going on between us a secret, keep it in the family, keep our bloodline strong, just like your mom, you do have some good ass pussy!

Ace laughed at her as he tried to reach up under his dresser to get a gun that were stashed at the bottom, her radar went up so as soon as he reached in that direction, she shot him in his other shoulder, pinning him to the floor.

Don't move motherfucker! I'm done playing these little games with you, I'm done answering questions, making your pain the topic of the day, now it's time for me to tell you what I want from you!

Bitch fuck you! I don't give a fuck what you want!

I know, you made that perfectly clear from the start! But I'm not asking you for shit big bro, I'm gone take it.

She shot him three times in the face, paused to see if he would show any signs of life, then she shot him three more times to make sure she finishes the job properly, no chance of making it through, as she stood over him looking at his lifeless body, she became filled with a strange sense of peace.

It's my turn now big bro to bring some order back to this family.

She walked to her phone that were sitting on the dresser picked it up and called 911 crying, she told the dispatch that she came to her brother's house to reunite with him after not seeing him in years and out of nowhere he attacked her, raped her and beat her with the intentions of taking her life, it the mist of the fight, by luck she was able to retrieve the weapon from his grip and turn it on him,

I told him to stop, he just kept coming, I didn't want him to kill me, O my God, I killed him, I didn't mean to kill him, she said as she screamed through the phone at the top of her lungs.

Before the police arrived, she was able to get everything in order that needed to be done from clearing out the safe to running her head into a mirror to make sure her injures were believable in the process, she needed all the pieces of the puzzle to fit in its own perfect place, the story hit big time on the News, every reporter in town fought hard to get inside the hospital to get an exclusive interview from her so they could get her side of the story. The Detectives felt that she was lying and felt it was much more to the story then was being told and unlike the reporter, she was not successful from stopping the Detectives from slipping through the cracks, they showed up three days in a row, sometimes two to three times a day, asking the same questions, mostly to see if her story would change the more pressure they applied to the situation. London had disappeared after giving her statement to the police, she told the Detectives she knew for a fact that Aiden didn't attack her, because he wasn't that type of guy, and that Myona had been wanting to kill him for a while now because she believed he had something to do with her mother's death. Grandma Vickie found out what London had done through the Detectives and so she paid London off to leave town before the Detectives could do a follow up interview with her.

Once Myona were released from the hospital, the Detectives placed her under arrest for the murder of Aiden Wright because of London's state she made but the charges didn't hold up because they were not able to get in touch with their main witness and Grandma Vickie turned in the journal to the chief Detective Cooper with her help, Detective Cooper were able to solve a lot of unsolved murders committed by Lamar and Aiden, though it put a bad reputation on the families name, it was enough to get Myona exonerated of all charges. While she was incarcerated, she began to get very ill, to the point she could barely keep any food down, after going to the doctor, they decided to run some test, still not able to find much of anything wrong with her the nurse suggested that maybe she should take a pregnancy test. She agreed and within five minutes the nurse came back into the room with the results.

Ms. Wright, I got your results back and all I could say is congratulations, you are 20 weeks pregnant, you are going to be a mommy!

TATE BLU
BE